Above All Else

Above All Else

Dana Alison Levy

Charlesbridge
TEEN

Published by Charlesbridge Teen, an imprint of Charlesbridge Publishing
9 Galen Street, Watertown, MA 02472
(617) 926-0329 • www.charlesbridgeteen.com

Library of Congress Cataloging-in-Publication Data
Names: Levy, Dana Alison, author.
Title: Above all else / Dana Alison Levy.
Description: Watertown, MA: Charlesbridge, [2020] | Audience: Ages 12+. |
    Summary: "Eighteen-year-olds Rose and Tate are long-time friends and
    climbing buddies, and now they are embarking on the greatest climb of all—
    Mount Everest—with Tate's father and another friend; but as the climbers
    encounter physical and emotional challenges the higher they go, the
    expedition starts to slide toward disaster, testing the teens' courage and
    determination"—Provided by publisher.
Identifiers: LCCN 2019034453 (print) | LCCN 2019034454 (ebook) | ISBN
    9781623541408 (hardcover) | ISBN 9781632899132 (ebook)
Subjects: LCSH: Mountaineering expeditions—Everest, Mount (China and
    Nepal)—Juvenile fiction. | Mountaineering accidents—Juvenile fiction. |
    Wilderness survival—Juvenile fiction. | Fathers and sons—Juvenile fiction. |
    Interpersonal relations—Juvenile fiction. | Everest, Mount (China and
    Nepal)—Juvenile fiction. | CYAC: Everest, Mount (China and Nepal)—
    Fiction. | Mountaineering—Fiction. | Survival—Fiction. | Fathers and
    sons—Fiction. | Love—Fiction.
Classification: LCC PZ7.L58257 Ab 2020 (print) | LCC PZ7.L58257 (ebook) |
    DDC 813.6 [Fic]—dc23
LC record available at https://lccn.loc.gov/2019034453
LC ebook record available at https://lccn.loc.gov/2019034454

Printed in the United States of America
(hc) 10 9 8 7 6 5 4 3 2 1

Display type set in Black Mountage by Sarid Ezra
Text type set in Arethusa Pro by AviationPartners
Printed by Berryville Graphics in Berryville, VA USA
Production supervision by Brian G. Walker
Designed by Diane M. Earley

*This one's for Kate, who walked up
the mountain with me again and again*

*The mountains are not fair or unfair;
they are just dangerous.*

—Reinhold Messner

March 1

Dear Jordan Russo, Tate Russo, Rose Keller, and
Paul Kirby,

*We are only one month away from your departure
for Nepal!*

*Climbing Mount Everest, or Sagarmatha, as it is
called in the Nepali language, is a challenge few will
attempt and even fewer will accomplish. We offer
top technological equipment, sophisticated weather
forecasting, expert guides, and comfortable Base
Camp facilities to help you reach your goal.*

*As you know, climbing Mount Everest is a
commitment of several months. In order to survive
the altitude at 29,035 feet, we require weeks to
acclimatize to the lack of oxygen. The best way to
do this is to move slowly up the mountain to Everest
Base Camp, which sits at 17,600 feet.*

*Base Camp will be our home for the next six to
eight weeks, as we commit to a training regimen*

that involves climbing to progressively higher and higher camps and returning to sleep at lower camps. "Climb high, sleep low" is our guiding principle, allowing the body to adapt to the reduced oxygen over time.

An expedition like this is a serious undertaking, and your safety is our priority. This climb is not for thrill seekers or daredevils but for those who hope to challenge themselves beyond what seems possible.

Thank you for entrusting us with your dream.

Sincerely,

Finjo Sherpa
Expedition Leader and Founder
Mountain Adventure Expedition Company

The only Nepali-owned organization to be rated in the top five Mount Everest outfitters by Lonely Planet!

Sagarmatha/Mount Everest
South Col Route

North Col
23,000' / 7010m

Khumbu
Icefall

Base Camp
17,600' / 5634m

Chapter One:

Rose

April 1
San Francisco airport
13 feet above sea level

The check-in line at the airport is ridiculously long. Even with my lists and special secret passport-and-foreign-currency pouch (which Tate keeps insisting is a fanny pack, but it's *not*), I'm still dithering around convinced I've lost my visa or something. It doesn't help that Mami is behind me, chattering in an upbeat, delighted sort of way about everything from the weather forecast in Kathmandu to the charm of the Buddhist temples we'll have to go see to the ice reports that are starting to be posted on the climbing blogs.

She should be coming with us. She should be photographing the temples and traversing the ice herself. I push this thought away and grab Tate. "Selfie time! Official trip documentation starts now!"

Tate obligingly puts bunny ears over my head and grins, then nudges me. "Yo. We're finally up."

I blink and rush toward the counter. We're already behind schedule, though in theory we still have plenty of time to make our flight. Or flights . . . two flights and thirty-two hours of travel await. San Francisco to Seoul, South Korea; Seoul to Kathmandu, Nepal. We're off to a tiny, rectangular country wedged in between Tibet and India, home to the highest peaks in the world, including the grand prize, Everest.

I hand over my paperwork to the bored check-in attendant and try to pay attention while she talks about our extra-luggage fees—it takes a metric ton of gear to climb, and that's before I sorted out which protein bars to bring—but Mami's still talking. She sounds so happy, like everything is going exactly according to plan, even though, in truth, nothing is. I'm heading off on this climb, this trip of a lifetime, and she's not.

This whole trip started with her. We have all climbed together for years, since Tate and I were little kids: RoseAndTate, best friends and climbing partners. But Mami was the one who made this trip happen, who pushed Everest from dream to reality, though the dream really started with Tate. He's always been the most into climbing of all of us, and Everest is the ultimate goal. Not that it was hard to convince Jordan, Tate's father. Jordan's pretty intense when it comes to bagging peaks. He's pretty intense in general. Tate is more chill than his dad, except about climbing. Ever-ready, ever-energized, up-for-any-mountain, that's Tate. Of course he's all about Everest. Especially since it got us out of our last few months of senior year. School's not exactly Tate's favorite place. Anyway, now we're heading off, and it's RoseAndTate, and Jordan, but no Mami.

Once we're done checking in, we shuffle ourselves out of the way of the crowds to say goodbye. Tate's mom, Sarah, is holding on to him like she might never let go, and Tate shoots me a half-panicked look over her shoulder. I shrug back, not sure how I'm supposed to help with her kraken-like grip.

"Sarah, we'll be fine," Jordan says, rubbing her back. "We are not the kind of mountaineers who are going to make the ultimate sacrifice. There's too much to come home to. We *will* see you in Kathmandu in June, and if we've summited Everest, great. If not, so be it, but either way, I promise you, we'll be there."

"I know! I know that," Sarah mumbles into Tate's shoulder. "But I can't help thinking—"

Jordan's voice quiets. "It was a fluke, what happened before. I promise, Sare. I'll keep him safe."

I turn and hug Dad. He looks baffled, as always, that this is something I want, but he hugs me hard and tells me he's proud of me. He has grown used to me and Mami heading off to points unknown, but I don't think it's ever easy for him. And this is the longest trip: almost three months. Without Mami. But if he worries, he doesn't tell me. Instead he just says again and again how proud he is, how much he loves me.

Next to me, Tate is still wrapped in his mother's arms. "I love you so much, Mama," I hear him whisper.

She squeezes him once, even tighter, then lets go fast.

"Be. Careful," she says, holding his chin and staring into his eyes as if she can burn the message into his brain. The whole family is white, but only Sarah has the kind of pale skin where you can see every freckle stand out. She's flushed and pink, her eyes a shiny, telltale red that means she's try-ing not to cry.

"Yes!" Jordan says, clearly relieved that the emotional part of the goodbye is over. "Let's break your 'Master of Disaster' track record, shall we? You'll need to really focus."

"I will! Jeez. I'm going to be climbing Mount Everest," Tate says. "I don't think my mind's going to wander."

Sarah interrupts. "I don't mean just climbing! Be careful on the streets in Nepal with those crazy drivers and on the trek up to Base Camp—my God! Be careful of the yak trains! I read about those giant groups of yaks that come barreling down the paths, loaded up with gear. You have to squeeze yourself against the inside, against the rock, or they can knock you right off the side of the mountain. Rose! Tell him!" She turns to me.

I nod solemnly. "I'm on it, Sarah. Trust me. It's not going to be like in La Paz—"

"I WAS TWELVE!" Tate pretend shouts, and we all laugh.

It's best that we laugh instead of thinking of what could happen. Like Dad, Sarah has never understood our climbs, but unlike Dad, she's never really been okay with it. When-ever we first get back from a trip, she clutches Tate like he's going to disappear. Now he's eighteen and off on the trip of a lifetime, so she's doing the best she can to suck it up. But I can see the fear in her eyes.

Mami is still smiling big and wide, her dark eyes crin-kled up. She looks so happy for us, but what is it like for her, to watch the rest of us head off to live her dream? She swears up and down she can't wait to meet us in Kathmandu when it's all over, that she's fine. And I try so hard to believe it. But my capital-D Dread, so enormous and gut-churning and constant, isn't easy to dismiss. It waits until I'm relaxing in my room or half-asleep in my bed. Then it tries to swallow me whole.

I push it away and hold up my phone. "Let's get a group shot, okay? Mami, I promise you, I'm going to send so many photos and videos and texts that you'll practically be there with us!"

"You'll have all the sights, none of the smells—so none of Rosie's high-altitude crop dusters! What could be better?" Tate says, and we laugh. Mami laughs loudest of all.

She grabs me in one last hug. "I am so excited for you," she says, her voice strong. "You, my love, are the most thoughtful, deliberate climber I've ever had the privilege of climbing with."

She looks at me with such intensity that I'm surprised flames don't crackle out from her eyes. "Savor every moment, Rosalita. I hope it is magical."

There's no judgment in her voice, no resentment. But I can't help thinking about every time I bitched about training or complained about missing too much school. I wanted this . . . but never as much as Mami. I can't help thinking that she should be doing this, not me.

I look more like my dad—a seriously tall, skinny white guy with blue eyes—than Mami, who is pretty short for a climber and has darker skin and deep, brown eyes. We're different enough that when I was a baby, people thought she was the nanny. But looking into her face is like looking into my own. Our connection is so strong it's like a rope strung between us. After staring into my eyes, she squeezes me once more, then lets go.

She turns and gives Jordan a quick hug, then swats him. "Jordan! Scram! The last thing I want to hear is a phone call once we get home and back into bed that you've missed the plane. Remember that time in Chile—"

"Again, I was TWELVE!" Tate says, and Mami laughs and hugs him.

"I know, I know. I'm teasing. You're an excellent climber, Tate. Just remember to take care of yourself the way you take care of Rose and you'll be fine." She pauses. "Take such care. We need you, my friend. Okay?"

Tate nods and hugs her tight, dwarfing her until she disappears in his arms.

We have one more round of hugs, and there's an attempt to actually head to security, but then we're delayed by a frantic realization that someone (Tate) forgot his e-reader in his mother's purse, followed by another round of hugs, and then we're off.

• • •

Twenty hours into our trip, I think Tate and I are the only ones awake. Jordan popped an Ambien the minute our second flight took off, and by the snores coming out of her, so did the woman in front of me. I keep turning around and around in my seat as though there were even the remotest chance of getting comfortable.

"Will you stop!" Tate whacks me on the arm. "It's like sitting next to a rotisserie chicken!"

I sigh. "Sorry! Sorry, sorry. I'm so tired. But I can't sleep."

He cracks his neck, then winces at the popping sound. "No, I'm sorry. I'm just edgy. Can't sleep, can't read, can't watch any more TV . . ."

"There are BBC channels. You can watch the baking show," I point out, my voice muffled. I've dropped the tray table and have face-planted on it, my head resting on a sweatshirt. "Will you draw pictures on my back?"

This is what we do in the tiny tents on climbing expeditions, where we get into our sleeping bags as soon as the cold bites. Depending on the climb and who else from our larger group is with us, I share a tent with either Tate or Mami. He snores way less than Mami, though I swear in high altitude it's like a contest to see which of our farts are worse. As an only child, I've always been fairly private, but sharing tents with Tate gives me some taste of what it might be like to have a brother. Even as we grew up, and the boy-girl thing could have been weird, we somehow managed to keep our friendship normal. Not that our friends at school totally believed it. Anyway, we have a deal: one night I tickle his arm until he falls asleep, the next he draws pictures on my back.

"'Course," he says, and starts to draw. I'm supposed to guess the pictures, but it's too hard to pay attention when I'm half-asleep and hypnotized by his light touch. The Dread falls asleep too. At least while he's drawing. This time he doesn't ask me to guess. He draws shapes that might be mountains, or waves, or rocket ships . . . with Tate, it could be anything.

"So, you okay? Saying goodbye to your mom and all?" he says finally.

I shrug, and he adds an accidental zigzag to whatever he's drawing. "It sucked. But . . . I mean, she's counting on me to go and totally live the experience, and I will. I'm not kidding that I'll send so many photos and stuff that she'll have a—I don't know—virtual reality version of the trip. So that makes it easier." I sigh. "I can't believe we're actually on our way. Do you realize we're done with high school? Hello, 'independent study!' But it's over. All our friends, and all that work . . . Honors Calculus, History . . . *done*." I sigh into my sweatshirt. "It feels weird, don't you think? We're going to miss all the fun senior spring stuff. "

He laughs softly. "Yeah, I'm not real nostalgic for high school. Maybe in twenty years. I'll take a trip to Nepal over sitting in those crappy chairs for six hours a day, anytime." He sighs. "You have no idea how pumped I am to be out of that place."

I snort. "It's not exactly a vacation. You know we'll be trying to stay alive in the death zone on Everest, right?"

His hands stop moving for a second, then start up again. "Yeah. I remember."

I sigh. "But I guess it's easy for you. You're the toughest of us all. Who barely gets jet lag? Who's the least sick from altitude? Who's the only one who made it up Engelhorn without puking? Also, was that a boat?" I ask, trying to stay awake.

"Shhh, no. It was an owl. Go to sleep; I'll keep drawing." Tate's fingers brush the skin of my neck for a minute, then they're gone.

I'm so tired. "Are you sure? I can stay up." My voice isn't very convincing.

"Go to sleep. I got this," Tate says, and I do.

Chapter Two:

(Five Months Earlier) December 19
Boorman Creek High School, California
7 feet above sea level

*I*t's entirely possible that the thing that will finally kill me won't be trying to ollie a stupid-wide gap on my skateboard or cracking my skull falling at El Capitan but will be . . . Advanced Seminar Literature. I wasn't going to take the class—I'm not an advanced kind of student, except for electives like Real-World Design Challenge—but my favorite teacher, Mr. Abrams, did that thing where he looked me in the eye and told me he reallyreallyreally thinks I can do it if I put my mind to it. He meant well, I'm sure, but now it's halfway through first term of senior year and all I hear while he's talking about persuasive arguments and fallacy of reason is the adult voices in the Charlie Brown specials: *Waah-waah WAAH-waah, wah-wah.* I have a feeling both Mr. Abrams and I are going to regret this by the time final grades are due.

I slide my sketchbook out from under my notebook and start to doodle. My brain's in that place where a million thoughts collide and crash into each other: Are we finally heading back to Mount Rainier in a few weeks even though the temps are going to be ball-shrinkingly freezing? Is Rose wearing yet another new necklace, and if so, how many necklaces does one human need? Is there a material light-weight and strong enough to build retractable wings on a small airplane, since realistically I think that's the only way we're going to get flying cars in my lifetime? The only thing that shuts off my brain is letting my fingers fly over my sketchbook.

Rose, who sits beside me, slides her foot under my desk and stomps on my toes. *"He's telling us what will be on the midterm,"* she whispers. *"TAKE. NOTES."*

I sigh. Flip her the finger discreetly behind my sketch-book. Slide it back under my notebook and dutifully try to take notes.

The thing is, school's easy for Rose. No. That's not true. She works incredibly hard, unlike our friend Ronan, who does dick-all and still mostly gets As. No, *working hard* is really easy for Rose. And not just in school. In every part of her life. She has color-coded calendars and bullet journals and list-making apps and whatever else it takes to juggle a million things and make it look effortless.

With climbing, like everything else, Rosie's a natural. That's what Dad said the first time he took us to the rock gym when we were ten, and he repeats it—feels like every single time we're out together. It's true: she clings to the rock like she grew there, like she has magnets in her hands that move automatically to the strongest hold on the moun-tain. And unlike at school, I am too. The two of us were phenoms at the rock gym when we were little, and now I've got six feet, three inches of reach that make it almost easy to monkey up stuff other people can barely touch. And the gnarlier it is, the better . . . It sends my mind into hyperfocus so that there's nothing to do or worry about except the next reach in front of me.

Somehow climbing went from one thing we do for fun—along with surfing (me), skateboarding (me), sketching (me), eating frightening amounts of fish tacos (me and Rose), buying necklaces (Rose), planning world domination via architecture (Rose)—to . . . *everything*. Every weekend filled with overnight, extreme-condition climbs in the Sierras or the Rockies. Every summer paycheck put into an account for climbing expenses. Every vacation's air miles cashed in for tickets to climbing playgrounds in South America, Canada, Europe. Every conversation leading to speculation about how long it will be until the big one: Nepal. Mount Everest. I love it.

Closing my eyes for a second, I imagine me and Rose and Dad and Maya, Rose's mom, on our way to Everest. Immediately my brain's overloaded with a million different images, facts, thoughts—like a beehive exploded in there. It's too much. Jimmy, the shrink I've seen since I was seven, would probably tell me to get a hold of my toolbox and figure out which tool was going to help me chill out. I've been trying to pull things out of that toolbox for ten years now. Sometimes it works, others not. But I get it now: I'm wired to be hyper.

We've been planning this trip for so long—longer than I have ever worked for anything in my life, by far. We were in fourth grade when I asked Rose and Maya and Dad if we could climb Mount Everest someday. I was hanging on an advanced route at Rockface, the gym where we started climbing, literally hanging in midair, because I could. Maya was belaying me, and Rose was on a route nearby, with Dad below. We both loved being roped in. When you're belaying, you're suspended by your climbing harness: even if you fall, you don't go anywhere, at least as long as you trust the person holding the rope. It's awesome knowing you can't fuck up if you try.

I asked her the question only because hanging there I could see this huge poster-sized photo of the gym owner on Everest, and it looked incredible. And Rosie said sure, like I was asking if she wanted to go to Mount Tam again this weekend. But Maya looked up at us, then at Dad, and shrugged and said, "Really? Would you?"

And we both said yes, and I don't know about Rose, but my heart was beating so fast, like someone was really asking me if I wanted to see dragons or travel to the moon. It seemed impossible, something that only climbing rock stars could ever consider, but that night over In-N-Out burgers, Maya pulled up some facts about Mount Everest, and the kind of climbers who did it, and said if we were serious, we could talk about planning for it.

I've never wanted anything so much in my life. School sucked, and fighting with my parents about school sucked worse, but when I was training to climb Mount Everest, I wasn't a school fuckup, I was a climber, someone working toward one of the most elite and extreme adventures on the planet. The more people we told, the more it felt like we were nailing down a promise. It felt impossible but also inevitable, like I *had* to do it.

With Maya's help there were bake sales every Thursday, with two hundred individually wrapped chocolate chip cookies and a cute handwritten sign saying *Cookies for Climbing: Help Us Reach the Top of the World*. And in fifth grade, a car wash every Saturday. And selling bags of popcorn every Friday lunch period in sixth. Maya was doing all the research, following each year's climbing season the way some people follow their favorite football teams. But I was the one who couldn't stop talking about it. And of course Dad was all in. He was climbing long before I came along. It was his idea to get me to Rockface in the first place. He said if I was going to climb the walls at home, I might as well learn how to do it right. But he was stoked that I love it so much and brags to all his friends about my climbing. It's cool to have *one* thing in common.

The bell rings, and I stare down at my language arts notebook, where I have the word *Everest* written in blocky, jagged letters that get larger in the middle, then taper down again. If the mountain needed a logo, this would be cool. But I'm pretty sure it has all the name recognition it needs. Crumpling the paper with a satisfying noise, I rip it out of the notebook and arc it toward the recycle bin.

Rose raises an eyebrow. "Were those your notes?"

I shake my head. "It was nothing," I say, not wanting to get into my poor note-taking skills. "Hey, we climbing today?" I try to keep my voice chill because Rose gets pissy when she thinks I'm nagging her. But the truth is that the trip of a lifetime is coming up in a few months, and I'm sorry, but her school yearbook/environmental club/unpaid internship/part-time job/AP course load all need to take a back seat. You can't half-ass training for Mount Everest.

"No, I can't." Rose peers down into her bag as we walk out of the room, and I put a hand on her back to steer her away from the wall. Sometimes she takes multitasking to dangerous new levels. "My mom has a doctor's appointment and needs a ride home after."

We're in the hallway now, pushing through the mob of people, and so many of them seem like babies. Was that really us, four years ago? I glance at Rose: climbing partner and best friend since the first-grade school bus. Four years ago she was five inches taller than me and had braces, but the summer after that year, all my guy friends started asking if they could climb with us sometime, and it wasn't because they all suddenly developed an interest in alpine ascents. She had turned into what Ronan called a "totally naturally occurring homegrown babe," which is, sure, maybe true but totally beside the point. We've both changed since first grade, but thank the god of whatever's up there, our friendship's stayed the same.

"Another one? Bummer," I say, trying to keep the annoyance out of my voice.

"Seriously. I don't know what the doctors are even looking for. I keep telling her—she's just getting old."

I laugh. "Yeah. Right. Your mom's like Wonder Woman . . . Thank God she's almost fifty, or we'd get our asses kicked every time we climb." It's true. Maya's literally a foot shorter than me, and thirty years older, but she's a total badass. Still, she's been achy and dizzy with some weird virus for ages, hence the endless doctor's appointments.

"I'll tell her you said so," Rose says. "But tomorrow, though, yeah? We'll go to Rockface?" She waves at a friend down the hall. "I'll bring the Twizzlers."

"Deal." I wave her off, then head toward the door, wondering if anyone's around to climb with me, not wanting to waste the day.

Chapter Three:

Rose

April 4
Kathmandu, Nepal
4,600 feet above sea level

"Watch out for the cow!"

It's not the first time Tate has said this since we got in the van outside the airport. The airport was total chaos between the baffling language gap at customs and trying to find Paul, our climbing partner, who left a few weeks before us to visit India, and whose flight was an hour late. We finally cleared security after several people shouted at us in Nepali for being in the wrong line. When our guide met us outside, holding a sign with our names, I was ready to jump into his arms.

Finjo is young, probably barely thirty—a fact that's a little alarming, given that he's the one leading the Everest expedition. But his company, Mountain Adventure, is one of the only full-service Mount Everest climbing expeditions that is owned by Nepalis, not Westerners. They have a great safety record and cost less than the better-known American and Australian groups that promise everything from Ping-Pong tables to fresh seafood at Base Camp. For the next few months, he and his staff of guides, porters, cooks, medics, weather forecasters, and support workers are going to be dedicated to helping us get up the tallest mountain in the world.

Finjo is all bright eyes and sly smiles and bossiness. Bossy is fine with me right now. Anyone who can navigate this place is my favorite person in the world. He took one look at our luggage and started talking fast in Nepali to the driver, who quickly abandoned his attempt to cram it in the van and instead started lifting it on top. There was nothing up there but a shallow cage, and as we bump over every pothole and crack, I imagine our bags bouncing off the roof and being lost forever.

"Are you seeing this?" Tate asks. "That one was in the middle of the road. We nearly hit it."

Paul grins. "'A whole new woooooorld!'" he starts to sing. "'Don't you dare close your eyes!' 'A new fantastic point of view!'"

We all groan. Paul's fondness for Disney movies is just one of those things, like the weird clicking Jordan does with his jaw, that we've learned to live with on our climbs. He insists that watching Disney movies at the hospital offers endless opportunities for psychological insights with his young patients, but I think he's just a mega fan.

Cows are sacred in the Hindu religion. I knew this. But somehow I never really extrapolated that fact to the reality of dozens and dozens of skinny cows wandering through the snarled and smoggy traffic of downtown Kathmandu, ignored by everyone from the traffic cops to the speeding motorcycles. Also ignored: families, children, old people, beggars, and monks who dart through the traffic, somehow knowing when to avoid being hit.

My eyes burn and sting from sheer exhaustion, and maybe from the fact that everyone in the airport appeared to be chain-smoking fistfuls of cigarettes all at once. I'm not even sure what day it is. The sun is so bright, and the horns . . . Drivers honk like mad here. It is a concerto of beeps—loud, lively, and constant. It's almost musical. I slouch against the van door, despite my fears that it will open up and dump me on the road.

"God, this is like some kind of amusement park ride in hell," I mumble to Tate, trying not to crash my head on the ceiling when we hit a pothole. "Remind me why we wanted to leave California?" Through the blaze of noise, of pollution, of exhaustion, I remember. Mami. With a groan I pull out my phone. "Hang on. I'm going to get some video." I turn it around so that it's filming me and the passing scenery. "Heyyyy, Mami and Dad! As you can see, we are here and happily ensconced in the local scene! Don't even worry about this van . . . While we don't seem to have seat belts, I'm sure it's totally roadworthy!" I turn it off, let the smile fall off my face, and wrap my arm through Tate's. "Don't let me fall out of this thing if the doors fall off," I mutter and drop my head on his shoulder.

"Rose. ROSE. We're here."

For a moment I am lost, hot, nauseated, and unsure where I am or who is calling me. Then I open my eyes to see a palace. An enormous building, wedding cake white and trimmed with frosting-like curls and flowers, is in front of me, surrounded by fountains and lush flowering plants. Off to the right, turquoise pool water is glistening.

"What . . . ?" I ask. "What happened to the—" I wave my hand to encompass everything: the noise, the dirt, the honking "—the cows?"

"This is the Hotel Shanker," Finjo says, smiling. "You're home. For now, anyway."

"This place is seriously swank. And we look like something the cat dragged in," Tate says, staring around. He turns to me and scrubs at his dark, shaggy hair, making it stand up like crazy. "Well, you look like something the cat dragged in. I look like something the cat dragged in, ate, then puked back up."

"Nice," I say, shooting him the finger and trying to smooth down my own hair, which has totally escaped its braids and is a mass of frizz and curl.

"It was a compliment. Kind of," he says, leaning over to mess up my hair.

Jordan sighs.

The hotel guy starts talking about our rooms, and Jordan is asking about timing for our first team briefing, while Tate is interrupting to ask if he can go crash, but I tune them all out. Beyond the lush green of the hotel gardens are smoggy sky and decrepit buildings. But beyond that, in the distance, are mountains. Dimmed by smog and barely there, but snowcapped and enormous against the sky. The Himalayas.

It's all starting. I try to imagine what it's like up there, two weeks' walking distance into the mountains, so far from home. Unbidden, my thoughts fly to Mami. She would love this. Love the roads with their chickens and cows and shrines, love the hotel with its wedding cake balconies, love the start of this adventure. My excitement dims, and the Dread shows up, strong enough that I must have made a noise because Tate glances over.

"You okay?" he asks, and I know he catches a whiff of it on my skin, fear so deep it feels bottomless.

I nod, take a deep breath, and reach for the excitement, fan it, coax it back into flames. I will love it enough for both of us. I will soak it all in and bring it home to her.

• • •

Noise and light and color. Kathmandu has a serious over-abundance of all of them. And traffic. In addition to the cows. Walking through Thamel, the main tourist district, is like being in a developing country made up of mostly white hippies and climbers. Every storefront promises *Everest View Trekking—Best Price* or *Mountain Panorama Helicopter Rides—Safety First* or sells fake North Face down jackets for five dollars. People follow us down the block, holding out trekking poles, water bottles, Mountain Hardwear gloves.

Tate realizes he forgot his water bottle on the plane and asks if we can stop for one, which has Jordan huffing in annoyance about the amount of gear Tate loses. But Paul makes a joke about Tate and leaving a trail of water bottle bread crumbs to follow home, and we all laugh. I'm reminded again that I'm glad to have him here. We've known Paul for years, when some friend-of-a-friend introduced him to Jordan before a climbing trip. He's younger than our parents and older than us, a peacemaker who always offers a welcome voice when we're getting on each other's nerves. But now, without Mami, I'm even more grateful he's with us. He's another grown-up for Jordan when Tate and I want to be by ourselves, another non-Russo for me when Tate and Jordan are squaring off. Maybe it's because he's a pediatric and adolescent psychiatrist, but he's able to calm the Russo

men down better than most. Listening to Tate and Jordan fight is not my favorite part of climbing.

Paul slows to wait for me.

"Can you believe this is really happening? Just being in Kathmandu is a dream come true, and we haven't even gotten close to the mountains yet!" He grins. "If only I could go back and tell my sad, bullied fourth-grade self that I'd be heading off to climb Mount Everest someday. Though maybe I should thank the jerks who made me so miserable. If it weren't for them, I wouldn't have run into the mountains every chance I got."

I put an arm around him. "I hate that anyone was mean to you. If you want, I'll fly back to Salt Lake City and beat them up. Or beat up their kids. Whatever."

He laughs. "Rose the Avenger. Thanks for the offer, but I think sending the article headlined 'Acclaimed Psychiatrist Aims for the Summit, Dedicates his Climb to LGBTQ Youth' to my alumni newsletter will allow enough gloating. Besides, that's all in the past. I need to—"

"If you sing 'Let It Go,' I swear . . ." I side-eye him. "Please. No."

"It's a great song!" His smile deepens. "I'm just really, really happy to be here." He looks around. "Hard to believe we're only a few minutes from the hotel. This is a different world."

"The real different world is when you get outside the tourist area," Finjo says. "But today we'll stay in Thamel and get our shopping done."

We nod obediently because that's our only option whenever Finjo tells us what to do. The bossiness continues unabated. Still, as he shepherds us forward, barking in Nepali to the map sellers who are encroaching, I can't help slowing

to stare. The streets are choked with cars and mopeds and the occasional cow, and the sidewalks have even less room, with tables of Buddha statues, prayer bowls, incense burners, and—oddly—old American DVDs for sale. Dust, thick and lung-punishing, hangs over the streets in a cloud, dimming the sun as though smoke from a fire were blowing. Adding to the dust is real smoke from storefronts that aren't stores but, instead, tiny makeshift restaurants with smoky grills that smell of delicious meat. No tourists stop; only crouching Nepali men grabbing a quick lunch. I can't help staring wistfully.

Finjo catches my eye. "No street food, ever. Okay? It will make you sick, and no getting sick before we climb." He looks fierce.

I nod, filming the street scene as I walk and nearly knocking over a rack of mountaineering maps. I'm taller than a lot of the men here, and the women only come up to my chest. I feel like a giantess laying waste to a village as I try not to trash the careful displays.

"Oops! Here, I wanted to get a few maps," Paul says. He has already stopped to buy an ornate Gurkha knife, a hand-hammered brass bowl, and some carved figurines. We've only gone around three blocks from the hotel—I can't imagine how he's going to get this stuff home. Now along with the maps he grabs more post cards, some to mail back to the kids he sees in the hospital, some for Drew, his husband, who will meet us here in Kathmandu when we return, along with Tate's and my families. I think about being back here in close to three months, having stood on the summit of Mount Everest. I try to imagine Mami's arms around me, her face when I display the photo proving that I held a picture of her at the top.

My head throbs a little from the noise and smog, and it's hard to see where I'm going while I film, but I keep at it, narrating the sights for Mami in the brightest voice I can muster. I'll have to edit before I send it to them. They don't need to hear me swearing when I realize I've stepped in a giant pile of cow manure.

We're stopped again, this time while Paul looks at a patchwork skirt for his niece. I pull Tate forward, trying to get him to stop staring at the wall of a sketchy little pharmacy. He appears to be reading an ad about male enhancement.

"Seriously? You know girls don't care about that stuff nearly as much as you think," I say, dragging him along to where Paul is finishing his transaction. "We always say, 'It's not the size of the dog in the fight, it's the size of the fight in the—'"

"Oh, shut up. I was . . . you know what? Never mind." He moves as though to give me a wet willy, but I duck, keeping my ears far away.

It's a comfortable seventy degrees or so, and I'm too warm in my long pants and boots. But I hadn't thought to pack any sandals, which was dumb. Kathmandu's at the same latitude as Florida—the cold only comes when we get up into the mountains. Still, I fit in here. Pretty much everyone in this part of town is decked out in climbing clothes. Tate snorts at a particularly geared-up blond guy who looks ready to start scaling a peak.

"What the hell? What's he going to do? Boulder up that two-story building?" he asks.

"He's just excited," I say. "Like us." But my voice makes it a question. I want to be excited, but I'm still so tired it's hard to think of anything other than sleep.

Tate doesn't answer.

"Hey," I press. "We are excited, right?" I knock lightly on the side of his head. "Right? You home in there?"

Tate swats my hand away. "Sto-ooop!" he fake whines. "You're messing up my hair!"

I laugh but keep staring at him. "Yeah? All good? You've been super quiet all day. And yesterday."

He nods. "All good. Still a little zonked."

I nod but keep looking at him. Tate notices and shoves me.

"I promise. Things are fine. I'm deliriously excited. Orgasmically excited. Radioactively—" He starts to spin around, *Sound of Music*–style, and almost knocks over a table of brass singing bowls.

"Fine!" I laugh, relieved. He is back. Endless-energy-constant-optimism Tate. The tiny knot of unease I hadn't really noticed dissolves. Normally Tate's bad moods are epic, more tantrums than moods, and they never last long. This quiet "just tired" attitude since we arrived in Nepal weirded me out a little and made me realize how much I count on him to keep our energy up.

We move slowly up the street.

"Did you see the poster?" he asks, after a minute.

"About male enhancement? Dude, I am *not* the person to talk to about this," I say.

"Dumbass. Next to it, for the missing climber."

I shake my head. "I didn't notice. What did it say?"

He shrugs, shouldering through the crowd. At six feet, three inches, Tate looms even higher than I do. I follow along easily.

"Tate?" I ask, trying to slow him down.

"Nothing. It was nothing. A Dutch dude last seen two weeks ago, heading toward Annapurna 1. I don't know why they bother putting up signs. If he hasn't been found by now, he's not going to be," he says, catching up to Jordan and Paul, who are standing outside a restaurant that Finjo has deemed acceptable for lunch.

I don't know what to say. Of course it's dangerous, climbing mountains. We know this.

"Tate . . . " I start, but I trail off.

"It's fine. It's too bad, that's all." He turns to me, his grin bright and real in his stubble-covered cheeks. "Hey, did I tell you? It was on CNN in the lobby this morning: a dog summited Everest!"

I blink at the change of subject, then scowl.

"That's bull. You totally made that up! Who's going to bring a dog twenty-nine thousand feet up a mountain! Humans can barely survive it, and most of them are wearing oxygen masks."

Tate takes his hand, puts it over his heart. "Scout's honor. It was a rescue dog. With its own tiny O2 canister hookup specially designed for him by a group of NASA technicians."

I look at him, skeptical. His brown eyes open wide, looking innocent. He shrugs.

"Okay, I made up the part about NASA, but the rest of it is true. Seriously, I saw it on the news. Ask Finjo." He turns and taps Finjo on the shoulder. "Didn't a dog summit Everest this week?"

Finjo snorts. "No summit. It was just to Base Camp. It was a Sherpa dog."

"That makes more sense," I say, comforted that I haven't been beaten to the summit by a canine.

"But the headline read 'First Dog to Summit Mount Everest!'—How is EBC a summit? It's not even eighteen thousand feet! Middle-aged tourists go there all the time." Tate snorts. "False advertising."

"Well, eighteen thousand feet is still something," I say. "Especially for a dog, I guess. After all, most mountains stop at that height. It's just that Everest starts there."

I glance over at Tate. We joke about the climb a lot, but we haven't talked about what it's really going to be like. Probably because—even with all the books and documentaries and live, in-real-time blogs—we don't really know. We don't know what it will take, only that it will challenge us in ways we've never been challenged before. That's the part of climbing I love best, solving a puzzle that's unfolding in front of me. The part I like least is the amount of time it takes, time that was increasingly hard to find as high school got harder and harder. Time that Mami had to remind me I owed to climbing, to our grand Everest plan. Time that I often gave all too grudgingly.

But everything is different now. Everest is unlike anything we've ever done, and Mami can't be here, but I can. I itch to start climbing, to push away the Dread and concentrate on the work ahead. I can't worry about Mami, or about anything, when I'm climbing. And right now that's exactly what I want.

All around us, Kathmandu roils and bustles, but I barely notice. Instead I'm seeing a route up through snow and ice, Tate beside me, roped in. We've climbed so many mountains together; maybe Everest will be just another peak. Maybe. But I can see it so clearly in my mind: me and Tate, arms around each other for the expected photo at the summit, sending it across the world to Mami in real time. Need like fire burns in me to do this, to *be* this.

Millions of tourists flock to Nepal every year, and most of them are there to gaze on Mount Everest. Getting to Everest Base Camp takes less than two weeks of walking—

not climbing or doing anything technical—and doesn't even have a view of the mountain, since it's so close. It's unimaginable to me, really. The idea of traveling so far and paying so much money to walk up and see the side of a glacier where climbers pitch their tents. The prize isn't there, among the junk left behind by the expeditions. The prize is at the top.

Chapter Four:

Tate

(Four Months Earlier) January 5
Paradise, Mount Rainier, Washington
5,400 feet above sea level

*I*t's a perfect climbing day, if brutal icy winds, frozen eye-lashes, and mild frostbite can be part of perfection. On Rainier in winter, it definitely can be. It's day one of our winter summit attempt; we'll make camp in a few hours and wake at midnight to push for the top. I grin, even though nobody's around yet. This is my happy place. I adjust my earbuds under my helmet and wait for the others to catch up.

Rose, when she gets to me, looks a little less pumped. "Argh! I think I'm in worse shape now than I've ever been! I'm sucking wind already." She takes a few deep breaths, and she groans.

"You've been slacking, Keller. I told you to keep training with me at Rockface. Time for beast mode." I keep my voice easy, trying not to sound like I'm saying *I told you so*. But

I'm totally saying it. She was so busy this fall with her millions of extracurriculars and honors classes and volunteer hours, all laser-pointed at getting her into Yale, that her climbing time definitely took a hit. It's fine—I can usually find someone to partner up with at the gym or even for a day trip into the mountains, but Rose is kidding herself if she thinks she can blow off training and zoom up Mount Everest in a few months. I glance at her, and her mouth's smashed together, which is Rose code for pissed off, usually at herself. So I lay off.

"At least you get to look at this view while you catch your breath. That doesn't suck, right?" I say, gesturing around me.

Below us, ribbons of white and fading-purple mountain peaks blaze in the late afternoon sun. I wave my hands around like a game show host or something, and finally Rose grins. So far we've barely climbed. We're just hauling ass up the trail. There are hikers and skiers and all kinds of outdoorsy types who have no intention of spending the night at 10,000 feet and leaving at midnight for the crux of the climb—a rocky and wind-scoured cliff. Suckers. They're missing the good stuff. The older we've gotten and the more we climb, the more it becomes the best part of my day, my week, my year. Unlike Rose, I'm not really looking for five hundred other things to do every minute of the day. Especially now that Everest is finally—*finally*—in our sights.

Partly to keep moving and partly to keep from bitching more about training to Rose, I bend down to make a snowball, and the next time she's looking all gooey-eyed at the view, I pelt her on the back of the head.

"Oh, it is ON!" She spins and starts hurling snow so fast her arms look like those cartoon circles. I duck, then figure it's easier to put her in the snow than the snow on her and pile-drive her. We both go down right as Dad and Maya join us. Maya used to lead, every single time, but lately whatever bug she's fighting keeps her slower than the rest of us. She tries to smile when she reaches us, but her hands are on her knees, and she's breathing hard.

"Tate! Enough with the games! This isn't exactly a playground." Dad is level-orange annoyed, despite the fact that we're on a plateau that is literally as safe as a playground. Probably safer, since there's none of that crappy mulch that always gets stuck everywhere.

"Chill out," I say, trying to get snow out of the neck of my jacket. Rose gestures for me to bend down and brushes it out, then I do the same for her. "We're all good. According to Rose's master plan, which is never wrong, we're still fine to get to Muir Camp by four thirty p.m. to set up. Rosie, I swear you have a bright future in trail guiding if architecture doesn't work out."

Dad snorts. "I'm sure she's been banging away at AP courses for four years so she can haul tourists up mountains. No, I suspect we'll be reading about her in either *Fast Company* or *Architectural Digest*, or both. I know you're holding out to get off the early decision waitlist for Yale, Rosie, but you'll have plenty of options. You, on the other hand, buddy . . . Well, hopefully we'll get some good news in the next few months. I hope your personal statement and recommendations are enough to let them see what you're actually capable of."

Maya and Rose both start talking at the same time.

Maya says, "Jordan, let's enjoy the view and worry about the future later," while Rose bursts out, "I'm sure schools will be all over him! Tate's an incredible artist and designer. He's a lot more likely to be famous than I am. The stuff he designs is real genius!"

I do love to design stuff, though I don't think it falls into genius range. First with Legos when we were little kids, now with fancy software (though let's be real: Legos are still completely dope). Somehow my whacked-out ADHD brain settles into some kind of holding pattern when I'm working on these kinds of projects, and I can totally focus. Hyper-focus, according to Jimmy the Shrink, and one of the reasons ADHD people can go on to greatness. I'm not counting on greatness; I'd settle for consistently decent.

Dad shakes his head and smiles a tight smile. "You two— maybe you should have written Tate's personal statement." But he stops. Maya changes the subject, and the two of them examine a crampon that has a busted strap. Maya's had my back forever, trying to tamp down the constant stream of Tate-Do-Better-Tate-Just-Concentrate-Tate-Can't-You-Please-Just-Put-Some-Effort-Into-It.

Now she grins at us, her smile like Rose's. "Last chance for photos. The cold is draining the battery something fierce. Better make it good!"

She points the camera toward us, and I immediately lean over and pretend to lick Rose's face.

"Don't lick my zipper! Remember what happens to a tongue on metal in this cold."

We both laugh. "Remember the ski lift?" I say. "Dad, you kept saying, 'Yank it off, son! Come on, we've got to get off the lift!' And I was all, 'Uh-uh!'" I mime shaking my head with my tongue stuck to the metal bar in front of me.

"They had to stop the lift and pour the lift guy's coffee on it," Dad sighs. "What a fiasco."

Maya looks at the sky. "We should keep moving. It's going to get dark fast, and we want to be well set up at camp by then."

The others agree, and we start moving again, a straight line of bulky bodies against the white of the mountain. Everyone's moving slower now. It's the slow, slogging parts that I hate.

Rose calls back to Dad. "I saw your email. Do you have all our flight details for Kathmandu yet? I still haven't really wrapped my head around how soon it is."

"Final flight info arrived a few days ago. We change planes in Seoul. Our flight to Seoul leaves early. I think it leaves at seven, which means—"

"Ugh, we have to get there at five in the morning! Which means getting out the door at four. That's brutal."

"Sorry, Rosie, we need to be there by four thirty or so," Dad says.

"Well, that's. Just. Wonderful." Rose makes her voice extra cranky, and we laugh.

"Weeks without a shower? No problem. Dehydrated food? Check. Hanging from a cliff face? She's good. But no waking up early. . . . That's our Rosie." Dad turns to Maya. "When they were younger, did you ever need to separate them in the mornings? When Rosie used to sleep over, I'd have to take Tate out to play in the park because otherwise he'd bug her until she either cried or punched him."

I do an accurate impression of my younger self: "Rose; hey, Rose; hey, Rose, are you awake? Hey, Rose, are you awake? Hey, wake up! Are you awake? Oh, sorry, did I wake you?"

Rose laughs harder than the joke deserves, but the mountain air is like a drug to her. She's always sillier, quicker to laugh and relax here. Her laughter makes me relax, reminds me that I want to be here, even with Dad's constant comments on my disappointing academics. My sunglasses fog with sweat, while the cold air works its way through my gear. I remember hanging upside down from the top bunk, trying to see if Rose's eyes were open, if she was up and ready to play.

She and Dad fall behind, talking logistics, while Maya and I keep moving.

"You doing okay?" Maya asks. She says it like maybe it's not the first time. She pauses, putting a hand on my shoulder.

I smile down at her. Thank God for Maya, my other mother, who always insists I'm as amazing in every way as Rose. Even though we all know Rose is another species altogether.

"Oh yeah. Spacing out, that's all," I say. I don't tell her that—truth?—I'm trying to figure out how many more days of school we have before I'm finally done, able to take off for Nepal, able to leave high school and all its constant, stressful bullshit behind forever.

Maya nods and grins.

"Camp Muir straight ahead! Let's camp above it. Should make the summit push easier."

I look back. Rose's sunglasses are hanging around her neck, and her face mask is pushed down.

"Wait for me!" she calls. "I want to find a good spot for our tents."

I wait for her to catch up, her cheeks red with cold, her mouth muffled back under her mask. But even so, I can see she's looking a little tired.

"Ugggggggh . . . everything is already sore! Remind me why we do this?" she asks.

I don't answer but start moving toward the camp. "Race you!" I say, knowing she can never resist a challenge.

"No fair! You have longer legs *and* you've been standing still waiting for me." Even as she's complaining, Rose is kicking into gear, her strong legs pushing off and her arms reaching to pole through the snow.

I laugh, then laugh harder when Rose grabs on to the back of my jacket and glides along the snow, letting me pull her. We are both barely able to breathe by the time we land in a pile, but Rose is laughing, and I'm glad. Glad to be here with Rose, like always.

Chapter Five:

Rose

April 5
Kathmandu
4,600 feet above sea level

*I*t's our last day in Kathmandu. Tomorrow we pack up and leave the luxurious Hotel Shanker, leaving behind hot showers and fresh fruit that we can safely eat, saying good-bye to real pillows and a refrigerator in our room. We'll fly out to Lukla, a tiny airstrip in the mountains far from any roads, then we'll start walking, acclimatizing to the altitude as we trek through small villages and outposts until we get to Everest Base Camp. The trek itself is easy. We just walk on a dirt trail, and if it weren't for the altitude, it would only take a few days. But we have to move slowly and take rest days, helping our bodies adjust. Not that we'll ever really get used to the thin air above Base Camp. If a person were dropped on the top of Mount Everest with no acclimatization, she'd be dead in three minutes. Moving slowly and letting our bodies adjust to the reduced oxygen is our best chance at reaching the top.

We've met the two other people on our team, though *team*'s not really the right word. We're not a unit working together so much as six people who have all decided to climb Everest with the same guide. They seem fine, but it's still weird . . . I'm used to climbing with people who are pretty much family, not strangers.

Anyway, Yoon Su Rhee and Lucien "Luc" Cartier are with us now. They're both young, probably midtwenties, which is why Finjo put them with our group. Yoon Su is Korean, though she speaks English with a posh British accent. She also informed us she speaks French, Italian, German, and Mandarin. She is shorter than me and probably thirty pounds lighter, gorgeous, and completely intimidating. Luc reminds me of a Texas cowboy by way of France, with a bandana around his neck and several days of stubble. He grew up in a small ski town in the Alps but from the sound of it has made it his life's work to travel the world and climb mountains, funded by family money. He's almost as big as Tate and speaks English with a strong French accent that, embarrassingly, makes me think of nothing so much as Pepé Le Pew, the skunk from the old cartoons. He and Jordan threw down with a macho-but-friendly discussion of summits tagged, routes explored, and gnarly near misses survived. By the end of our first dinner, they had officially bonded.

Today we're heading to a Buddhist stupa, and Finjo ushers Yoon Su, Tate, and me into one taxi, following behind in another with everyone else. Soon we're rolling through the garbage and chaos of the streets, horn honking wildly. I try to pan my phone out the window, but the bumps are so bad it flies out of my hand onto the floor of the car.

"Do you think the horns work extra hard because the brakes don't work for shit?" Tate asks, bracing against the seat as we slide to the side of the car. Our driver merges into packed roundabouts by going full speed and holding his hand on the horn. We haven't been hit yet.

"Don't talk. I'm too busy trying not to panic," I say. People say climbing is scary, but it doesn't scare me. I'm in control, setting the pace. Not like in a car, where I fly around at the mercy of our driver and every other person on the road. I don't even like it when Tate drives, but this . . . This makes me wish Tate were at the wheel. "This must not be as dangerous as it seems, right?" I try to stifle a scream as we round a corner and nearly hit the stopped traffic in front of us.

Yoon Su looks up from her phone. "All the shrines along the road are for the people who die in car accidents," she states calmly, before starting to text again.

I stare at her. She flashes a fast smile, and I decide not to ask if she was kidding or not.

Soon we are at the gate of Boudhanath, one of the largest Buddhist temples in the world. It sits huge and white and domed against the deep-blue sky. Rising from the dome is a dull golden pyramid, brightly painted eyes gleaming over the edge. Strung down from the tip, thousands and thousands of colorful prayer flags flutter in the wind. It is massive, endless, timeless, beautiful.

"This was definitely worth the ride, since we survived," I say, standing still. It is quiet within the gates of the stupa, quieter than anywhere else I've been in Kathmandu. It's almost its own small city in here, with a few guest houses, restaurants, and shops tucked among the religious statues. Pilgrims and Buddhist monks walk clockwise around the massive structure, rolling the cylindrical brass prayer wheels that line the edge. All around us are buildings with pots of orange flowers and statues of Buddha.

"We start the tour?" our guide, Ram, asks, joining us. He is an official city guide, unlike Finjo, who can only guide in the mountains. Ram meets us at all the tourist sites, wearing a rakish purple scarf and smoking constantly.

Before we can answer him, he starts speaking. "I can tell you all about it. This is the largest stupa in Nepal, sacred to Tibetans and Buddhists. There are over five hundred prayer wheels, all engraved with the mantra *om mani padme hum*, which means 'the jewel in the heart of the lotus.' It is also one of the most ancient—"

Yoon Su makes a dismissive sound and interrupts his monologue. "First we will look around by ourselves. Then you can tell us everything when Finjo and the rest arrive." She doesn't look at me or Tate for approval, but I can't help being relieved. I want to soak it in.

Tate leans over. "Holy shit," he whispers. "She's even bossier than Finjo."

I give him the big eyes to tell him to shut up. I'm liking Yoon Su more and more. "Want to walk a bit?" I ask her. "Before the others get here?"

She nods. "Definitely. We will wander and meet back here. Can you please tell Finjo?" she tells Ram, then starts walking before he can answer.

Ram looks a little disgruntled, but he agrees.

Silently Yoon Su, Tate, and I start to circle the enormous building. There's less dust and smog here, and the noise of the city is hidden behind the walls. Mostly it is the quiet murmur of prayers and the slow footsteps of pilgrims.

I jump a little when Yoon Su speaks. "How are you feeling about the expedition?" she asks. "Are you ready?"

Tate glances at me, shrugging, but I nod. "Definitely! We've been planning this since we were in fourth grade. In fact . . ." I pause, pulling out my phone. "Time to capture this for posterity!" I take a photo of the stupa, then a selfie with prayer wheels behind me.

"How did you decide to summit Everest?" Yoon Su asks. "It is an unusual goal, even today, when so many are crowding the mountain."

I tense a little. The full truth about this trip is more complicated than I want to get into. I settle for the easy version. "We had been climbing for a while, with my mom and Tate's dad. First in California, where we're from, but then in Europe and South America. We were still pretty young when we decided to train for Mount Everest. And here we are."

I leave out all the stuff in between. The endless fundraising and the ongoing, grueling training. I leave out Dad's worries and Mami's reassurance that we would be fine. I leave out Mami and our arguments over whether I was training hard enough. I leave out her pointed silences when I struggled on a climb, which felt louder than an I-told-you-so, and my grudging return to the training schedule.

I glance at Tate, wondering if he'll have more to add to my abbreviated version. He catches my eye.

"We've been dreaming about this for a long time," he says. "It's Mount Everest! Is there any climber in the world who doesn't want to bag this one?" He smiles but it looks forced, and I wonder if he too is thinking about Mami and her plans. "What about you?"

Yoon Su flashes her quick grin again. "I read about this mountain when I was a little girl, in boarding school in Switzerland, and decided that someday I would be one of the few who climb it. In Switzerland it was easy to train because climbing was so common. At home hiking is very popular, but climbing Mount Everest? That's harder for people to understand. And a woman climbing? That can be even more difficult to explain."

She and I share a look. I've spent enough time on high peaks where bro dudes act like I'm there to hand them their beers and laugh at their jokes to guess at what she's not saying. And that's not even getting into the everyday harassment and sexism on the streets in towns where we travel. I'm white-passing, but Mami, who's Puerto Rican, would get additional attitude: in places where the lodge workers were Latinx or even just dark-skinned, other climbers would often assume she worked there. She never complained about it, but I always felt a weird kind of guilt, like I was getting away with something I didn't deserve.

I wonder about Yoon Su. As an Asian woman, she probably has another level of crap to deal with. I wonder what it will be like for her, and me, on the trail up to Everest. So far though, Nepal has been refreshingly uninterested in me as female. If anything, people are excited that another woman wants to summit, since so far only around five hundred of the total five thousand people who have made it up Everest have been women. We have some catching up to do. As though reading my mind, Yoon Su says, "I have heard good things about climbing in Nepal. At least here I hope not to be called 'China doll' or told I can't possibly know how to use the gear I'm carrying." She sighs, then changes the subject. "Jordan is Tate's father, yes? So where is your mother?"

I swallow, trying to make the story easy to tell, easy to hear. Tell it like it was history, over and done, not something that still roils, digs, hurts.

"She has some health issues and couldn't come." I leave it at that.

Yoon Su looks at me. "Ah. I am sorry to hear that."

No need to talk about the bad days. No need to talk about the pain. No need to talk about the end of Everest. But not for me. Not for the rest of us, because Mami would never *ever* be the one who took it away from us. No matter if I used to complain about the training, I definitely want it now, want to succeed twice as much, for Mami, for me. The Dread bites at me, and I push it back, think about the summit, think about what it will mean to be there, to share it with her. Yoon Su is still looking at me, her face pitying, and I need to stop talking about this. Pulling out my phone, I start filming, moving slowly in a circle and narrating some of the facts Ram told us about the site.

Tate's hand lands on my shoulder, fast and heavy, squeezes a little. Then he asks Yoon Su about some technological advance in high-altitude gear. She answers quickly, and I'm relieved. The Dread retreats back as I finish up my video by blowing kisses into the phone, then tuck it back into my pocket. I look up at the burning whiteness of the temple, prayer flags flapping wildly, and breathe deeply, in and out.

Yoon Su turns back to me. "It's nice to be out of the smog. Nice to breathe."

"Seriously," I say, and something in my voice makes Tate look over.

"Oxygen. You're going to miss it, huh?" he says. Altitude never bothers him the way it bothers me, although of course we've never been near the death zone—above 26,000 feet. And now it's right around the corner.

I don't want to sound scared in front of Yoon Su, but the fact is I'm not psyched about it. "Yeah. Well . . . Thin air isn't my favorite, you know. I'm a little freaked, actually."

"I'm sure you will be fine," Yoon Su says, so firmly that I almost believe her. "There will be plenty of bottled oxygen, and the guides, well, that is their job. To help us."

"And worse comes to worst, you know, if you're feeling bad, I'll carry you. No problem," Tate says, grinning his wild this-is-supposed-to-be-fun smile. "See? Easy!"

Before I can move, he jumps in front of me and pulls my arms over his shoulders, yanking me off the ground and into piggyback position. I yelp and laugh, trying desperately to hang on.

"Are you eating rocks again, Keller? Jeez, when did you last weigh yourself?" he groans, lurching back and forth. He staggers and nearly runs right into a group of monks.

Three young guys with shaved heads and dark-maroon robes move carefully out of our way. I try to apologize, but I can't stop laughing. They smile in return.

"Tate! Cut it out. NOW." It's Jordan, who has caught up just in time to see our near religious collision.

"Hey!" Tate protests, setting me gently on the ground. "You could say, 'We're here.' No need for such aggression."

Luc laughs. "He cannot help himself! Who can, when it comes to a beautiful woman?"

My cheeks burn hot and red. I ignore Luc and try to pull myself together. Finjo, Paul, Luc, and Jordan are all here, along with Ram, the city guide. I hope we didn't look like total idiots.

Jordan's talking about respect and religious monuments,

and I know he's right, but I'm still grateful, as always, that Tate made me laugh before I cried. Even if we did almost knock over a monk.

But that's Tate. Brightness and fun and energy and happiness and always more and more and more, until the thunderheads break through and that hyper energy turns from hilarity to anger. Though most of the thunder-and-lightning anger ended in middle school. Now it's more likely to be the endless daydreaming, the late-to-everything, the Tate-would-do-better-if-he-only-applied-himself fights.

Finally, Jordan winds down, and we keep walking. Next to me Tate is coiled and angry. Ram walks behind us, spouting facts about the prayer wheels, the monks, the burning incense that sticks out of holders in the stones. I reach out and grab Tate's hand.

"You okay?" I ask.

"Spectacular." He spits the word out.

"Hey. Don't think about Jordan. Think about the climb. Tomorrow! We're finally off into the mountains! That's something, right?"

"Right. Endless acclimatization climbs, frigid wind-blasted tents, no oxygen, frostbite and hypothermia . . . It sounds super," he says.

I pause. He's not wrong, obviously. Climbing Mount Everest is going to be the most brutal thing we'll probably ever put our bodies through. But even so . . . He's always been the one who loves this stuff. He never complains.

"Hey," I start, but I'm not sure what to say. A slow ooze of unease spreads through me. Tate Angry equals Rose Unplugged.

He looks at me and gives a turning-on-the-light smile, all crinkled, brown eyes and white teeth and gleam. "KIDDING.

Kidding, of course. Of course I'm pumped! This is the big moment!" He gives a quick glance over his shoulder, then whispers, in a perfect imitation of Luc's accent, "*Zis ees ҳe moment ҳat separates ҳe boys from ҳe men!*"

I close my eyes for a second, relieved. Battery-Powered Rose, powered by Endlessly Energized Tate. The adventure of a lifetime, unfolding ahead of us. As it all should be.

Chapter Six:

Tate

(Four Months Earlier) January 6
Camp Muir, Mount Rainier
10,200 feet above sea level

*I*t's go time: time to stow all our gear in the total darkness, get our boots back on, jam some food down our throats, and start to climb. It's also 2:00 a.m., which isn't ideal, but still. The sky's totally black, lit only by the quarter moon and the absolutely wild splash of stars. It's beautiful. The snow gleams bright white in the moonlight, and farther down the slope, a few tents show signs of life as other climbers start their preparations. Like Maya planned, we're slightly above them, giving us a better position to push for the summit.

I've been awake for hours. There are times when I seriously hate these tents, these stupid, shitty, claustrophobic tents.

My eyes burn like I've been surfing, but there's no sun or sand or salt here, just exhaustion and darkness and a fierce wind that rips at my skin. I pull at my laces and snarl as they refuse to give up their knots.

"Here, want me to do it?" Rose is by my shoulder, already zipped and buckled and pulled together. Of course.

"I'm fine," I mutter.

"I know you're fine, but do you want a hand? We should be moving in ten—"

"Dammit, I can do it!" My voice is louder than I mean it to be. Immediately the hot itch of frustration—with my laces, with Rose for being ready, with my shitty night's sleep—mixes with a wave of embarrassment that only makes it worse.

"Okay." She smiles, a real Rose smile, to let me know she's not mad. "Come get me when you're ready." She walks away, disappearing almost immediately in the darkness.

I sigh, and some of the anger drains away. It's only a stupid bootlace. I take another deep breath, or whatever passes for a deep breath at 10,000 feet. The edginess fades more, and I'm grateful, for the millionth time, that I have a best friend who knows not to bark back at me when I'm being an asshole. It's fine. I'm fine. This is where I want to be. Another deep breath, and I go.

The darkness presses in on all sides as we stand in our tiny group. Our tents and gear are packed up for us to pick up on the way down; looking back there's no sign we were ever here.

"Ready!" I say, and I make my voice sound energized. "Sorry for being a ferret, Rosie."

Rose gives me the thumbs-up. "Apology accepted. I know the feeling. Two a.m. is a great time to be home, sound asleep in my awesome bed."

Maya sighs. "Enough with the martyrdom, Rosie."

"The journey is the reward. Yah, I know. Got it." Rose's voice is clipped and pissy, and I roll my eyes. Obviously I'm Team Rose, but sometimes she still acts like a sullen eleven-year-old around Maya, and it's getting old. "Let's get this party started, okay, boss?" I say and start walking.

Rose follows, and we head up, headlamps bobbing in the darkness. Four thousand two hundred feet above us is the summit. Crampons crunching into the hard snow, we begin to climb. It's quiet except for the stomp of our boots and the heavy sound of my breath in my ears. I slept with my iPod in my sleeping bag to keep the battery alive, and now I turn it on, letting the music amp me up for this climb. Loud guitar chords blast into my ears, drowning out all other sounds. I try to forget Rose's crankiness, Maya's frustration, and Dad's nagging and let my body take over.

In the darkness I can barely tell white snow from dark rock, but even so, the movements are automatic. The tread of Rose's footsteps in front of me marks our time. I pull out my earbuds and tuck them into my collar, and there's only the scream of the headwinds and the blackness of a mountain sky above us.

We stomp along the glacier until we get to the ledges that give our route, Gibraltar Ledges, its name. The giant Gibraltar Rock looms over our shoulders on the right, and the darkness of the rocky ledge drops down on the left. Dawn's barely beginning. This is the technical part, requiring ropes and real climbing, and the adrenaline starts to thrum as I contemplate the route. Rose and I stop to add extra layers to protect us from the winds that will try to rip us off the mountain as soon as we round the edge. We tie ourselves together, leaving plenty of slack rope, then double-check our ice axes, extra line, and helmets before starting up. Dad and Maya are still behind us. Maya must be feeling like crap because they're moving slower than ever.

"You ready?" Rose asks, her voice muffled beneath her mask. "We'll head up until Camp Comfort, which, if I remember, is the most poorly named spot on the mountain, then take a break. Okay?"

I nod, glad I can't see her face beneath her goggles, helmet, and mask. I know from her voice she's still in a shitty mood, and I can feel myself tense up in response, can feel my jaw working and my neck tightening against my shoulders. I try to roll my neck, make myself smile to see if, as Dr. Jimmy always says, smiling actually changes your mood. Shaking my arms and legs to warm them, I start up after Rose.

After a few minutes I stop, my body held tight against the rock. "Rosie. Check out the view." I can't pull my eyes away.

The sunrise, crazy beautiful, is blazing hot orange and pink and red, striping the sky and glinting off the far-distant ocean.

"It's gorgeous." She smiles and shakes her head. "Ridiculously gorgeous."

I bat her with my mitten. "Right? Worth the trip?"

She rolls her eyes but nods. "Yes, Mom, it's always worth the trip! That's why I'm here instead of in my delicious bed. Anyway, we should keep moving. Lots of cautionary tales about rockfall and seracs crashing down on this chute." She starts to climb again.

I follow, and soon we're alternating between steep, hard-packed snow pitches and small level stretches that give us a chance to catch our breath. Dad and Maya eventually catch up to us as we rest at Camp Comfort, which is comfortably out of the wind but still icy and miserable. Displaying my usual expertise and skill, I drop my mitten trying to get a cough drop.

"Tate, for God's sake," Dad says, his voice tired, like it's too much work even to yell at me.

"It's fine! It caught on the lip of that serac, so you're in luck," Maya says, trying to be cheerful, as always.

I resist the urge to tell her how lucky I feel and start down the snow to reclaim my mitten. While I'm walking, a gust of wind knocks my helmet off the spot where I parked it and sends it hurtling down toward me.

"Oops! Better grab that while you're there," Rose calls. "Anything else you want me to drop, so you don't have to make a separate trip?"

I give her the finger with my mitten-less hand and retrieve all my gear. "Sure, sure," I say, huffing my way back up to them. "Make fun of the loser. Typical."

Rose shoves me, and I shove her back, while Maya looks at the view and Dad looks disgusted. Time to go.

"Okay, Captain. Let's tag this bad boy and get down. I'm hungry," I say, and Rose agrees.

Waving to the others, who are still fixing crampons and dicking around with their ice axes, we start to climb.

Shoving the earbuds back into my ears, I start up behind Rose. She's a splash of yellow high above me already, but I'll catch up quickly. I've got almost six inches of reach on her, so she never stays far ahead for long. I adjust my ice axe and dig my right crampon into the crusty snow, pushing off. Crunch, shove, crunch, shove, crunch . . . The snow shifts between crunchy and soft, making it hard to know how much pressure to use. Twice my foot slides loose, but I catch it before I shift my weight. Soon all that's in my brain is the smash and thrash of the music in my ears and the pause, step, pause, step of my feet. Up ahead the spot of yellow stops as Rosie waits for me on the edge of the glacier. The wind's unbelievable, howling and screaming around us. I give up on the music again and rip the earbuds out. The iPod will be dead before I get back anywhere that I can hear it.

"How's it looking?" I ask when I'm close enough to shout in her ear.

She shrugs. "Not great. We're going to need to tap dance through this crud. That warm week really screwed with the glacier."

She's right, as usual. Even from here I can see the crevasses, some two or three feet across, some only a few jagged inches, all standing between us and the finish line. I nod, resigned. I hate this part, when there's no vertical, just these little old-lady steps and stopping to check the integrity of the ice every few seconds. It's barely climbing. Give me a chute any day. Still, it's my job to look on the bright side. "Sure, but a little more of this and we'll be at the summit crater. And from there . . . the summit!" I throw my arms up like a champion, and she laughs.

We push forward slowly, and the impatience moves through me like an itch. Jimmy always tries to get me to notice how my body's turning on me, siding with my ADHD brain, by making me take short breaths or hunch my shoulders or clench my fists. He's all into yoga breathing and stuff, which does kind of help, although I laughed my ass off the first time he lay down on the floor and told me to try belly-breathing. Anyway, I try it now, or at least as much as I can at 13,000 feet.

Doesn't work.

My footsteps get faster, and sure, they're probably too fast for this crap we're skating on, but I need to get off of this, need to get somewhere where I can climb, or stop, or anything but this. Moving faster still, I glance up for a second to see how far ahead Rose is.

I take one more step without looking down.

Chapter Seven:

Rose

April 6
Lukla, Nepal
9,380 feet above sea level

"Did you know this airstrip was on the Discovery Channel's special on the world's deadliest places to fly into? It was number one." My voice sounds weird, even to me. "The landing strip actually runs uphill to help the planes cut their speed, but it stops right against the mountain. I guess takeoff is the worst, right? I mean, thinking statistically—"

"Rose. Shut the fuck up. Please. I've never puked on a plane, and I would really like to keep my record." Tate doesn't look at me.

The Soviet-era plane, which only seats around sixteen people and gives a definite impression of age—with duct-taped upholstery and a ripped, sagging ceiling—is bouncing badly. Making things worse—much worse—is that out one side of the plane, the mountains are reallyreallyreally close. Like, reach out and touch them close.

Next to me, Tate squeezes his eyes shut.

"You okay? You never get sick. Are you—"

"PLEASE!" His voice comes out kind of as a yelp.

I shut up and place a mint in his hand, which he puts in his mouth without opening his eyes.

"Sorry. That helped," he says finally.

"You're doing better than those two," I say, gesturing toward the back of the plane, where two New Zealand women, trekkers who are going to some monastery, are wailing and shrieking.

"At least Luc stopped yelling 'Ahhhhh *merdemerdemerde!*' a few minutes ago," I say. Luc had been ridiculously excited about the whole roller-coaster effect.

Tate sighs, dropping his head on my shoulder. "I'm going to be really happy to get off this plane."

But when we finally land, staggering off the plane onto the cracked concrete, he doesn't look much better. I feel fine as soon as my feet are on the ground. We are only at 9,000 feet, barely an altitude gain by Himalayas standards, and we're officially in the mountains. Peaks surround us on three sides, glorious and huge, sending long shadows over the tiny airport. As with every climb, the bureaucracy takes forever, and we're ushered inside while Finjo and the other guides deal with five hundred pages of permits and paperwork. Tate slumps on a bench.

"I'm fine," he says, anticipating my question. "Just glad to be off that stupid plane. And ready for a nap."

I hand him my water, and he gulps it down while I stare around me. Finjo and his minions are all huddled in a corner. In fact, now that I look up, every single Nepali and a few Western guides are in that corner too.

"What's going on?" I poke Tate, who is leaning against me while I tickle his arm.

"Mmmmm?"

"Wake up. Seriously. Do you think something's wrong? What if the permits aren't ready? Doesn't that happen sometimes?"

Jordan, who also looks a little pale from the flight, stands up. "I'm sure the permits are fine, Rosie. Let's not assume the worst. I'll see what I can find out."

I stare around at the tiny room. "Not much of an airport, is it? I want a Starbucks."

Paul looks up from his book. "Actually, there's apparently a fake one, right here in Lukla! I read about it in the guidebook."

We are laughing over the response I would get if I ordered a grande no-foam skim mocha latte when Jordan's voice breaks through the room.

"Jesus Christ! How bad is it?"

Everyone turns to stare. I am halfway across the room, Tate right behind me, when Paul calls us back.

"But—," I start.

"Wait. Let's hold tight," he says, and maybe it's his professional therapist voice, but we all do what he says.

Voices buzz like swarms of wasps, rising to high pitches and dropping again, but I can't understand any of it. My stomach twists, and the Dread shows up, hungry. Could there be news from home? Were there messages waiting for us?

Finally, Finjo and Jordan walk over. With them are Dawa, Asha, and Bishal, three of the other Sherpas who'll be guiding us up the mountain. No one is smiling, not even Finjo, whose Cheshire Cat grin is his most constant feature.

"So." Finjo rocks back on his heels, looking around. "There has been a very bad accident. A tragedy. The Icefall Doctors—the group of Sherpas who set all the fixed ropes up the route to the summit before we arrive—they have encountered an avalanche."

He pauses, and no one says anything. No one wants to ask the question.

"There are two confirmed dead, several more still missing," he continues finally.

"Oh no." On cue, my eyes fill. I swipe at them, frustrated. I have what Tate nicely calls overactive tear ducts, welling up at Christmas specials, musical numbers sung by children, and weddings of complete strangers. But this time it's real. This time my tears don't count enough.

Finjo nods. "Those whose bodies can be found are being brought down now for cremation and funeral. And the search effort is still ongoing. It is a very hard thing, a very sad thing."

No one speaks, and there is no sound except for my sniffling. I bite the inside of my mouth, hard.

Finally Yoon Su speaks. "This is a terrible tragedy. I'm so very sorry to hear of these deaths, and I will pray for them." She pauses. "But now I have to ask. Is there reason for us to reconsider our expedition? This is a very inauspicious beginning."

I feel Tate twitch against my shoulder and put a hand on his arm. I know without him saying anything what he's thinking; it's blazing bright in his eyes. People died. How can it be about us? But I can't pretend to be shocked. Climbing Everest requires big stakes, big money, and a very short window of time to reach the summit. It doesn't stop for any-thing.

Finjo nods like she's asked a reasonable question. "You are correct to ask. But as you know, we will take almost two weeks to acclimatize as we trek up to Base Camp, and even more time will pass before we are on the fixed lines. The Icefall Doctors will continue their work—"

"Once they find the rest of the bodies, I guess," Tate mutters. I can feel him vibrating with something—rage or sadness—against me.

Finjo continues as though he hasn't heard. "And by the time we need them, the fixed ropes will be perfect. This tragedy, it was an accident of nature. There was no wrong-doing, no way to know. The storm that arrived, it was not expected."

"But there will be all kinds of accurate weather-forecasting technology up there when we arrive, *n'est-ce pas?*" Luc says, speaking for the first time. "God rest the souls of those men, but when our asses are hanging on those ropes— *excusez-moi, Rose et Yoon Su*—I hope you will have only the best weather tools."

Tate pushes past me and runs out the door to the airstrip. Falling to his knees, he throws up in the dirt.

• • •

Inside, everyone's discussing the news. There are delays, of course. Two of the guides, Dawa and Mingma, turn out to be cousins with one of the Sherpas killed on the moun-tain. Also, the funerals are being held tomorrow in the village that we're supposed to get to the following day, so there will be no rooms for us. I walk to find Tate crouched over, swigging water from his bottle and spitting into the bushes.

"You okay?" I ask, trying to keep my voice steady.

He shrugs. "Fine. Queasy from the flight, I guess." He stands up, stretching and wincing. Around us, the village of Lukla is going about its business: more flights with trekkers and climbers arriving, Nepalis lining up against the fence, offering their services as porters and guides. Overhead a massive bird wheels and dips against the almost navy-blue sky. It is post card–beautiful, with jagged mountains in the background and picturesque prayer wheels along the trail in front of us.

"Yeah. It was pretty bad," I say, but I don't know if I'm talking about the flight or the accident.

Tate turns to look at me. "You okay? I mean, with all the . . ." He pauses. "Death? Jesus. That sounds grim."

I make myself nod, quick and sure. "Yeah. Of course. You know me. Waterworks. It's sad, that's all." Despite my best efforts, my eyes fill back up. "Sorry. God, I'm ridiculous." I wipe at my face.

"Rose," Tate says, pulling my hand down. "A bunch of people just died. Dawa and Mingma lost their cousin. It's not ridiculous to cry when you hear that these poor bastards, who are paid fuck-all to do the hardest and most dangerous job on the mountain, lost their lives so we can have an adventure."

It feels like he slapped me. Heat floods my face, and I pull back. "Is that . . . Do you think we're selfish? Like we have no right to be here? Because my mom spent a ton of time making sure she found a Nepali-owned expedition, one that pays fair wages and offers women equal opportun—"

Tate puts his hands up. "Stop! Rose, I'm sorry. You're not

selfish. And Maya's probably the best person I know. I didn't mean that. It's really fucking sad, that's all."

I sigh, long and deep, and lean against him. "Yeah. It is."

He bends down toward me. "Here. You've got a big smudge of dirt. Right . . . here." He reaches forward and presses his fingers against my cheekbone. His hand is gentle and cool on my hot cheek.

Why is he still touching my face?

And why am I blushing?

"I should take some photos of the airstrip. For my mom," I say, but I don't move.

"Tate! Rose!" Jordan calls from the doorway. "Come on back. We're going to head out to a lodge around ten minutes down the trail. We'll stay there tonight and figure out the rest of the delay from there." He turns and walks back in.

Tate drops his hand like he's been burned, but he doesn't move away.

I close my eyes, then open them again. He's still right there. "Well. We'd better . . . I mean, risk is part of the mountains, you know? This is part of the deal."

Tate blinks and nods. "Sure. That's the price of climbing big peaks. People die. Though I don't know, Rose. I don't know. Like, that sounds simple, I guess, but did the sisters and kids and parents of those poor fuckers agree to that price?"

Before I can say anything, he shakes his head a little and holds out his arm, like he's going to escort me back in. "Never mind. I'm being . . . whatever. You ready?"

I stare at him for a second, trying to see if he's okay. If I'm okay.

But, finally, I take his arm. "I was born ready," I say, and he laughs, just as I planned.

"You screw that up every time, Keller. You got to say it with more growl in your voice: 'I was *born* ready!' Go on, try it again."

I hip-bump him, and he shoves me as we walk inside, and we both pretend to forget what happened high above us in the mountains.

Chapter Eight:

Tate

(Four Months Earlier) January 6
Gibraltar Rock, Mount Rainier
12,660 feet above sea level

FearFastFallingFUCKFUCKFUCK

SILENCE.

Then Rose, screaming. "TATE? TATE, ANSWER ME, DAMMIT! TATE, PLEASE ANSWER!" But it's faint, so faint-and-faraway.

I answer. I swear I do. But she keeps screaming. So maybe I don't.

I try again.

And again.

somuchpainowowowowowowowowow

I work sososohard to make words. To keep Rose from screaming like she's in pain. Rose can't hurt like that. So . . . words. I push my head against the ice, and the cold brings me back to myself, just enough for the horror to wrap around my throat.

Panic.

Words for Rose.

"Rosie, I fell. I, uh." More ice on my face. Wake up, Tate. "I think I broke my arm. Arms?"

She hears me, and her voice is closebutnotcloseenough.

"GOD! Okay, that's okay. But . . . Do you know why the rope's slack?"

I want to close my eyes, but Rose asked a question. Rose needs an answer. I try. Like school. ConcentrateTate!Focus!

"My ice axes. On my belt. They both caught on the edges of the crevasse, and I'm . . . kind of . . . hanging here."

Rose gasps, and she's soclosesoclose that I can picture her face except that she's not close, not really. She says, "Wow! That's . . . that's lucky."

I'm not moving, I don't think, but maybe I am, because her voice is farther now, and I know I can't reach her. "Funny, I don't feel that lucky . . . " I let my eyes close, which is goodsogood.

I can hear them above me, but I'm gone, not-here-not-there-not-anywhere.

"We'll have to go down and get him."

"I'm the lightest."

"Are you sure the rope is strong enough?"

"Let's get him up! NOW!"

Then I hear Rose, closer and louder, and I try to wake up. "Hey, Tate, I'm coming down to get you, and by the way, remember when I told you that someone on the track team said she'd totally have sex with you, and I refused to tell you who? Well, maybe, if you're awake, I'll tell you!"

She keeps talkingtalkingtalking about the hottest-seniors lists on the bathroom wall and a girl named Anya, and I want to answer, want to laugh with Rose, but I can't.

There's a horrible groaning sound echoing around me. And I realize it's me.

Then someone kicks me in the head.

FUCK.

That definitely wakes me up.

"Jesus Christ! I've already fallen. Do you have to kick my head in?"

And there's Rose, bravest of the brave, with blood and tears washing down her face like rain while she thumps and shoves and—owowowowowowowow—positions me behind her, tries to wrap my arms around her neck, but I scream somuchpainowowow, and she works the ropes, tying the knots we've both known by heart since we were kids.

I want to help, but every movement is black-and-gold blasts of pain, and I can't, I can't, I—

A massive lurch that sends pain sparking through me, and we start to ascend, and I want to say thank you, but I can't, I . . .

• • •

So much noise. It's bizarre how loud it is, people screaming and shouting, doors slamming, sirens drilling into my head. I want to tell everyone to shut the fuck up, that they need to be quiet, but as I open my mouth, a wall of pain and nausea slams into me. I throw up, and the pain feels like fire. Softly, so much quieter than anything else, I hear Rose's voice whisper my name. Then it's black again.

• • •

The next time I wake up can't be much later, because all I smell is puke. It's almost enough to make me hurl again, but

I breathe through my mouth and try not to think about it. I'm not moving anymore; I'm strapped to a dolly—no, not that but the other wheelie thing they use in hospitals. And I seem to be parked in a hallway. I can't move my head, and for a second I panic, the nausea rolling back over me, and my body jerks.

I hear Mom now. Most of the noise is quieter, but she is screaming. Screaming at Dad. The words fade in and out.

"What do you think will happen if you keep pushing him up these mountains?" she shrieks. "Are you waiting for him to die?"

"*Pushing him?* It's all he wants to do! It's the only thing he feels good about, Sarah. What am I supposed to do, tell him to quit?"

I want to tell her no, that it's not Dad's fault. But all I can do is moan.

Rose's hand touches mine.

"You're okay. You're going to be okay," she whispers.

I stare straight up at the ceiling, dirty and pockmarked. "I can't move," I say, and even the words hurt, but now the hurt is blurred, faded. The panic's faded too. My eyes are shutting, the ceiling farther away. I can hear Dad, his voice low and angry, but it's fainter now.

"The doctors put a neck brace on you. And . . . and some other things. That's why. You're safe now. You're—"

"Stay," I tell her. The wheelie thing's disappearing too, and I'm floating, just my body, in the air. It somehow seems important to tell her this before I'm totally gone. "Stay."

Her hand's on top of mine, keeping me from floating off completely. "I'm right here," she says. Her voice is strong. "I'm not going anywhere."

• • •

When I finally wake up for real, I hurt so much I almost laugh. It seems like a fucking joke, like a cartoon where the Coyote gets run over chasing the Road Runner, then peels himself off the highway.

Dad's sitting in the chair opposite the bed, his head back, snoring. At this I really do laugh, but it turns into a moan.

"You're up."

I whip my head around to the voice, which was a shitty idea. Pain shoots up my neck and into my forehead so hard I literally see stars. I close my eyes for a second, trying hard not to puke again.

"Rose? What . . . ?" It's as far as I get. God. I'm so tired. I worry for a second that I'll fall back asleep before she answers. I go to pinch myself, a longtime trick to try and keep myself focused, but both my hands and arms are wrapped like mummies.

She sighs, and I see her, really see her, for the first time. She's got big, black Frankenstein's-monster-style stitches on her hairline and a bruise on her cheekbone. Her eyes are so bloodshot that they're a bright, scary blue, and her hair's a wild, frizzy mess. She looks so tired and worn out. I've never seen her like this. It scares me. One of the machines I'm hooked up to beeps as my heart starts to race.

"What?" I ask. "What's going on?"

She leans forward, her face even more worried. "It's okay, Tate. Your arms will be—"

I cut her off. "Not me, you. Why do you look like that?"

She reaches her hand up to touch her stitches, then winces. "Oh. Seriously, it's barely anything. I bumped it against the ice. That's all, but it wouldn't stop bleeding, so the paramedic had to sew it in the ambulance." She tries to smooth her face out, but it still doesn't look like her.

"What happened?" I ask.

"You . . . It was a crevasse. We were moving fast, and . . ." She trails off. "But your ice axes caught on the sides, and we were able to get you out. Amazingly, you only have one bad break. Everything else, well, the doctors will tell you, but you're mostly bruised and sprained. The rescue guys said you were the luckiest they'd ever seen. They're going to set your arm in a little while, so you need to rest now."

"What else? What's wrong?" She looks . . . undone. I scrabble, trying to sit up, but the pain hits, and I gasp.

"Nothing. My mom's feeling crappy again, but that's because we had to rush to get down. I swear, I'm fine."

There's a sound in the corner, and I turn my head, carefully this time, to see Dad looking at us. If Rose looks old and worn, he looks like the undead. He hasn't shaved, and I'd never noticed how gray his beard has gotten. He looks flimsy and broken.

"Dad," I say but stop. I was going to say sorry, but that seems weird. I want to ask what really happened, why I fell, what's wrong with me. But I don't. I let my eyes slide shut, seeing Rose's hand on my bandaged arm before the blackness comes back.

Chapter Nine:

Rose

April 9
Namche, Nepal
11,290 feet above sea level

I don't even know what day of the week it is; me, who loves a calendar almost as much as I love a list. It is day three on the trail, three days since we sat in a smoky lodge in Lukla and tried not to think about the bodies being cremated a day's walk away. All of our guides and porters left, rushing off to make the laborious uphill walk as fast as possible so that they could pay their respects before turning around and walking back down to meet us. Search teams found two more bodies in the Icefall, and, amazingly, two survivors. Now the funerals are over, and everyone's back to business as usual, back to the business of climbing Mount Everest.

It's horrible, and I'm ashamed, but excitement drums through me, hot and fierce and stronger than before. We are far from home, far from all the stress and Dread and worry, and I take photo after photo, sending them to Mami in the lodges when the Wi-Fi works, turning off my phone after to conserve battery. It feels great to share as many moments of this trip as possible with her, almost like she's seeing it herself. It feels great to share my excitement, so long as I don't let myself think about how frustrated she was with my lack of excitement before. It feels even better to turn my phone off and disappear, leaving Mami and her illness and my guilt far behind. I can love this for her, I remind myself. I can give her that, at least.

Every day we walk, usually only around five hours or so, acclimatizing to the altitude and soaking in the local culture. We walk by Buddhist prayer wheels and piles of mani stones, rocks painted with the now-familiar mantra *om mani padme hum*, the jewel in the heart of the lotus. And above us literally thousands of multicolored prayer flags are strung between buildings and trees and temples and flap wildly in the wind. Porters wearing flip-flops and carrying huge loads on their backs, held in place by a tumpline—a rope across their foreheads—pass us at twice our speed. We walk through crowded villages filled with young children and puppies and small storefronts selling Coke and Sprite to thirsty trekkers. We cross the Dudh Koshi, a winding turquoise river, on high suspension bridges that dip and sway as we walk across them. We move to the side of the trail as dozens of donkeys with bells and headdresses and massive loads push past us on their way to deliver goods to the villages above. The landscape changes from lush green terraced fields and flowering bushes to drier, browner land with a few wind-twisted trees.

It is surreal to be here. I've seen photos of these villages, seen documentaries about everyone from Tenzing Norgay to

Sir Edmund Hillary, the first guys to summit Mount Everest in the fifties, to today's top climbers, all standing in the same places I'm standing. Almost everything from home has been dismissed, erased like it never mattered. Gone is homework, worrying about my GPA, trying to remember to put gas in the car—even the frustrating exercise of refreshing my inbox to see if I've moved off the waitlist at Yale. I've left everything but Tate. He alone is my anchor, laughing over remember-whens, wondering if our friends Will and Gus ever hooked up, pondering scenarios where Ronan had finally made his move on Chessa. I am breathless from laughter. Laughter plus altitude equals burning lungs, but I don't care.

• • •

Today we arrive in Namche Bazaar, the largest Sherpa village in the region, complete with an Irish pub, Italian coffee, and internet—all at 10,000 feet and many days' walk away from any roads. Everything here is brought up by porters and donkeys, a fact that makes the occasional expensive glass bottle of Sprite feel more than a little guilt-inducing. We will stay here for two days to acclimatize before going higher. It feels good to settle in.

"Well, this is pretty much the nicest place I've seen since the Shenker," Tate says, dropping his pack in our room. The room, like the others we've stayed in on the trek, is basic: plywood walls, two twin platform beds, a shelf by the window, and a row of hooks. But it's large and well-built, with huge windows that open up to a ridiculously gorgeous mountain panorama.

I sit on one of the beds. "Ooh, this is good," I say. "The mattress is actually more than a few inches thick." Lying down, I stretch long and hard, twisting my back this way and that to release the tension from the day's walk. Namche is bowl-shaped, and our lodge is at the tip-top rim of the bowl. We thought we'd arrived thirty minutes earlier, and the endlessly ongoing walk up the dozens and dozens of stone stairs through the bustling village has nearly worn me out. I try not to think about the altitude waiting for me. I lie back, waiting until the blood stops pounding in my skull.

I look over at Tate, who is lying facedown on his own bed. "I heard there are solar showers here. Which is good. Because I stink like whoa, and if I can smell me, I can't imagine what you're smelling."

Wrinkling my nose, I turn toward my armpit and sniff. Ugh. Definitely not the right choice. Baby wipes and deodorant only go so far.

"Showers sound good," he mumbles, facedown. "But so does napping."

I don't expect to be this tired, this soon. A tiny sliver of fear darts through me. Like a mantra, I run through the mountains we've climbed to train: Rainier, Denali, Aconcagua. We can do this. I can do this. I can do this for me and Mami. I am strong enough.

A knock on the door sends me flying. Apparently, I fell asleep, boots still dangling over the edge of the bed. Tate's out cold.

"Yeah?" I call, moving upright. "It's open."

Silence, then the door opens a crack. "Hello? I don't want to interrupt . . . " It's Yoon Su.

I open the door wider. "You're fine. I'm up and Tate's out. We'd have to work harder than this to wake him. Come on in."

From his face-plant position, Tate mumbles, "Notasleep-I'mtotallyawake. Don'tgotalkingaboutme."

I look at Yoon Su. "Whatever. What's up?"

She glances over at Tate and smiles her fast smile again. "Luc and I are walking back down to the village. He wants to see the sights, and I will buy a few supplies. Namche is the best-stocked spot until we are back in Kathmandu. If you want anything—from post cards to chocolate bars— now is the time."

I groan a little. Those stone steps, waiting for me. But I do want to get a few things. "Sure. Sounds good," I say, trying to sound less pathetic. Yoon Su has moved fast up the trail every day, often ahead of our porters. She's the first to finish our tea breaks on the trail, first to jump up and start walking again, as though she can push us to Base Camp by the sheer force of her will. I'm not used to lagging behind.

"Bring me a Snickers," Tate mutters. Then adds, "Please."

I roll my eyes at Yoon Su. "His mama raised him right, but he's still lazy," I say, grabbing my down vest. It is warm, hot even, in the late afternoon sun, but I've learned the hard way that as soon as the sun goes down, it will be freezing.

We clomp out of the lodge, meeting Luc by the door. Luc has been insistently friendly since we left Kathmandu. Like me, he's clearly delighted to be here, and his booming "*Salut demoiselles!*" to me and Yoon Su makes me smile.

"Getting to walk with not one but two beautiful women—if only ze men back home could see me now," he says, trying to put an arm around each of our shoulders.

I shrug him off without saying anything, but Yoon Su stops and puts her hands on her hips, facing him. "We are not here for decoration!" She gives a little hiss of annoyance. "Honestly! Would you say this to Tate, who is also lovely to look at?"

I grin at the expression on Luc's face. He's so bug-eyed it's almost funny.

"But he is a *man*!"

"And I am a woman! And a climber! So. Think of us as you think of Tate or Jordan or Paul. As climbers. Okay?" She starts to walk again, and after a second Luc scrambles after her.

I follow, vowing to buy Yoon Su all the chocolate bars I can afford.

As we walk down, Luc bounces back from Yoon Su's comments. He seems less sophisticated as he points out the bakeries, espresso bars, and other wonders of Namche, reminding me of a big shaggy dog—all enthusiasm and energy. When he darts off to buy post cards, Yoon Su and I wait in the sunshine, watching the path fill up with tourists, porters, climbers, and the occasional donkey. It's warm and friendly and full of everyday life.

The Sherpas are an ethnic group who have lived in the high Himalayas of Nepal for centuries. Like in some of the other places we've climbed around the world, the people who live here are very poor, though the money that flows in from tourists and climbers helps add to the subsistence farms and tiny trade outposts. Sometimes in our travels, that wealth gap leads to uncomfortably aggressive tip grubbing and sales pitches, but not here. So far the Sherpa guides and villagers we meet are more like gracious hosts, sharing their gorgeous countryside. Even so, the whiplash from seeing trekkers with a few thousand dollars' worth of gear staying at lodges where the owners average a yearly income of $1,000 is deeply uncomfortable. It's a part of traveling I never get used to, mostly because I have no idea what to do about it. Isn't it better if we come and spend some money? Maybe I'm just making excuses.

It is glorious here. Hard to imagine that if we didn't have

to move slowly for acclimatization, we would be at Base Camp in a few days. I turn to Yoon Su. "I can't believe how close we are. It doesn't seem real."

She smiles, and this time her smile lasts, spreading over her face, like she's finally given it permission to stick around. "Oh, it is very real! It is a lifelong dream, being here. But for me, being so close to a dream is a serious thing. The celebration will wait until I come down."

I nod. I know what she means. "Do you have family coming over to meet you at the end?"

"Yes, my younger sister and my parents will meet me in Kathmandu."

"How old is your sister?" I ask.

"She is sixteen and at boarding school in Switzerland. She is an excellent climber, like me."

I smile a little. Modesty is not Yoon Su's strong suit.

She continues, "It is her dream that we'll climb Everest together in a few years." Yoon Su looks up at me and beams. "I told her about you and about how young you are. Now she's hoping we might attempt an Everest summit when she's eighteen."

My own smile broadens. I'm embarrassed but also thrilled.

Luc rejoins us, breathless and smelling slightly of chocolate. "*Alors*, I think it's the perfect time to find a pub. Will either of you ladies join me?"

I hesitate, looking at Yoon Su. I've already stopped for what I need and have no agenda, beyond hunting down more chocolate bars. "Sure," I say. "Why not?"

Luc whoops and claps me on the back, then turns to Yoon Su and starts to get down on his knees, hands held up, pleading.

"Stop it. So dirty!" Yoon Su scolds. "And look, the donkeys are coming." Sure enough, dozens of heavily laden donkeys with loudly ringing bells are pushing their way through the center of town. "Here, move out of the way."

She pulls us toward a storefront, and we all press against the racks of hiking clothes until the donkeys pass.

"I will come. For a short time," Yoon Su says, and she starts to walk quickly behind the donkeys, stepping neatly out of the way of the dirt they leave behind. Luc and I rush to follow.

Inside, we hand over our wrinkled rupees in exchange for three enormous Everest beers. Luc tips his back and drinks for several long seconds, while Yoon Su and I both take a sip, grimace slightly at the warm, flat taste, and set them down.

"This is better," Luc says, leaning back in his chair. "So far there has been very little . . . How do you say? *Camaraderie*. Everyone sticks to themselves."

I open my mouth to answer, then close it again. The truth is that Mami was always the one who organized games, started conversations with strangers in lodges, grew friendly with everyone around us.

Without her, we are all quieter. Once again, missing her threatens to swallow me.

Yoon Su notices my silence and pats my hand, a hard, quick tap that is somehow comforting. "Phhhht! We are not on a party cruise. We're approaching Base Camp, which should make any *thinking* person turn inward and mentally prepare for what's ahead." She shakes her head at Luc but smiles—quick, then gone—to take the sting from her words. "It is foolish to underestimate our challenges."

Luc shrugs, a big French shrug. "Of course it is dangerous!

That is part of the fun, *n'est-ce pas*? Why would we climb, if not for the whiff of death that accompanies it?"

I look at him. Luc is the ultimate climber bro, but when he stops laughing, his eyes are dark and shadowed. I remember reading somewhere how mountaineers are rarely thrill seekers but, more often, people seeking control, seeking to rein in their emotions. I wonder what brought Luc here.

As though reading my mind, Yoon Su leans forward. "So, what leads you to chase this 'whiff of death' up the mountains? How did you decide to climb?"

Luc shrugs again. "There is no place on Earth that makes me happier than the mountains. I used to ski more, but mountaineering has captured me. In life, much of what we do has little meaning. You travel, you drink good wine, you enjoy the company of beautiful women, but always there is a question of why. When you climb, the questions disappear. The only question is what the next move will be, and the only answer that matters is the one that keeps you alive." He grins. "And when we answer incorrectly, when life is at risk, and all could be lost . . . Well, you never feel more alive than that!"

I gape for a moment. I hadn't expected an existentialist answer, but maybe that's how French climber dudes roll. But then he laughs.

"Of course, it doesn't hurt with the women either. It is impressive, *non*, to stare down death and ascend, godlike, up the rock."

I roll my eyes. "Oh yeah . . . I'm sure that ladies line up at the mention of it."

He grins. "But *non* . . . I am no longer a . . . How do you call it? A hound dog? Just months before we arrived here, I met a woman, Amelie, who is . . . very special. So we shall see." His cheeks flush, and he looks downright goofy as he stares down at the table, trying not to smile.

"Yeah?" It's my turn to grin. I glance at Yoon Su and raise an eyebrow. "What's so special about her?"

He shrugs. "She is beautiful. Of course. But also very strong and brave, like you women! She does not climb, but she skis, and *mon dieu*, she is like a warrior on skis. And she is kind, and she makes me laugh." He laughs. "And she does not complain when I say I am leaving for months to climb Mount Everest! She says, 'Maybe next time I will go with you!' That's a woman worth holding on to, no?"

Yoon Su and I both agree, exchanging a quick smile.

Before we can ask anything more, he leans forward and changes the subject back to climbing. Yoon Su and Luc have done many of the same routes in the Alps, and Luc once spent a summer climbing in California, and soon we are laughing and reliving these other, safely finished climbs.

" . . . And when we are finally able to see each other in daylight the next morning, after I've guided him down, he looks at me, very surprised, and says, 'Interesting. You don't look Italian!' You see, I learned Italian at boarding school and had been speaking Italian with him all night. He had no idea I was Korean!"

Yoon Su is funny, with a sly kind of humor that only comes out in her stories. Luc shakes his head in admiration.

"You women are . . . like the Americans say . . . fierce! Most French women are not so strong or brave."

I close my eyes. "Luc, you know that's sexist and stereotypical, right? I mean, to generalize about French women? What about Amelie?"

He looks surprised. "But I am complimenting you! And her! How is that sexist?"

I sigh and look at Yoon Su, and we work together to educate him as we walk up the stone steps. To his credit he listens, and soon we are all laughing as I try to explain that the expression "ovaries of steel" is better than "balls of steel," and I barely notice when we reach the top.

Chapter Ten:

Tate

(Four Months Earlier) January 12
Palo Alto, California
30 feet above sea level

I started talking. I had to. Christ, the way they were freaking out with shrinks and occupational therapists and neurologists and who the hell knows who else, I figured if I didn't talk, I was probably headed toward shock therapy. So I said something.

I said, "Do you want my pudding?"

It was like I lit a bomb and threw it. Everyone started freaking out at once, except Rose. She was the one I was talking to. She looked at me, her bruise blooming to a spectacular purple blue that was actually a cool color but not for skin. And she said, "Sure," and picked up the pudding cup and started to eat.

Then she looked at me again, and her eyebrows crumpled up in the mad-but-not-mad way, and I couldn't help it, I laughed, even though my ribs burned like fire. But that was all it took for her to lose it, so *she* started laughing too, silently at first, then out loud. Then her laughter turned to sobs, and I must have looked horrified because for all her weepiness, she never *really* cries, and whatever *I* looked like, it made her laugh again, which made me laugh even with the rib pain and every single thing in my life being so fucked up and wrong.

• • •

The first day after surgery was easy because nobody expected me to say much. But as the days went on and I got stronger, the doctors started saying how amazingly lucky I was. I knew what the next questions out of Dad's mouth would be:

"What about Everest?"

"Will he be able to go?"

"Can he still climb?"

• • •

I don't want to ask the questions because I don't know what I want to hear. I mean, thank God for miracles and ice axes and the fact that "all things considered" I'm in excellent shape. Of course I'm psyched it's not worse. But when I first came to and the doctor told me I was miracle-level lucky, that I'd be as good as new, the relief was mixed with a kind of panicked disappointment, a bottomless horror like I had gotten awful news.

What the fuck? I've taken bad falls before, and yeah, pain sucks. I know that. But I've always bounced back. I've always *wanted* to bounce back, frustrated at having to wait before I could climb again. And this wasn't so bad. It could have been, but it wasn't, and I'm fine, which means I'm hoping I'm fine for Everest, this trip that we've been planning forever. Right? I have *always* wanted to climb. But somehow this time as I sit in the hospital, I feel like I've woken up from some spell, like I can see clearly for the first time. And what I'm seeing is that I have no idea why I'd want to do this. It's probably just a weird aftereffect of the adrenaline leaving my body or something.

It has to be.

Anyway, when I am finally dismissed, the doctor says he wants to see me in three weeks "to assess," and my parents just nod, like that means something important. Maybe it does. Maybe I'll still be all broken and fucked up in three weeks, and he'll tell me there's no way he can clear me to go. That thought should be sour and shitty, a lifetime dream lost. But it leaves me numb.

• • •

At least the talking got me out of the hospital. All I have is a broken arm, a sprained wrist, cracked ribs, a fractured ankle, and some good old contusions and bruises and scrapes, although none look as intense as that Frankenstein gash on Rose's head. After the pudding and the laughter and the relief that, yes, I know how to talk, it took barely two hours until we were home in my basement TV room.

Not so much laughing now. Rose is staring at the wall like she's waiting for a secret portal to appear.

"Well," she says finally. "Here we are."

My parents have—with great relief, I think—left us

alone. That week in the hospital was more togetherness than any of us wanted. Other than climbing with Dad, I don't spend much time with them these days. When we're together, it's usually for another round of you-need-to-try-harder/ I-am-doing-the-best-that-I-can—a game I'm really fucking sick of playing. I'm four months from graduation. Since my sister, Hillary, is already through college and barely even comes home for vacations anymore, I kind of feel like they're waiting for the door to hit my ass on the way out. It's fine. I'm waiting too.

Rose still looks exhausted. I try to sound normal.

"So, what did I miss? Any news on Ronan and the hot barista?" I ask.

"Not much," she answers. "Ronan found out her name— it's Chessa Bond. And Mr. Abrams gave me some books he thought you'd like and said not to worry about catching up."

She glances at me, and I look away. "So what gives?" Rose asks finally. "Why weren't you talking? Your parents were freaking out. It freaked me out too."

I think of the sickening jolt and blackness of the crevasse and close my eyes. It turns me upside-fucking-down even to remember it—the nauseating, sweaty fear's waiting to climb into me and own me the second I let it cross my mind. I shake my head and open my eyes because I can't—I won't— go back to that place.

I turn my head and stare at the wall behind the couch. There's a huge map of Nepal taped up there, with a red string along the famous southern route we'll take to the summit of Everest. The path we're supposed to take. The path I honestly don't know if I can do.

I stay silent, my face turned away. I want to tell Rose everything, tell her that I don't even know what the doctors are thinking, that I'm too chickenshit to even ask them, that I don't know what I want to hear. I look up finally. Her face has gone white, almost greenish, and the blue bruise is horror-show bright.

"What?" she says, and her voice is a whisper. "What's going on? Are you hurt worse? I mean, I thought you were fine. Is there something else that you're not telling me?"

I shake my head again, too hard, and my neck throbs. "No! No, I'm fine. I mean, other than the ribs, bruises, scrapes, sprains, and the fact I literally pissed myself I was so scared when I fell. But that's enough. I don't . . ." I trail off. It feels too melodramatic to say I'm not willing to die for this. But it's the truth.

"*What?*" she whispers.

More silence. More pain, but not the same kind. Now it's the pain of bending your best friend's heart, not breaking it, not yet, but maybe pushing it. Not a kind of pain I'd ever experienced before because even though I've frustrated and annoyed Rose around a million times, nothing I've done will hurt her like this will.

I'm a fucking coward. Finally I have to break the hideous silence. I look right at her white face. "Nothing. I was just exhausted. And who knows?" I say, trying to sound normal. "Who knows if the doctors will even clear me to climb?"

Her face smooths out a little. "God, no wonder you're upset. But it's still a couple months until we leave, and then there's weeks and weeks of acclimatization and trekking before we even get close to any mountaineering. And you've climbed pretty quickly after past falls. Why on Earth wouldn't they let you?"

I shrug and my ribs protest, but not as much as my brain does. *Tell her you're freaking out*, my brain screams, but I don't say anything. Even the hellish, terrifying, pain-swirling ride down from the mountain seems better than telling my best friend I'm a wimp who wants to bail on the trip of a lifetime. The trip of her dreams—and mine, once.

"Who knows?" I say finally. "Who the hell knows?" I let my eyes slide shut.

"Should I let you rest?" Rose asks, and her voice sounds defeated.

I nod. "Sorry to be such a loser," I mutter.

"Not a loser. Healing," Rose says. She stands, and through half-closed eyes I watch her cross in front of me and bend down, covering me with the ratty 49ers blanket that lives on the back of the couch. "Sleep and feel better. I'll talk to you tomorrow."

I feel a barely there breeze as she walks by, then hear the thud of her footsteps up the stairs.

She's gone.

And I'm alone.

Chapter Eleven:

Rose

April 10
Namche, Nepal
11,290 feet above sea level

One perk of Namche is reliable internet, so after dinner I sit down at the lodge computer and try to reach Mami and Dad on Skype. It's early at home, and for a second the Dread surfaces as I wonder if Mami is feeling okay, if her face will be pinched and crumbled with pain, even as she tries to smile. Part of me wants to cut the connection before they even answer. But when the picture comes up, she and Dad are beaming.

"Rose! We were going to try to get you today! Because, drumroll, please! . . . You got a certain email!" He holds up a sheet of printed paper, and there it is, the Yale crest. I had given them my email log-in, in case I was unable to get on-line, and somehow today, the one day I haven't checked, is the day.

"IT IS GOOD NEWS! THEY AREN'T IDIOTS, THOSE ADMISSIONS PEOPLE!" Mami yells. She's so loud that Finjo and Tate, who are still in the dining room, come over.

I scream. "READ IT!"

Dad puts on his reading glasses with great ceremony. "'Dear Ms. Keller, Welcome!'" he starts, but I can't hear the rest because Mami has starting singing and clapping, and I can't help it, I laugh and turn to the rest of the dining room and yell, "I GOT INTO YALE!"

Everyone—including a tour group of British trekkers and a few American backpackers—bursts into applause. Mami keeps singing, and Dad, crouching so close to the screen that all I can see of him is his cheek, tries to read the rest of the letter.

Tears stream down my face. "I can't believe it. I didn't think . . ." I'm smiling so hard my cheeks hurt.

Tate, who gave a wild YEEHAW when I shouted, is now trying to lift me off the bench.

"VICTORY LAP!" he shouts. "BE RIGHT BACK, MAYA AND CARL!"

I scream but let him grab me and run me once around the room flung over his shoulder.

"High five! Give the newest Yalie a high five!" he yells, and smiling white-haired British tourists do, one after another. Finally he flings me back on the bench, collapsing next to me.

"Whew. That's a lot easier at sea level." He puts his head down and pants like a dog.

"Mami? Dad? You still there?" I ask, focusing back on the screen.

"Of course! We are so glad to celebrate this with you! Isn't technology amazing? We can all be together!" Mami says, and she means it, I know.

But still, a little of the joy leaks away, and I lean forward. "I miss you so much, I wish—" I shut up, but not fast enough.

Mami looks, just for a second, desperately sad, then her smile is back. Dad puts an arm around her.

I make myself think about Yale, about this news. Next to me, Tate rubs my shoulder. "Hey, guys, hope you're eating fish tacos and avocado and fresh fruit every single day!" he says. "Also, Carl, feel free to take my surfboard out if you're looking to shred some gnarly waves while I'm gone!"

We all laugh, especially Dad, who would never surf in a million years. And everything is okay again.

We talk for a few minutes, and they promise to reply to the email with my acceptance and forward the information about start dates and roommates and dorms. The excitement thrums again, and I can give them a real smile before we blow kisses and say goodbye.

Afterward, I lean against Tate, staring at the fire in the woodstove. It's late, and there are only embers left. The room is cold and getting colder, and we're the only ones here.

He holds out a fist, and I bump it. "Yalie. Way to rock it, Keller."

I shrug, feeling weird. Tate hasn't gotten in anywhere but State yet, and I can't help wondering if he's . . . not jealous, because he wouldn't want to go to Yale. But worried. Or something.

◆ ◆ ◆

Later, once we're each in our mummy bags on either side of our room, I try to ask him. He's been there for me through all of it . . . the stress over scholarship applications, the freakouts over Mami. And I want to make sure he knows he can talk to me. Lying in the dark, staring at the ceiling, it's embarrassingly hard to figure out what to say. RoseAndTate, as always, but somehow the words still won't come. Finally I speak.

"Are you . . . Have you checked with your mom lately to see if there's been any news?"

He grunts. "Nothing good. One waitlist. One rejection."

I'm silent, trying to figure out what to say that's not patronizing or stupid.

He speaks again. "It's fine. I don't care, Rose. Seriously. State's got some good programs, if that's where I end up."

I lean on one elbow. "I know. There's actually a higher percentage of Fortune 500 entrepreneurs from state universities than—" But he cuts me off.

"I told you. It's fine. I'm psyched for you, but I'm not worried."

I sigh, wanting to leave it. But it's Tate, and I need to try. "But you *are* worried. I mean, you're barely sleeping—I know you're awake, because I hear you get up and walk around and read with your flashlight! And when you *do* sleep, you're having nightma—"

"ROSE. Fuck! Enough." He shuffles around and turns on his headlamp, blinding me for a second before pointing it at himself. He's trying to smile, but I can tell he's annoyed, Tate on the Edge.

My stomach clenches. Rose the Unhelpful.

"Seriously. This is the face of someone who's not freaking out about college, okay? I swear." He takes a deep breath—in through the nose, out through the mouth—then smiles. He doesn't look mad anymore, but still.

I don't believe him. Tate the Impervious, Tate Always Energized has been thrashing and whimpering in his sleep.

And when we're not talking and laughing, he's Tate Drained and Depleted, staring at nothing until I nudge him and we start to talk again. But he doesn't want to talk about it, and okay, maybe a best friend who just got into the college of her dreams isn't the best person to talk to.

Or maybe I'm a chicken.

"Fine! You're perfect in every way. Put out the light already," I say, making my voice light. "This is the face of someone who wants to go to sleep!"

"God, getting into Yale has made you so bossy," he says, turning out the light. But I can hear the smile in his voice.

"Good night, Yale girl. You're awesome; you know that, right?" he says, once we are both snuggled back into the darkness.

I smile. "Whatever. Yale's later. Right now it's you and me and Mount Everest. Everything else—even Yale—is going to have to wait until after the summit." That's all I say, but I hope he hears what I mean, that I don't want to be anywhere but here, that for the moment, everything else is less important than RoseAndTate, getting to the top, together.

Chapter Twelve:

Tate

(Four Months Earlier) January 30
Palo Alto, California
30 feet above sea level

I'm the luckiest guy on Earth, according to everyone at the hospital and school. And I'm really trying to be that guy. I go back to classes, bug Ronan about whether he's got moves smooth enough for Chessa the Barista, and do my physical therapy like a good boy.

Also, I try to stay away from Rose so I don't have to look at her and lie about how Oh. So. Lucky. I feel.

I hurt all over. It's like my own personal hell, complete with little Hieronymus Bosch devils poking and prodding and putting me in liquids that are too cold or too hot for comfort. Alas, the orgies aren't part of my physical therapy program. Insurance regulations, probably.

I've been coming to Bradford Rehabilitation Center for the past two weeks. Even though the banner outside the building says they're the official rehab center of the 49ers, there are no football players here. Nor cheerleaders who sustained a pulled groin doing a split, either, which is what Ronan and I dreamed might be waiting for me when he drove me here my first day. No, everyone's ancient. Broken hips, mostly, although there are a few youngsters with knee replacements. Today's my last appointment, my graduation day, before they send me away to break myself into pieces on another mountain.

"You want me to hang around?" Ronan asks when he drops me off. "I can chill here if you need me. I brought Veronica." Ronan named his computer after his favorite porn star, which I find hilarious, since he's usually working on his novel, a weird super-religious epic that takes place in ancient Ireland.

I give him a fist bump. "Nah, you're good to go. My dad's picking me up, and we're doing dinner. You know, bonding time."

Ronan grimaces. He knows Dad well enough to know there's an agenda here. It's always a variation on the theme of Come-on-Tate-time-to-man-up.

Of course the irony is that he's right. I need to get over myself and figure this out. Every night's a repeat: shitty nightmares where I fall again and again, stumbling on the sidewalk or walking down stairs but continuing to drop, until I spiral into a full-on panic. But I will not be that guy, the guy who—once again—needs the shrink, the extra help, the sympathy and understanding. I fucking won't do it. I can't tell him, and I can't tell Rose.

I get out of Ronan's SUV, slowly lowering myself down from the seat, trying not to land hard on my ankle, which is still weak and feels shitty. As Ronan peels out of the parking lot, I see a baby-blue car turning in.

Rose. She drives through the crowded lot before sliding the car into a spot way down by the corner. I stand like someone planted me, watching her. We've seen each other plenty these past few weeks. We've had class together, where I arrive just in time to slide into my seat before the bell. We've sat in the cafeteria, where I make sure to sit at least two seats away from her. We've stood around after school with a group of friends and bantered. But we haven't been alone since she left my basement, the day I got home after the accident.

She walks toward me, and it takes forever. Tall and thin and broad-shouldered, she walks like she always does, fast and strong, her crazy long legs moving toward me while I stand here like some broken-down car. I don't watch her much, I realize. Truthfully, I don't stand still much, and if I'm standing still with Rose, it's probably because she's way above me on the other side of a rope. But as she gets nearer, I can see each detail of her, each freckle on her face, the way her wrists stick out of her long-sleeve tee shirt because her arms are always too long for normal sleeves (monkey arms, she calls them), her braided leather belt she bought in Bolivia when we climbed there last summer. The bruise on her cheek is almost gone, and her curls are held back by a turquoise headscarf thing that is the same bright blue as her eyes. She's chewing hard on a cuticle, really gnawing on it.

"Hey," she says, when she gets close. "Thought you might want company in there."

She's trying to be casual, but I can tell she's nervous. Her nervousness makes me feel weird. Are we both avoiding each other? Why is she avoiding me? I smile and offer my arm, like we're going to a fancy event.

"How nice to have an escort. I should have brought you a corsage," I say, and we start in. She walks slowly to match my pathetic pace. Rose has been here with me before. In tenth grade I broke my arm, not climbing but messing around after school. I was freaking out over not being able to climb or play ball or anything, but Rose came with me to meet the physical therapist so she could see how my exercises were supposed to be done. She worked with me on those exercises every night. I was back climbing a full month before any doctor thought I would be. I wonder if she thinks she can whip me back into shape again.

As we get to the automatic doors, Rose stops abruptly. Since her arm's through mine, I stop too. We're so close to the entrance that the doors open in a blast of air conditioning but then when we don't move, close again.

"Tate, I . . . " She pauses.

Open. Close. We stand at the threshold.

"I'm sorry I haven't been around. My mom's been feeling really bad . . . but that's no excuse." She stops again.

The doors keep doing their thing. I'm ready to grab her and walk through them already, but I want to hear what she's trying to say.

"I'm sorry though. I've been a shitty friend," she says finally. She looks up at me. "I guess I thought you wanted time, but I should have, I should be there for you—"

I cut her off. "Rose, stop. You didn't do anything wrong. I wanted to be left alone. I can't . . ." The words almost break out of me. *I can't climb Everest.* But I don't say it. The truth is I could. I just don't want to.

"I don't know if I want to do this anymore," I say, but I'm chickenshit, and I say it quietly, so quietly that Rose moves forward to hear me.

The receptionist has apparently gotten upset with our disregard of the neurotically oversensitive doors, which keep opening and closing. She swings out the door toward us, her face stormy.

"If you don't mind—" she starts.

"We're coming in," Rose says, as I'm about to say she should leave and spare us any more of this hideous awkwardness. "Tate has an appointment, and I'll be staying with him."

Inside, I watch her watching me, her eyebrows mushed together as she takes note of how the therapist makes me lift and lower, again and again, until my arm trembles and sweat drips down my face. And in a rush I realize, with an icy wave of fear, that no matter what I do, no matter whether I climb or quit, she'll be on Everest, facing whatever it throws at her. She's still going. And I'd be left behind, scared shitless that something will happen to her.

"What's wrong? Tate? Hey, stop the exercises for a minute!" Rose says, up from her seat and crouching down in front of the torture chair I'm strapped into.

"Nothing. I'm fine," I say.

The PT glances up from my chart for a second and shrugs. "We're about finished anyway," he says and glances over at Rose. "Did you have any other questions? Are you thinking about a career in physical therapy?"

Rose shakes her head, eyes still on me. "No. I just wanted to see how Tate is doing. I wanted to make sure he's okay."

I stand, and I'm pissed that my legs won't stop trembling. It's been a brutal session, and, if I'm honest, I know I worked harder than I needed to and probably should have. I wanted Rose to see me working that hard. I want her to know I'm trying.

• • •

Dinner with Dad is predictably annoying. I don't think he *means* to be a parody of douchey fatherhood, but somehow when he opens his mouth, Jordan Russo is incapable of stopping the flow of bullshit. First come the "interested questions about life" so that I know he cares about me. Then he segues into "when I was your age" tales from the past. Finally, we move on to the "barely veiled frustration" section of the evening, when he presses me again and again on working harder, reaching out to colleges to see if I can turn in additional portfolios, and other ways that I could do better if I only tried.

I attempt to keep my temper, but my answers get shorter and shorter until I snap out, "Mind your own business and leave me to my fucking life!" and we finish our pho in silence.

Awesome.

In the car on the way home, he talks on and on about how soon we leave for Nepal, how amazing it will be to actually see Everest, how he can't wait to see me tackle that mountain like the beast that I am. It's his idea of an apology, I guess. But it feels like he's handing me a box of scorpions.

I'm down in the basement after, using Xbox like the soothing drug that it is, when Rose stops by the house. Something's happened, something bad, that's clear. But she asks about dinner, about my sore muscles, about homework, until I interrupt.

"Enough. What's wrong?" I lean forward on the couch.

"It can wait. How are you feeling?" she asks, but her face is grim.

"Seriously, you're a crap liar, Rose. What is it? Did you hear back from Yale?"

She shakes her head, but her eyes are bleak, and I can

feel my heart beating faster, and, fuck, everything still hurts so much. Today's PT session was definitely overkill.

"I'm imagining a hundred seriously awful things, so can you just tell me?" I say finally.

Rose straightens her back, moving away from me. "It's . . . Mami finally got a diagnosis. And . . ." She shakes her head, tears pooling in her eyes.

Fuck. No. Not Maya. Not a giant universe-shaped hole in Rose's world. I reach a hand out, but Rose twists her fingers together in her lap.

"It's not . . . I mean, it could be worse. But it's . . . not good. She's got MS. Multiple sclerosis."

I take a breath and my ribs burn. "I don't . . . sorry. What exactly is that?"

Rose shakes her head. "MS is when the body's immune system attacks the nerve coatings in the brain and spinal cord. There are times that are bad and times when everything's in remission, but there's no cure. And it can get progressively worse. Sometimes it's not that bad, but sometimes . . ." She stops talking.

Then she looks at me. "She can't climb anymore, Tate. It affects her mobility, and she can't . . . She won't ever . . ." She clamps her lips shut and bites down hard, but tears pour down her cheeks.

Without thinking about my ribs or sprained wrist, I lean forward and grab her, and she falls into me like she's been waiting, barely surviving, until she can collapse. My muscles are so sore, but I hold her as tightly as I can, rubbing her back with my nonsplinted arm, trying to think of something to say.

And I'm an asshole, the worst kind of friend in the world, really, because even as my best friend's heart is breaking and a woman I've known my whole life gets a horrible life-changing diagnosis, there's a tiny part of my brain exploding with hope. Because maybe this—this terrible, unwanted, shitty thing that has nothing to do with me—maybe it's enough to keep me from having to rope in and climb again.

But Rose's voice, muffled into my shoulder, knocks back any selfish hope I was feeling. "We're still going, Tate, that's a definite. The first thing Mami said was that there was no way on this Earth she would let us give this up. She made me promise. But God, Tate, going without her . . ." She breaks down and sobs some more.

And I tighten my arm around her and try to take deep breaths because it's clear, it's crystal fucking clear, that I'm going to climb this mountain with Rose.

Chapter Thirteen:

April 11
Namche, Nepal
11,290 feet above sea level

So far, since we got to Nepal, I've almost convinced myself that I'm on vacation, that all we're doing is trekking up crowded trails with way too many middle-aged tourists and guides and porters carrying crap tons of gear on their backs. That it's a gift—a get-out-of-jail-free card for the last months of high school, a chance for me and Rose to laugh and eat our carefully rationed Twizzlers and talk do-you-remember for hours. The altitude bugs me less than it bugs anyone else, and other than the occasional nightmare, it's all good. Really good.

But today we're climbing.

The climb's nothing—a bullshit simple technical climb that I could have done when I was twelve. We're only a few hours' walk from the village, and the mountain's barely a pimple compared with the giant peaks around us. But Finjo wanted us to get some ice-climbing practice while we're acclimatizing, and this spot is close enough that we can climb for a few hours and be back in our lodge before dark. We're all here: me, Rose, Paul, Dad, Luc, and Yoon Su, along with Dawa and Finjo and Asha. Dawa sticks to the rear with Dad, while Asha, in a kind of Girl Power move, leads Yoon Su and Rose at the front of the pack. The three of them are moving fast, though I should be moving faster. It's supposed to be an easy climb.

Kick off, grab the rock, pull. I've been doing this practically forever, and the muscle memory usually takes over. It used to be that the pull and grab chilled me out, shut up my brain, and let my body do what it's trained for. I used to love this.

But not now. Now a fucked-up hum of panic buzzes the whole time, fear and adrenaline making my tongue thick in my mouth and my skin crawl. My hands sweat and shake, and I hesitate before the simplest holds.

Terror.

I had no idea.

No fucking idea what people meant when they said climbing was scary, that they could never hang off a rock face like I do. Today I get it—sweat like icy water runs down my spine, and I get a sick drowning pit in my gut when I look down. I don't know what the fuck this is, but I can't do it. I try to take deep breaths, but the air is thin and dusty, and I cough and cough.

"*Ça va?* Are you okay?"

Luc's behind me, waiting for me to move off the ropes. I give a thumbs-up, coughing too hard to answer.

"Okay then. We will keep going?" he asks. Hard to know

if he's being nice or a dick, and it doesn't really matter because I'm stuck.

"Pass me," I say. And it hurts to say it. Hurts because my throat's raw and dry and because hanging out on the ropes, feet jammed into the rock, while Luc goes up like he's running up a line at a climbing gym, sucks. But I move out of the way, and he scampers by me.

Rose is ahead, already at a rest point and probably gazing out at the panorama of mountains and gabbing with Yoon Su. They've been bonding, sharing the British fashion magazines Yoon Su brought and giggling over some secret topic that I suspect has to do with Rose trying to braid her leg hairs. But right now I have nothing in common with them, and not because of secret girl things. I'm halfway up the rock, and I don't think I can keep going.

"Hey! Zoom zoom! We need to keep moving, okay?" It's Finjo, bringing up the rear. I look behind him, but peering down the ice face makes spots dance in front of my eyes, and I lurch on the ropes.

"Where's my dad?" I ask, once I'm sure I can keep my voice steady. "He hasn't passed me."

Finjo shakes his head. "I sent him back down with Dawa. He was not feeling good, and though he says he is fine to climb, I took a look at him and said no."

This is not good news. We're barely at the edge of the expedition and Dad's already hurting with some virus that's clogging his lungs and making him more susceptible to altitude. He started taking Diamox, the prescription drug that's supposed to help with altitude sickness, but so far it hasn't done much. Apparently, you can also take Viagra, but my guess is he hasn't tried that yet. Or if he is, he's not talking about it. Thank God.

All at once I see a way out. I turn to Finjo. "I'd better go down. I'm worried about him."

Finjo shakes his head definitively. "No need. Dawa is with him, and you should be training. Zoom zoom, right?" He motions for me to head up, but I don't move.

"He's my father, man. If he's down, I'm going down," I say. This is bullshit, of course, and Finjo, who's been with us for almost two weeks, probably thinks so too. He probably noticed that father-son bonding isn't really our thing . . . My fault, really, since Dad's so delighted to be here that instead of nagging me, he's kept up a consistent stream of hey-buddy-you-got-this pep talks that are almost worse.

But Finjo's not about to mess with paternal loyalty. Finally, with his blessing, I start down, trying not to think about what this retreat means.

• • •

When I get back to the lodge, Dad's sitting in the smoky dining room, waving off offers of more tea. He raises his eyebrows when I walk in.

"Why are you back?" he asks, his voice cracked from coughing.

I hesitate. The odds he'll believe I want to check on him are slim. I go with a partial lie. "I wasn't feeling great. I'm just . . . not feeling the climb today." I slump next to him, avoiding his gaze.

Silence for a second, then he speaks, trying to sound casual. But his hand tightens on his empty mug. "Really? Because you've seemed fine skipping up these trails. This is Mount Everest, son. Come on . . . If you're not willing to push yourself now, when the hell are you going to?"

I don't want to answer. I want to squeeze a frozen orange or punch the heavy bag hanging in our basement or any of the other techniques Jimmy's been getting me to use over the years. But I'm stuck here. There's nothing I'm going to say that won't piss him off, so I stay silent.

He coughs, then pauses, taking a deep breath, and I know the next volley is coming.

"The truth is I love you, but I'm worried. You don't push yourself. You coast along waiting for things to get easy. I know you're sick of hearing it, but when I was your age, I was working two jobs, one after school and one on the weekends, and trying to figure out how the hell to pay for college. You're getting the trip of a lifetime paid for. And you won't put in the effort to make sure you're as prepared as possible. I'm telling you, buddy, given those first few college responses, I hesitated over this trip. You have *got* to learn to work for things."

I try to let his words wash over me, but at this my eyes fly open. All the exhaustion combines with a surge of anger so strong I almost lift out of my seat.

"You have no fucking idea how hard I'm working," I snarl, and in some far-off part of my mind, I know I'm too angry to be as careful as I should be. "I *have* worked hard. Every. Fucking. Day. I work hard not to lose track of shit. I work hard to keep staring at the massive pile of studying in front of me and not get up and go shoot hoops in the yard. I work so hard to hold it together, and now I'm working even harder trying not to break—" I stop. My hands are balled into fists so tight the veins have popped up.

We're both silent. I breathe in through my nose, out through my mouth. I repeat the mantra: Smell the flower, blow out the candle. I almost smile, thinking of Ronan and

Rose, who would whisper, "Flower, candle. Flower, candle," when they saw me getting stressed. My hands unclench slightly.

"Break what?" Dad asks, and his voice is quieter now. Defeated. I hate this part. The part when we both stop being mad and start being sorry that we have failed to be decent to each other yet again.

I look at him. He looks exhausted, and we're not even a week out of Kathmandu.

I sigh, letting my head rest in my hands. The sweat from the failed climb is long gone, and I'm cold. My mind travels to Rose. Break a promise. Break down. But I don't say that.

"Nothing," I say. "I'm in, Dad. Seriously. I'm . . . You know. Taking it slow."

He nods, not like he believes me but like he's willing to be done with this conversation.

"Okay," he says. "Okay then. Do you want some tea?" He waves to the porter who's been texting on his phone in the corner, and within minutes the lodge owner comes in with steaming tea.

She smiles and exclaims over how exciting it is to see a father and son head off together to climb Everest. We nod and smile, not meeting each other's eyes.

◆ ◆ ◆

Soon Dad heads off to rest. Guilt and resentment swirl through me. I feel trapped. There's nothing here, nothing to do except prepare for the climb of a lifetime. My mind flies to Rose, who's climbing while roped in with someone else and who's got her phone and GoPro going so constantly that Finjo jokes that the Nepali government's going to think she's a spy. To Yoon Su, who takes photos of herself and Rose in every lodge, each of them trying to make a sillier face than the other, cracking up until they have to slump against the wall laughing. And to Luc, who calls Rose La Rosinator, after the Terminator, and has started joking with her about stealing her Twizzlers while she sleeps. What the fuck is my role here? What good am I if I can't even climb?

I need to move, to go somewhere, even though I don't have any idea where. I leave the lodge and walk up the yak path that leads to a helicopter landing pad. The views here are stupid gorgeous, a sweep of the world's highest mountains from end to end. Above them all looms Everest, an ugly black triangle jutting up above the rest. Snow crystals blown by the jet stream fly off one end. It's unearthly, inhuman, other. I have no desire to be there. And though I know I used to want it so badly, I can't remember why.

It seemed as obvious as breathing, once. I was a climber. I bagged peaks. That was the best and easiest way to think of myself, especially once we got to high school, where Ronan and Rose and most of my other friends barreled through honors and AP classes like the overachievers they are, and I sat in my extra study halls and guided study sessions and felt like a total tool. Climbing was the best, most fun, most natural thing for me to be excellent at. And Everest. Everest is the grand prize, the one that, when you drop the name, even nonclimbers are amazed. Going for it felt as natural as grabbing for the next hold on the wall at Rockface.

But now . . . now it doesn't feel obvious or natural or even remotely possible. Now I'm here, and I can't imagine spending fucking brutal days and weeks hanging on the ice, hoping to survive. I can't do it. And I don't even know who I am without it.

I stay up on the helipad, shivering as the sun drops. The mountains turn amber, then deep pink and orange in the sunset. It's a sight that belongs on a Sierra Club calendar or on an inspirational poster in Paul's office—one that reminds us to ask for the strength to change what we can, the tranquility to accept what we can't, and the wisdom to know the difference—but it's not where I belong. Nothing about this place is where I belong.

• • •

Rose finds me there, hunched and cold, staring out at the fading sky. It gets dark faster than seems reasonable here, all light swallowed up by the mountains once the sun drops.

"Hey," she says quietly, standing behind me, pressing her legs against my back. She radiates heat, even through her thick leggings and boots. "I brought you this." Bending, she drapes my down parka around me, as though it were a blanket.

"Thanks," I say. I don't look at her. Instead I stare out at the impossible mountains, now just a silhouette in the near-total darkness. The sky's the color of a bruise, of Rose's cheek after she rescued me.

Slowly she lowers herself next to me. My back's cold where she had been standing.

"You okay?" she asks.

I shrug and try to smile. "Just nerves or something. Nothing major."

"Nerves?" she asks, and her voice is careful, neutral, more doctor voice than Rose voice.

I squeeze my eyes shut. "I . . . there's a lot of shit to think about. There are so many fucking things that can go wrong."

My voice rises in spite of myself, and I shut my eyes tighter, trying not to see the endless blackness around us. "And I know I'm the Master of Disaster and always fucking up, but anyone can take a bad step, or shit can break down on the Icefall even if you do everything right! Everything can kill you up there. Do you get that? EVERYTHING!"

I'm almost shouting, but I don't care. I can't help it because it's like someone's decided to show a greatest hits movie deep inside my head, reminding me of what it feels like to fall, to fuck up, to miss a step or not arrest a slide, and the fear's right here trying to grab hold of me.

"Hey, it's okay," Rose says, her eyes wide and worried. She turns to face me, up on her knees, her hands on my shoulders as though she can anchor me. "It's okay, Tate. You'll be fine."

I shake my head. I want to shut up, stop spewing all this, but the stench of my fear is everywhere, and I can't. I can't stop my words, and I can't stop leaning forward until I am pressed against her, wrapping myself around her, her arms folded in against my chest. "No, it's not okay," I say, and I try not to shout. "It's not okay because it's not only about me. It doesn't really help if I'm okay because if something happens to you . . ."

I stop talking. And she is so close, her eyes wide and worried, her mouth open as though she has more to say, tiny hairs escaping from her hat and flying into my face. And I lean down and kiss her open mouth, just like that, like it's exactly what I'm supposed to do, like we're made to do this.

She kisses me back. Her lips are so soft, so incredibly soft, and they are nothing like the rest of Rose and exactly like everything I know about Rose all at once. We kiss for only a second, or for many long minutes, a bad gum commercial come to life in front of the mountains. I have no idea.

Holy shit. I kissed Rose.

"Oh." One tiny word, a barely-there word, is all she says.

I should lean away from her, give her some space, but I can't let go quite yet. I run my fingers lightly down her back, feeling the sharpness of her spine through her jacket. "That was . . . I should have probably—"

"No! I mean, I don't know," Rose says. She looks right at me, and her expression's unsure. "But did you mean it?"

I close my eyes and hold her tighter, tucking my head into her neck and breathing in sweat and incense and lavender moisturizer. She's brave. Always.

"Yes," I say finally, letting her go but grabbing on to her hand. "I could not possibly have meant it more."

We stay up there in the darkness until the cold drives us back down. Neither of us says anything. I'm not sure what I can possibly say. We're here. This is happening. All of it's happening, and I can't control anything, I just fall.

Chapter Fourteen:

Rose

April 12
Tengboche
12,660 feet above sea level

*B*reathing like thunder, silence like mountains, newness like nothing has ever been new before. Tate's skin endlessly hot, so hot that even when we are walking up the trail, many feet apart, I feel it blazing, pulling, calling.

I keep away.

We are friends. Best friends. We always rolled our eyes at classmates who whisper-gossiped in our ears, asking what's *really* going on. How can this be happening to us now? Was this always there? Or did it grow here, out in the mountain air? I had been so clear, so sure, that it wasn't like that with me and Tate. It wasn't even worth discussing when friends brought it up. I don't think I was lying, except now,

now it would be a lie. But what is this new thing? And will it survive the journey home? Ex-RoseAndTate, ex-friends, experience extinguished . . . unimaginable.

Kissing Tate in the first darkness of night by the mountains is magic, and I don't know if there's room here for magic. Not when I'm short of breath from climbing the stairs to our room, not when I spend dinnertime scooping dal, or lentils, into my mouth without noticing what I'm eating because Finjo is going over the acclimatization schedule at Base Camp; not when soon, so soon, we will be on the climb of our lives.

I try and explain this to Tate, in our room, which has never felt smaller, all walls and closed doors and beds that grow by the second until they are practically pressing us into each other. My back against the wall, I tell him that no, we are RoseAndTate, we are about to summit Mount Everest, our dream, our biggest climb ever, and we have to concentrate. Have to keep our eyes on the prize. I actually say "eyes on the prize," and I wonder if my face could light my scarf on fire, it is burning so hot and red as I talk.

Tate just nods. Then he walks over to me, only two short steps in our tiny room, until he is right in front of me, all stubble and heat and dark eyes and lips.

"Maybe not now. But sometime. Soon. All right?" is all he says, and then he bends and kisses me, once, and flames grab my knees, my chest, my whole body, and I want nothing more than to melt into him. But I don't, and he backs up, still watching me, still grinning his isn't-this-fun electricity-everywhere grin.

I open the door and run to the empty, freezing hallway, breathing hard, hoping no one is around to ask questions. My heart pounds so fiercely I am afraid I will fall, afraid I am already gone, somewhere I can never get back from. I stay away until I know he will be asleep. Then return to move around our room in silence, listening to his steady breath.

• • •

Now I stay close to Yoon Su, pushing my pace to walk with her, listening to her talk about her life at home, her two cats and part-time job teaching at a girls' school. She blogs constantly, writing updates to her students, and sometimes she asks me or Luc to write a few words, to describe the scenery or our lodges. Luc surprises me, jumping into this task with enthusiasm usually only seen in kindergarten teachers. Apparently, he has a bunch of nieces and nephews at home, and he is the ultimate favorite uncle. He writes painstaking descriptions of the puppies and kittens we befriend along the trail, photographing them in his jacket pocket or, once, in his hood until Yoon Su yelled at him about fleas.

Her students love our posts and write comments, cheering us all on and asking Yoon Su to take photos with their school banner at the top. I swear Yoon Su starts moving faster each time she hears from them, like she can race to the summit and dazzle them all.

I take similar photos and videos, sending them to Mami, trying to send every detail her way. But now when I'm writing, I try to think of words that are not *kiss* and *hot* and *want* and *need*. Now when I film the landscape for Mami I have to keep moving my camera away from Tate, like he's true north and I'm the magnet, incapable of staying away.

Yoon Su is still faster than me, and I'm breathless trying to keep up, breathless trying not to stare at Tate, who is always, always looking at me. Sometime. Soon. I keep my eyes forward and think of the mountains ahead.

• • •

Today is a walk to Tengboche, a famous Buddhist monastery on the way up to Base Camp. I barely notice the trail, and suddenly we are there, in front of a massive, gorgeous temple looming against the mountains. It's a cluster of buildings, really, all built around a central temple that rises against Ama Dablam, Lhotse, and of course, Everest. They still look endlessly far away, though we are only days from Base Camp. Pulling my eyes away from the peaks, I take in the temple and the masses of mani stones and prayer wheels that surround it.

"It's so new," Luc says from beside me. "I thought it was *ancient*, this place."

Yoon Su answers. "It was old. Then it was destroyed in an avalanche in 1933. They rebuilt. Then a fire in 1989 destroyed it again. It is only in the 1990s that it was rebuilt again."

Luc laughs. "That is stubborn! Maybe their gods were telling them that this is not the place." He continues in a high, silly voice, "'Move ze temple! I will smite it! This is your last warning! *Écoutez!* I really mean it this time!' Right? Not the smartest thing to do."

I can't help laughing at his exaggerated gestures of confusion. Luc remains as politically incorrect as possible, maybe because it makes Yoon Su nuts. Sure enough, she starts lecturing him, and the two of them move forward, toward the huge red gate.

I stare at the buildings, which manage to look both medieval and modern at the same time. There's a steady stream of tourists walking in—probably Everest expedition climbers. Ever since Norgay and Hillary's famous first ascent up this route to the summit in 1953, climbers have been stopping here to light candles and receive a blessing from the lama for safe passage. Of course, it doesn't always work, but that doesn't stop people—Sherpas and tourists alike—from being superstitious.

I'm not ready to enter the monastery, to begin the official ritual that will mark our move up the mountain toward Base Camp. Everything changes here. I want to think about the path ahead, but instead I close my eyes and relive Tate's lips, soft and hot against my own.

"Are you meditating?" Tate's voice comes from right over my shoulder, and I nearly fall over in surprise.

When I open my eyes, he is right next to me, and my body wants to move without my permission, to lean into him and breathe him in. I look away. Red Hot Rose, melting the mountains with the heat of her cheeks.

"Or maybe not meditating?" Tate says, even closer to my ear. "Maybe thinking about—"

I cut him off. "Paul's here." I wave over Tate's shoulder as he steps away from me, leaving cold air where he had been.

"What are you two whispering about?" Paul asks, joining us. "Is there nefarious planning happening? If so, tell me all about it!"

"Nothing!" I say, as Tate says, "Just enjoying the views." My cheeks flame even hotter.

Paul looks at us. "Okaaay," he says. But he doesn't ask anything else. Instead he turns to the monastery. "Here we go! This is the official beginning, right? Or at least the beginning of the beginning. So, we ready to go in?" He starts humming.

Tate moves along the path. "I don't even know that one. Dude, you're getting a little esoteric in your choices."

Paul stops humming. "'I'll Make a Man Out of You!' *Mulan*! Exploring gender norms, discrimination, civil disobedience . . . right, Rosie? Back me up on this one."

I shake my head. Sometimes Paul and his Disney chatter is way too much for me. "I'm going to . . . I need to walk around a bit." I head off before they can answer. I can't tell if I'm grateful or pissed that Paul showed up before I did anything too stupid to be undone.

I start to walk around the temple. In theory, I was going to take some notes and try to say something intelligent about indigenous design and architecture of the Khumbu region, but that hasn't happened yet. And since I can't stop watching Tate, I'm not likely to get much done now. Walking around the compound, I spin the prayer wheels that line the sides. *Om mani padme hum.* The jewel in the heart of the lotus. I try to take deep, calming breaths, try to feel the spirit of the place penetrate me, calm me, center me. I want to truly be here, immersed in this place. Instead my mind is flying ahead, to the increasingly cold and thin-aired lodges to come, to Everest Base Camp, which is only a week away. To Tate, kissing me as though our mouths belong together as easily as the rest of us. To me, kissing him back, his touch answering questions I only now realize I've been asking. The wanting threatens to flood my brain, and I push it away.

Sometime. Soon. What can that even mean? Tate and I have this climb, this dream-come-true Everest summit, and then what? Summer? College? Unless he's gotten more news than he's shared, State's the only place he got in.

My chest knots, and I want to tear my brain out of my head. What the hell is wrong with me? I'm in the most beautiful spot on the planet, about to embark on the adventure of a lifetime. But all I can do is worry about whether Tate should have studied harder in American History last year so that his GPA was a little higher.

"You seem unquiet."

The voice startles me, and I have to stifle a scream. It's Asha. I put my hand over my racing heart. I've walked almost halfway around the buildings, barely taking notice of the tall prayer flags and mani stones. Clouds have rolled in, hiding the mountain peaks and highlighting the bright red of the gates against the browns and grays: brown earth, pale buildings, gray rock.

"I, too, thought to take a walk, to meditate a bit. But then I saw you, stomping—" here she breaks off to imitate me, scowl on my face, storming along the path "—and I thought I would see that all is okay." She smiles.

I like Asha. When Mami and I researched expedition companies, Mountain Adventure was one of the few that trained and supported women Sherpas to guide, and Asha will do her first Everest summit with us. She's probably five years older than me but seems so grown-up that I feel like a kid next to her. A really tall kid.

I start to answer but don't really know what to say. I shrug, then look ahead. Beyond us Yoon Su is also walking, but at a fast pace. She spins the prayer wheels so hard I can hear the whir from here.

Asha's eyes follow mine. "She's impatient, I think."

I nod. Yoon Su has been impatient from our first dinner. She gets visibly upset if we're behind schedule, even by a few hours. I thought I was bad, but at least here I know I can't go any faster than the guides—and the mountains—let us. I once asked her why she was in such a rush, since we can't climb until we've acclimatized, until the weather window opens, until a million details come together. But she just shrugged and said something about no time to waste.

I turn to Asha. "Why do you want to climb Everest? Why does it matter to you?"

She laughs a surprised laugh. "Money. The guides who summit Everest earn more than anyone else. This will be my first Everest summit, though I have already summited Lhotse and Cho Oyu." She names two of the ten highest mountains in the world, which are part of the same range as Everest. "I am lucky that Finjo was willing to train me, as many companies do not want women guides. But as a guide, I earn good money. My oldest brother died several years ago, and my middle brother is here, at the monastery, as a monk. After Everest, our family will be much better off."

I nod, unsure of what to say. I know how poor most of the country is, of course. And I told Tate the truth: Mami researched and found a Nepali-owned expedition that pays fair wages and life insurance and helps the local economy, which some of the other companies definitely don't do. But with my dreams of the summit, I never thought about Everest as a source of a pay raise. At home, tagging peaks is all about the bragging rights, not about the payout. Sure, pro climbers try to set more and more exciting routes to get sponsors, but most of us spend huge, once-in-a-lifetime sums for the challenge, the excitement, the rush we get from climbing.

Asha looks at me. "Can I ask you why you are climbing?"

I'm embarrassed, trying to think of an answer that doesn't sound self-indulgent and spoiled. It seemed really cool? I want to knock it off my bucket list? I can't quite think of how to answer.

"Tate and I have climbed since we were kids. And my mom," I begin but then stop. Because I'm trying to remember, trying to think back to the steps that landed me here. RoseAndTate, climbing partners forever. Mami, loving climbing with me, her monkey-mama arms reaching higher than seemed possible, always packing chocolate for the celebrations at the top. It seemed natural that we'd climb more and more challenging peaks, that we would set our sights on Everest, the top of the world.

I try not to think about how I resented the hours of training, how Mami would ask me, an edge in her voice, if I was *sure*, really certain that I wanted to do this, and how I'd answer, a matching edge in my own, that obviously I wanted it, but she needed to chill out and stop nagging. I've always wanted this, but I never had to think about how much until Mami stopped being the wind at my back, pushing me up the mountain. Until suddenly I'm here, preparing to climb, and Mami isn't.

"I don't know," I say finally. "The challenge, I guess. And the beauty. If you love to climb, climbing to the summit of the earth seems an obvious thing to want." I speak slowly, more to myself than to Asha.

"My mom is . . . was . . . a climber too. And she got sick and can't climb anymore. So if I can do this, then in a way, she gets to do it too, you know? Because she's so excited for me." I don't say the rest, which is that secretly, shamefully, it's far less scary to be here, half a world away from Mami's pain and the endless waiting Dread that whispers in my ear that she could get sicker, she could die, she could leave me forever. Climbing, with all the exhaustion and risk, is easier.

"I'm sorry about your older brother," I say. "How did he die?"

"Climbing," Asha says simply.

I nod, but I don't say anything else because I don't know what to say.

We walk in silence for a few more minutes, until we are back at the entrance.

"Are you ready to enter?" Asha asks.

A thin, young monk waves at us, grinning from inside the doorway. He's holding a cell phone in one hand, incongruous with his shaved head and burgundy-and-saffron robes.

"My brother," she says, and her smile is big and bright. "Come on."

We go in, and at once I'm struck by the riot of colors, bright reds, vivid oranges, deep blues, and greens that cover every inch of the space. Ceilings, columns, floors—they are all painted in wild designs that almost burn my eyes after the dull gray of the landscape.

I smile and nod at Asha's brother and follow obediently as he walks us through the richly decorated temple to the modern information display. But my mind is racing ahead. We will be at Base Camp in a few days. As I stare, unseeing, at the board in front of me, my mind is not on the climb. It is on Tate, whose eyes burn into me from across the room.

I try to look away.

Chapter Fifteen:

Tate

April 13
Tengboche
12,600 feet above sea level

We're way above the tree line now, above anything alive. Here it's only scrubby, low bushes and dirt and hundreds of damn yaks that churn up crazy amounts of dust. It's like walking through a continuous dust storm, and we leave our buffs over our mouths to keep from breathing it all in. I can tell Rose is starting to feel the altitude. She moves a little more slowly, talks a little less, pauses at the top of a steep ascent with her hands on her knees for a few seconds.

I feel fine. Great, actually, at least in terms of the altitude. I'd feel even better if I could kiss Rose again, if I didn't have to force myself to leave her alone. I want to be all caveman crazy, pulling her to me and holding her by her shoulders until she looks me in the eye and kisses me like she did that first night, until I get to kiss her neck and her wrists and every other tiny flash of skin that I see through slitted eyes when she silently slides into her sleeping bag, thinking I'm asleep.

I'm spending a lot of alone time in the tiny ice-cold spigots that pass for showers in the lodges. Jesus.

Wanting Rose is totally new, swallowing everything else in my brain. It's not that I haven't thought about it, though not nearly as much as Ronan and the other guys assume. He used to beg me to spill Letters to Penthouse–worthy stories about me and Rose sharing a tent. And yes, Rose is hot, and yes, I've seen her mostly naked before, in tents or on climbs or at the beach. But it's Rose, and there's a wall in my mind that kept all those thoughts on the far side, with golf and cat barf and other desire-killing items. But now wanting her is unlike wanting any girl, even my girlfriends, such as they were. Most of my girlfriends have been pretty short-term. After all, whoever I was dating had to deal with the fact that I still spent most of my time with Rose.

We're heading into Pangboche, a village where we'll stop in to see some famous religious guy for a blessing. It's apparently an honor—we actually go to this old guy's home, and he escaped from Tibet to live here. Definitely cool, but I'd rather skip it. I'm not really in the mood for some spiritual moment. I want to keep moving.

Moving's the only time my brain quiets, the only time I'm not worrying, not freaking out about Rose, about climbing, about whatever happens next. I put one foot ahead of the other, watching the swirl of dust fly up past my boot. The landscape's empty, sky and peaks and the occasional prayer flag–covered stupa.

It's easy to walk. If I could, I'd walk for days, for months, for years, just keep walking, spending nights in tiny rooms with Rose, then waking up and doing it again. No need for plans or looking out for the occasional emails when we get internet for a few hours, which will only tell me I've been rejected from another college.

Long before I'm ready to stop, we're here. Yoon Su and Rose talk in low voices as we walk in, everyone slow and solemn.

"Lama Geshe, *namaste*," Finjo says, and bows.

A tiny, old man with a bald head shining like a brown cue ball smiles at us. "*Namaste*," he says, bringing his hands together and bowing low. "Welcome. And thank you."

We take our seats in his crowded living room, and his wife and daughter pass us small cups of tea. We're all silent, and I slurp my tea.

"GAH!" I work really hard not to spit the tea back out, but it's a challenge.

Lama Dude bursts out laughing. "Salted yak butter tea. Is it not to your liking?" he asks, and by the sly look in his eyes, I'm guessing I'm not the first guest to be surprised by the greasy, salty mess.

Dad's looking at me, his eyes narrowed in his don't-embarrass-me stare. But I was raised right, even if my host gave me sink backwash for a cocktail.

"It's delicious, thank you," I say, "just a little hot." I take another sip, breathing through my mouth until it's safely down my throat.

Everyone else, warned by my canary-in-a-coal-mine move, takes careful sips. Lama Geshe winks at me, like it was all part of a good joke.

"Last week, an old friend of mine came, a Canadian scientist, and he brought with him a group of graduate students from his university, here to research our glaciers.

One of them was clearly unhappy. He moved slowly and heavily. He had no smile, even when others smiled at him. He did not carry as big a load as the others. Truly he was uncomfortable. The other students, they called him 'Doughboy' and did not seem to enjoy his company. So I gave him some tea." He grins. "He spit it—splat! On the floor. He says, loudly, 'TOO SALTY!' My friend, he escorted that boy outside. I hear quiet voices, then loud ones. I never saw Doughboy again."

He looks around at us and laughs his big laugh again. "I am glad there are no Doughboys here today."

Well, that pretty much breaks the ice. We all start talking and laughing, and Luc imitates my face when I tasted the tea. But after a few minutes of this, Lama Geshe rings a small brass bell, and we all fall silent.

He gives us his blessing, asking the mountain gods for permission to climb and for safety for the climbers. Then he walks to each of us and drops a silk *kata*, a white ceremonial scarf, on us, hands us a little written blessing, then puts a red string around our necks.

I'm last in line. When he gets to me, he holds me by the shoulders and pulls me forward so that our foreheads bump together. I want to rub my head; he bumped me pretty hard. But I'm no Doughboy.

He doesn't let go right away but keeps hold of my shoulders, peering into my face. I try not to look away, but I'm all done with this. It's hot and stuffy, with the incense burning and making my eyes sting, and I want out.

But still he holds on.

"What?" I say finally. "I mean, um, thank you."

He smiles again, and when he speaks, his voice is quiet, only for me. "You will not look me in the eye, and you move around like you want to be anywhere but here. I think maybe you do not wish me to ask the gods for you to pass. Is it because you don't believe in them or don't believe in this journey?"

I don't answer. I stood here, taking the scarf, the blessing, the whole thing, same as everyone. I don't know what else he wants.

Lama Geshe pulls me close one more time. "You must choose what peak you aim to summit. You must tame your mind before you tame the mountain." Then he pushes me back and turns away.

"*Namaste*," he says loudly, gathering everyone around one last time. "Send me your photos, your summit photos with your blessings, and I will put them on the wall. I look forward to your safe return."

I glance at the wall behind him, where hundreds of photos show climbers, Sherpas and tourists alike, standing at the summit with their tiny prayer cards held up to the camera. I shudder.

"Are you ready? Let's go," I say to Rose and head toward the door.

Dad hangs back, talking to the lama in a quiet voice. He breaks off into a thick, choking coughing jag that makes me cringe. It's been bad the whole trek, but now it sounds nasty.

"*Namaste*, Tate," Lama Geshe says, "and good luck."

I bow one last time and head out into the cold, empty air.

• • •

Later that afternoon, after another ice climbing attempt that I muscle through with barely clamped-down fear, we slump around the fire in the lodge. Dad's cough is worse, and he's running a fever; he made it up this practice climb but it totally wiped him out, and now we're waiting for Finjo to tell us what's supposed to happen next.

He comes into the smoky room and claps his hands. "So, we will have a slight change in our plans. As you know, we were planning to spend tomorrow and the next day in Dingboche. But instead we will detour slightly and travel to Pheriche. There is a medical clinic there. I would like them to assess Jordan's lungs, to decide if he needs to descend or perhaps needs a different antibiotic."

We all turn to look at Dad, who scowls and clears his throat like he's trying not to cough. A second later a cough rips out of him. I wince. He never gets sick and has no patience with anyone else who is. This must suck for him.

"Does this put us behind schedule?" Yoon Su asks. "It seems unfortunate that so early in our trip we must delay."

Finjo shakes his head. "No problem! It is not a delay, just a change in the plan. Either way we will travel up, and either way we must stay there two nights to acclimatize. You have your porters, and if you wish, you can go—zoom zoom!—straight to Dingboche. But it makes no difference. Either way we are on schedule."

Yoon Su nods.

"It's nothing," Dad says, sounding pissy. "I'm fine. I just need to shake this virus. I'm still ready to climb." As though in direct contradiction to his words, he coughs again, but he scowls, daring anyone to say anything.

He sounds so sure of himself, even with the shitty cough. It must be fucking *great* to feel that sure. I glance at Rose, expecting, as usual, to find her looking anywhere but at me. But she's staring at Dad like she's watching some kind of horrible news channel, like something bad is happening that only she can see. As everyone begins to discuss times for dinner and hot tea, Rose bolts from the room, muttering something about needing to change.

I follow her. I know I shouldn't. I know her not-now-Tate rules still stand, but I can't help wondering, can't help worrying, can't help making sure she's okay. We're still friends, no matter what else.

In our tiny ice-cube-cold room, Rose is on her bed, face-down and sobbing. I lurch back in surprise.

"What happened?" It comes out in a half whisper. I drop to my knees next to her bed. "What the hell, Rosie? What's going on?"

The room's dim, the lodge conserving its solar-powered electricity until it's fully night, and I can barely see her face when she looks up.

"God. It's nothing, really. I'm being so stupid. I think it must be a side effect of altitude—" she starts, but I put out a hand to stop her.

"No. Fuck that. What is it?"

She takes a deep, shuddering sigh and sits up, leaning against the wall. Without thinking, I sit next to her, pushing against her so that we're squeezed on the tiny bed. She presses into me, sliding down until her head is on my shoulder. Same as always, except now it's dangerous and radioactive. I try and ignore the heat of her against me, which is like trying to ignore someone lighting me on fire.

"It really is stupid. But listening to your dad coughing, swearing he'll be fine . . . It was a weird déjà vu, you know? He's fine, I get it, but I couldn't help remembering . . ."

"Your mom," I say, understanding. Maya went from Wonder Woman to sick so fast. Though looking back, I wonder how bad the pain had been, and for how long.

"Yeah. I know it's different, obviously. But . . . This was going to be the four of us, you know? And now she's out. And if Jordan really does get sick . . ." She trails off. "I never imagined we would be here without her, you know?"

I nod. Rose's breath is warm on my shoulder, and I keep my body still, keep myself from pulling her against me, pulling her face up to mine and running my hands along her back. I think of her tears and of the climb ahead and Maya left behind.

I close my eyes. Try to will myself to move, to put distance between us.

Rose's hand touches my face, whisper-light. "I think . . ." she says, and her voice is low, so low that I have to bend to hear her, so that her words are warm against my ear.

"I think I was wrong. You know, about us. About . . . this." And she slides her body up until her lips are right above mine, lowering them so gently that I barely feel the pressure at first, until realization hits and I grab at her like it will save my life.

Chapter Sixteen:

Rose

April 13
Tengboche
12,600 feet above sea level

Tate pulls me against him, then stops. He is an open flame, the skin at his neck hot against my cheek.

"Jesus," Tate says, and, in the faint light from the window, I can see his eyes, dark and endless. "Jesus, Rose."

I pull him to me, wanting to swallow him, wanting to hold him as close to me as I can possibly manage. My lips find his skin, his head first, then his rough cheek, and finally back to his mouth. I kiss him hard, blocking out anything that is not us, not right now.

"Are you sure? I—"

Grabbing his hands, I bring them up to my lips, kissing his wrists, letting my tongue lick at the strong pulse beating against my mouth. Tate makes a noise in the back of his throat, and I pull him to me, on top of me, never taking my lips off him: his arms, his neck, his rough cheek, smelling of sweat and dirt and Tate.

"Yes," I murmur against his neck. "I'm sure." I press myself against him, unwilling to let any space come between us.

Tate pushes back against me, just as hard, and kisses me as though I am food and water and air. I gasp and grab him, touching as much of him as I can reach. The buckle on his climbing pants digs into me, and I move blindly, trying to make it disappear, wanting anything that's between him and me to be gone. Once it's undone and his shirt pulled off, I move my hands away from his body just long enough to pull my shirt over my head. A jolt like an electric shock runs through me when my skin touches his.

He groans and finds my mouth again. Lips against mine, he whispers, "Rose. I want . . . I want this so much. Are you sure? I mean, can we . . . ?" His voice trails off into a gasp as I bite his lower lip.

I nod without moving my mouth away from his, and his kisses push harder against me as we struggle to undress.

"Remember? I've had the implant forever," I say into his chest, which is damp with sweat, even in the chill of the room. "I'm sure," I say. And I mean it. This is Tate, my best friend, the person who knows everything about me. Almost everything. Until now. My hands tremble as they reach for him, wanting to bring him closer, as close as I possibly can. I want to live inside his heat, smother it like a thick wool blanket over flames, absorb it into myself.

Tate's skin. Every scar and freckle I've seen and some I haven't, all mine to touch and explore as I hold him tighter, wrapping my legs around him and kissing him again and again, swallowing his voice as it rises. The voice that makes me laugh now makes me blush, want and need and love all there as he calls my name, soft at first, then louder. Until I can't think anymore, and it is only my body, rocking against him, answering him best.

We finish, exhausted, breathing heavily and slick with sweat. In the dim room, I can feel and taste but not see the dampness on his neck. My heart is slowing down, and the unreality of the moment makes me dizzy. Outside our windows, the tall Himalayan peaks blaze orange in the very last of the day's light. Inside, I am naked with Tate, every inch of his skin, which I thought I knew so well, now exposed to me in a different way.

We lie still, my legs tangled up in Tate's long, heavy ones. He runs his hands across my hips, my waist, my legs, tracing the shape of my body. His hands linger on my scars: a long puckered ugly one on my thigh from a bad fall at Yosemite, a big one on my knee, a smaller one on my wrist.

"I'm damaged goods," I say, and my voice is low and raspy. I hope we were quiet enough to avoid being heard in the lodge.

Tate laughs a little. "Please. I think I have you beat on that one." He lies back, and I look at him, really look at him. His body is a map of accidents—bike skids on steep hills, missed skateboard jumps, falls on rock. The Master of Disaster, put back together again and again.

"Yeah. You win." I keep my eyes down, tracing the scars and lines on his thigh.

"Hey. You okay?" Tate asks. He lifts my face until he's staring at me. "With . . . You know." He raises his eyebrows. "That."

I smile and nod. Being with Tate is easy, easier—and better—than anyone else I've been with. Not that there have been many. There was my first, a misguided month-long "relationship" that started during spring break of junior year, and then my only boyfriend, who Tate insisted on calling Ben Boring. But my mind is replaying our conversation, and I'm suddenly embarrassed, not that we had sex but that my weepiness turned into my tearing his clothes off. I start to roll away from him, curling up in a ball, but Tate's arm stops me and pulls me tight against his chest. I sigh and stretch out, leaning back in his arms.

"I can't imagine anything better than being here with you," I say quietly. There's no way to explain to Tate, to make him understand that he is the rope, tethering me, keeping the Dread away.

Tate's arms tighten around me, but he doesn't say anything. Together we stare out the window as the last light slips away.

"I want to be with you," he whispers into my hair. "I want to give you everything you need." His hands move against me, and I push into them, turning until I am facing him again. His face falls into shadow, so I hear him but don't see him as he says, again, "I want you—"

I kiss him as deeply and slowly as I can, until the only sound is the gasp of his breath.

It is hours before we stop, hours as we skip dinner and push aside all thoughts of anything outside this room, hours before we sleep, and, when we do at last, we cram ourselves together, arms and legs tangled, in one tiny bed. The room as always is freezing, but Tate's heat is a live thing, wrapping around me. I sleep hard, barely dreaming at all, waking only the next morning when a knock on the door sends Tate flailing across the room to his own bed, an icy blast of air slamming against me where his body had been.

Chapter
Seventeen:

Tate

April 14–15
Tengboche to Pheriche
14,300 feet above sea level

I wake up psyched, a kind of Christmas morning–level excitement thrumming through my veins that makes no sense, until I remember. Rose. Rose and me.

At breakfast I feel like I've got a giant sign over my head—one that says, *Hey, I skipped dinner to have incredible sex with Rose last night!* But nobody's saying anything, so maybe not. Still, I can't take my eyes away from her. From her long fingers, wrapped around her coffee cup, to her lips, squeezed together to blow on the hot drink, to her—

"Dude. Are you even listening?" She's peering at me, her eyebrows all wrinkled up.

"Yah. I was listening. I was . . . Actually, no. No idea what you were talking about. Sorry." I smile at her, and I don't know, maybe my smile says something along the lines of "hey-put-down-that-coffee-and-let-me-kiss-you-hard," because she blushes fast and red. I love making Rose blush.

"Stop it," she says, but there's a smile in her voice and her gaze softens.

Looking around quickly, I see that everyone's busy with their guidebooks and novels and morning oatmeal. I lean down and pull her finger into my mouth, sucking hard. Rose jerks like I electrocuted her, her mouth opening in a gasp that she bites back. I lick her finger one last time, then move it away, wrapping it back around her mug.

"I . . . ah. I don't remember what I was saying," she says, and her cheeks are a wild and totally sexy red.

A clatter behind us sends us both bolting back against our chairs. Paul slides into his seat, scraping it against the floor, and reaches toward the coffee.

"Morning. You both feeling better? You flaked out hard last night," he says.

Rose nods, pretending to be busy with her oatmeal. But I grin at Paul. I slept nightmare-free, and I'm allowed to lean over and kiss any part of Rose I want, which means everything else can go screw.

Rose glances over, and her face turns red. I'm pretty sure my telepathic messages are working.

"Well, I need some time to . . . you know . . . write post cards and stuff. Before we leave, I mean. So I'm going to . . ." She trails off, gesturing behind her as she slides out of her chair.

"Yup. Me too." I stand up and turn quickly. "Later, Paul."

I catch the swinging door that leads out of the dining hall as it slams behind Rose. It's still cold, and I rush to get to her, wanting her heat and touch so badly that everything else feels unimportant and distant.

Inside our room I pull her against me, running my hands up the warmth of her bare back under her shirt.

"Tell me you aren't really planning to write post cards," I say into her ear. "You can't possibly have anything so pressing to say. Please tell me that. Please tell me you came in here so I could do this." I kiss her neck. "And this." I run my hands up the front of her shirt, feeling her shudder against me.

"Tate, I . . ." Her words drift away as my mouth travels over her, my hands pushing her toward the nearest bed. "I want you to be sure . . . because last night . . . oh, God."

We are lying down now, and I want to tell her that of course I'm sure about her, that I've been sure of her since she sat with me on the otherwise-scary bus in first grade, since I saw her in her bathing suit the summer after ninth grade, since I trusted her to hold my life in her hands whenever we climbed. I've always been sure of Rose. But I don't say any of that because I'm holding her as tight as I can, trying to show her how much I need her.

When we're still again, when I'm busy looking at the bite marks on my shoulder Rose made when I whispered for her to be quiet, when she's half-asleep with her hair in a wild tangle around her, I ask her.

"What did you want to ask me?"

"Hmmm?" Her voice is slow. "We'd better get up. We've got to pack up and head out in an hour or so."

"We've got time. That wasn't . . . Well, let's say it hasn't been that long since we came in here. But it's not my fault. You can't touch me the way you do and expect staying power," I say, running my fingers lightly across her stomach.

She laughs. "I'm not complaining." As she groans and stretches, rolling over into a sitting position, I ask her again.

"Oh, yeah. I . . . last night was . . . I mean, I was upset. And then I kind of jumped you—"

"Thank GOD," I interrupt.

"ANYWAY," she goes on. "That's kind of my point. I didn't want you to think . . . You know." She blushes and walks away to pull on her hiking pants and fleece. Dressed like this, her hands moving fast to pull her hair back into braids, she looks the same as always, not like the Rose who was naked next to me. I miss that Rose.

"Hey." I walk over to her and pull her to me. I kiss her head, her hair smelling of lust and sweat. "I don't know. Tell me what you're talking about."

"I didn't want you to think I was . . . ugh . . . trying to use sex to make this all about me," she says, her face buried in my chest. "I felt like I was throwing myself at you right when I was so upset, like it was your job to comfort me . . . You know what? Forget it."

I tilt her face up until I can look into her blue eyes. Rose, who wants me, who wants to be close to me as we climb the tallest mountain in the world, who looks embarrassed, like she got caught breaking a rule. She needs me. I can do this.

My heart's whacking away at my chest, the kind of tight, fast excitement that I can't control even if I want to. And right now I don't want to. Fuck it. I'm happy in a way that I can't remember ever being.

"Rosie," I say. "This is what I want. You're what I want. I wasn't being nice because you were crying; you know that, right? You can throw yourself at me anytime you want. Really."

She looks at me. "Really? This isn't too weird?"

I kiss her again, but my legs are jittering, ready to walk. Ready to move. "Not too weird. Just weird enough. The perfect amount of weird."

My good mood lasts through our trek up to Pheriche, through the chance to move slowly through the village with Rose, pulling her against an empty old stone shack so that I can kiss her until we're both gasping for air. It lasts through the afternoon's ritual cup of tea, where we sit by the fire while Dad and Finjo head to the clinic. Then Paul and I walk over to the clinic to see Dad, and the fun and games dissolve around me, gone as fast as the sun, which disappeared under low swirling clouds.

It's colder, snow drifting around but never landing. The wind shifts, and the massive mountains show through the gray. They look fucking ominous, stock photography out of an action movie where the good guy bites it in the end. Lama Geshe's words run around in my head. I believe in the mountain gods. I think they're vicious, nasty sons of bitches who think of us the way a dog might think about fleas climbing up its back. I shake my head and walk faster.

Paul leaves me at the entrance to the clinic, wandering off to pick up more high-altitude tips at today's workshop. First thing I notice is the pictures—wordless first-aid instructions that show everything from dealing with a choking baby to how to splint a leg. Walking past a seriously gruesome one that shows how to pull someone out of a fire—something I would have thought was fairly obvious—I look around for any signs of life.

"You looking for Jordan?" someone asks, and I jump.

The voice turns out to be attached to an insanely tall dude with a white doctor's coat and a shaved head who'd been crouched down under a desk by a filing cabinet.

"I'm Dr. Walker. You can call me Bo, though," he says

and offers his hand. His hands are massive; mine looks like a tiny kid's when I shake.

"You must be his son," he says, walking quickly back out the door and along the covered walkway that connects a bunch of different rooms. "He's a terrific guy. And fit too. I wouldn't figure him to have a kid your age, by looking at him. He should be good to go in a day or two," Tall Dude—Bo—continues. He ducks his head and walks through a doorway. I follow, not ducking.

"He should be . . . Shoot. Well, they must have brought him for one last O2 test before discharging him. He'll be back shortly," he says as we stand in an empty room.

"Oh. Okay, well, I can wait," I say. I'm unsure what to make of this guy.

The room's quiet, and I realize that he's waiting for me to say something.

"Uh . . . Sorry. What was that?"

He laughs. "I said you should come back and wait with me in the main room. That way you won't miss him if he's being discharged."

I nod, feeling like an asshole. We make our way back to the cramped front office with the scary first-aid pictures.

"So, you look like you're in pretty good shape. Do you feel ready?" Bo says.

"Ready for what?" I say stupidly.

He laughs again, big and loud. "You're either really confident or really out of it. Not sure which. Everest, man! Isn't that why you're here? The big father-son climb? And your friends too, right? Rose and Paul? Jordan was telling me all about it. He's stoked. Wasn't going to let a little chest infection mess with his moment. He's seizing the day, man. He's all *carpe diem!*"

I don't answer, walking around the tiny space instead. When I come to a bunch of photos, I stop and look at them: a group of doctors, I assume, sitting in the clinic. Then the same people climbing, and lots of happy group shots of them eating somewhere. Bo is the only Black guy in the bunch, not to mention a foot taller than some of the others. I turn to him.

"So, how'd you end up here? I mean—"

He interrupts, laughing his big laugh again. "I know what you mean. You probably noticed I don't look like most of the Western doctors around here?"

I laugh. "Yeah, I noticed. You're pretty . . . tall."

He grins. "Yup. And pretty Black. You probably noticed that too." He continues, "Despite my vertical, I always wanted to be a doctor, and to the disappointment of high school coaches, I was better at chemistry than point guard, so I went to med school. And then a good friend of mine got a real bad lung disease . . . She was dying by inches, and every breath was hard. I started studying her disease and realized it was a lot like the effects of high-altitude sickness, so I started researching high-altitude medicine, and . . . Well, here I am."

He holds his arms out wide and grins again. But I wonder what pieces he left out of the story. Like what happened to that friend that made going 6,000 miles away seem like a good idea.

"Anyway, it's been fun. The Sherpas thought I was some kind of bald Black yeti at first, and I thought they were little pocket-sized people, but we're all good now. They're some tough dudes. You know, the actual Sherpa people, the ones whose families have lived at higher altitude for generations, they've got some supercharged ways of using oxygen that make hitting those peaks easier for them, at least up to twenty-three thousand feet or so. After that, in the death zone, all bets are off. But they're like fuel-efficient cars, using less gas to get better mileage. But the porters and support staff who come from lower villages and do the grunt work at Base Camp? They don't have any special genetic benefits for climbing; they don't have better lung capacity than you or any other flatlander. So how do they get to Base Camp and work so hard, you ask? Fucking toughness, pardon my French. They're just tougher than most." He nods. "Anyway, what about it? You feeling tough enough?"

I can't help it, I snort. "Probably not."

Bo starts to laugh again, but as he looks at me, his face sobers. "Wait, seriously? Your daddy . . ."

"Yeah, I know." My daddy indeed.

As if summoned, he walks into the room.

"Tate! Did Dr. Bo tell you I'm good to go? Should be able to *run* up to our next village tomorrow, right, Doctor?" he says, coming over and grabbing Bo's hand and shoulder in the universal bromance half hug.

"I heard," I say, forcing a grin. "That's awesome. You look good." It's true, sort of. He looks better rested, at least, and he obviously showered. But he's still scarily skinny, given that he's not even at Base Camp, and when he stops talking, he coughs, a quick, sharp hack.

"We're getting there, T-Man. Thanks to these guys, we'll be at Base Camp in a few days. You ready?"

"Me?" I say. "I'm not the one getting IV drugs in the clinic. I'm all good." I avoid Bo's eyes when I talk.

"That's right. You're the beast! You're going to be awesome. But it's game time, buddy. No more messing around, deal?"

"Deal." I try and walk to the door, but he grabs my arm.

"Not so fast. Before we go anywhere, I've got to let the

good doctor here give me one last checkup and get me some pills. And cough syrup. You've got more of that, right?" My dad turns to Bo, but the good doctor is staring right at me.

He seems cool, but the last thing I need is a chat about Tate's lack of balls.

Finally, Bo looks back at my dad. "Hmmm? Oh, yeah. We'll load you up with the good stuff and see how that works for you." He pauses, and his dark eyes flash back to mine. "But you know, Jordan, you still got to take it easy for a bit, let the meds do their work, right? You can't charge out of here like some kind of wild man."

He pauses again, and I can see he's trying to say something carefully, something I really doubt I want to hear.

At last he continues. "I cannot stress this enough: this mountain . . . this climb, it is *not* forgiving. A little cough. A stomach bug. A moment's distraction . . . You know any of them can be the catalyst that leads to it all unraveling. And the higher you go, the faster a small problem compounds into a huge one. On Everest people die, not because of catastrophes but because of a small mistake." He looks at me like he wants to say more, but he's said enough. I hear him, loud and clear.

"Boy, you're upbeat today, Doctor! Why the doom and gloom?" my dad asks. "You sure *you're* feeling okay?"

Dr. Bo smiles a big easy grin and slaps my father gently on the back. "Yeah, yeah. I'm fine. Just trying to talk some sense into you and your boy before you charge up the mountainside. That's all."

Dad looks at me and wrinkles his forehead, considering. "That's good. It's good for Tate to hear this. This is no joke, son. This is the big time."

I've had enough. Shoving through the crowded office, I pull open the door. "Like you said, I'm a beast. This is what

I'm built for, right?" I make myself look at Bo. "Nice to meet you, Doctor."

Bo's eyes stay on me, even as I try to look away. "Nice to meet you too, Tate. Good luck," he says.

I mutter an answer and wait outside as my father says his triumphant goodbyes. Tomorrow we leave for our next rest stop, Lobuche, the next day for Base Camp. No jokes, except the hilarious fucking joke that now, when we're finally here, I'd rather be anywhere else. As we start the walk down the empty dirt trail to the lodge, I picture Rose, waiting for me, and realize that I'm wrong. I don't want to be anywhere else. Not while she's here. If she's climbing, I want to be with her. That much, at least, I'm sure of.

Chapter Eighteen:

Rose

April 17–19
Lobuche to Everest Base Camp
16,200–17,600 feet above sea level

*I*t is much colder now, colder and emptier, with nothing but deep-blue skies and devastatingly gorgeous mountain peaks all around us. Our lunch stops are even rougher than the lodges where we spend the night; they're small, smoky rooms that pretty much serve the basic *dal bhat*, or rice and lentils, and maybe eggs if we're lucky. Lobuche is a wind-blown maze of stone walls and narrow paths. Unlike the villages farther down the mountain, this exists only for expeditions heading up to Base Camp. In the late afternoons, our lodge is dim, the only heat coming from the smoky fire in the main room.

"Phew, what is that stench?" Tate asks, throwing down his hat and gloves on a table.

"It's the fire," I answer, too weary to do anything more than slump in the nearest chair. "Now that we're above the tree line, the lodges have to burn yak dung, which—"

"Which smells exactly like what it is," Tate interrupts. "Burnt shit. Oh well, at least it's still freezing."

He's right. The fire is small and barely giving off any heat. A young girl comes in and—with a quick, shy nod—adds more dung chips, which makes it smoke worse than ever. Tate groans.

"Come on, let's go to our room for now," I say, even though I'm so bone-weary it takes two tries before I even get out of the chair. "This room will warm up, and the smoke will get better in a bit, but for now I'm going to climb into my sleeping bag."

We head down the dark hallway to our room, where our packs lie waiting on our beds. No matter what time we arrive, the porters have already dropped off our stuff. Now I pull my massive down sleeping bag from its stuff sack and, barely stopping to pull off my filthy pants, climb in. Within minutes, the delicious heat starts to relax me.

"Shove over." Tate collapses next to me on the bed, face-first. He wraps one arm around me and cups my face with his hand.

"Come here," he says and pulls my face toward him, his lips finding my neck. "It's been hours. Hours of walking behind you, listening to you and Paul talk about how architecture can better serve mental institutions, and all that time I wanted to do this." He kisses me harder.

My heart stutters. He is lying against me, his body heavy and warm, and I can't help it—I turn toward him and kick out of the sleeping bag, wrapping myself around him. Rose the Invasive Vine, twining tighter. A low groan comes from his throat, and I let my hands move over him, mapping his skin, my fatigue fading away.

A knock on the door sends us flying apart.

"Argblaergleonesecondyeahwhat'sup?!!" Tate calls in a strangled voice. He's now curled up on his bed, facing away from the door.

I laugh, though my hands are shaking as I pull my tee shirt down and try to smooth my hair. We didn't even lock the door. I still have my filthy dust-covered shirt on. I blush, thinking about where Tate's hands were, where I wish they still were. Bending over to hide my face, I take off my socks, wincing a little at the smell.

"Kids? Are you already settled in? Did you want to take first showers? There are two, and I paid for the four of us," Paul says, still outside the door.

My mood instantly brightens. Solar hot showers. Lobuche is looking up.

"Go ahead," Tate says. "We'll stay dirty a while."

"Great. I'll come get you when we're done. Enjoy the downtime."

I wait silently until the footsteps fade away, then turn to Tate with a sigh.

"Well, that was potentially hideous. We'd better—"

"Lock the door? I couldn't agree more," Tate says, springing up from the other bed and flicking the latch on the door before launching himself at me. "Then I can get back to doing this—" he pauses and runs his hand under my tee shirt, along my back "—and this." He pauses again and kisses my neck, hot and wet and openmouthed until I gasp. "And . . . Jesus, Rose."

His kisses move through me like fast-working venom. I had been planning on moving away, on telling him how there was dust on my neck and in my ears and everywhere else he was kissing, planning on reminding him that there were showers to be had. But I close my eyes and kiss him back.

• • •

After we shower, which feels almost as amazing as kissing Tate, we return to the dining room. The fire is blazing, still smoky but now throwing off warmth that makes the whole place cozy, and everyone is here.

Paul looks up when we enter. "Well, you both look refreshed! Those showers must have agreed with you."

Predictably, I blush. It is amazing to me that on the trail, to Paul and Yoon Su and even Jordan, who has known me since I was six, we are still RoseAndTate, still best friends, hanging out together. Of course, Jordan has other things on his mind, like breathing.

"I never asked you, what did you think of the Himalayan Rescue Clinic?" I ask. "Did you think they helped Jordan?"

Paul's face lights up. "It's a great spot. They do a daily information session on altitude and mountain medication. The head doctor seems like a terrific guy, which made me feel a lot better. I think Jordan's definitely on the mend." He glances at Tate. "Did your dad tell you we got your mom on Skype? She was worried about him, of course, but thrilled to hear that it's been going well so far."

"Nice. Did she have any news from home?" Tate asks, yanking out a chair and sitting down backward.

"Well, Rose, she said your folks are both doing well, that they had dinner last week, and that she and Hillary would bring you Twizzlers. That was about it." Paul looks at Tate. "No news from colleges, bud. I asked."

Tate shrugs and turns toward the rest of our group, who are all seated around a big table near the fire. "Who's up for a game of Uno?" he asks. "Luc? You playing?"

Uno, the easy color-and-number card game of our childhood, has turned into our group's favorite game. Tate, me, Luc, Paul, and Jordan always play, and, despite not speaking much English, several of the assistant guides and porters usually join in. Two of them, Bishal and Kami, play with us most nights, and sometimes even Finjo and Dawa jump in. Only Yoon Su refuses, rolling her eyes and saying that it's for children. Not even Paul batting his eyes and singing, "'Do you want to build a snowman?'" has gotten her to join.

"When are you going to let us play for money, *mon ami*?" Luc says, pushing aside his book. "What is it they say in your American south? Cards without gambling is like kissing your sister!"

Tate shoots me a fast glance, and my cheeks flame red once again. But Luc isn't looking. He turns to Yoon Su.

"And you? Ze fastest girl on the mountain, but never cards? Perhaps you do not know the rules. Or are afraid to learn?"

Tate and Paul start up a chorus of *oooohs*, like Luc has thrown down some major insult. Yoon Su bursts out laughing.

"You really think such silly taunts will work on me? You are all completely ridiculous!"

"Chick. En. Chick. En," Tate starts, and Paul begins clucking.

"Ahhh! I give in. Fine. I'll play your silly children's game. And I will beat you at it so hard that you will beg me to leave you alone next time," she says, putting down her e-reader.

We all whoop.

"Deal zem," Luc says, throwing down the brightly colored cards.

With a shy grin, Asha starts dealing.

And as the wind howls outside and the barely there electric lights of the lodge come on, we pass the cards around, laughing far too much at silly jokes, teaching each other insults in all the languages we know.

Bishal hands me a plus-four card with an apologetic smile. I'm asking him how to say 'you suck' in Nepali when Tate slips his hand beneath the table and onto my leg. I stutter and nearly drop my cards, which has the rest of the group staring at me, but I don't even care. Everything—okay, almost everything—I want is in one place, tucked in at 16,000 feet, a day's walk away from Everest Base Camp. I am perfectly, endlessly happy.

• • •

The next day all of us except Jordan, who is still resting, do an acclimatization hike up to Kala Patthar, a nearby 18,500-foot peak with some of the best views of Everest. As if in answer to my mood, the clouds lift, and all at once we're under a deep-blue sky, with the Himalayan peaks surrounding us in a glorious array. I move in a slow circle, taking yet more video to send home, wondering if Mami considers it enough of a consolation prize. I try to show how happy I am, hoping it makes Mami glad to see me enjoying it so much, hoping that she doesn't wonder where all that joy was when we were climbing together. I push away the guilt and make myself smile even bigger, praying she will understand.

"*C'est magnifique*," Luc says as we bask in the sun for one of our frequent water breaks. He holds out his hand for a high five and I slap it, feeling a little silly. Luc is all about the high fives, the fist bumps, the bro hugs, as Tate calls the one-armed man hugs Luc seems to favor. Still, his good mood is contagious.

"Yoon Su!" he calls. "Take a photo for Amelie and your students! *Regarde!* The strongest Frenchman in the world delivers them Mount Everest!" He flattens out his hand to rest under the famous peak so that it looks like he's holding it on display.

Yoon Su laughs and snaps the photo, then grabs me and Luc to take a selfie. "Eh, your big head is blocking Everest. Try again," she chides, pushing him over.

Our laughter echoes over the empty sky.

A panorama of high peaks—Nuptse, Changtse, and others—blazes through the clouds, ghostly and magical in the swirling mist.

"The moon is changing, and so we have snow. But it will be nice weather for our trip to Base Camp," Dawa says, watching the few flakes spin and fly around us.

Dawa is the oldest of the guides, and Finjo's uncle, even though Finjo is the boss. He has a web of wrinkles around his eyes, probably from squinting in the mountain sun, and he doesn't talk a lot, but for me at least, his quiet inspires confidence. I catch his eye and smile.

He smiles back. "We are almost there! This will be my fourth summit but my first time climbing with such young people. My daughter is only two years younger than you. Maybe when we return to Lukla at the end of the expedition, you will come to my home and meet her."

I nod. "I would love that." I wonder if she wants to climb someday or if she wants to go away to school. I wonder what her choices are, but I don't ask, unsure if I will say the wrong thing. What does it mean to have your father off on his fourth attempt to summit Mount Everest? Are you proud? Or terrified that his luck is going to run out?

• • •

Slowly and steadily, we keep moving toward Base Camp. Finjo has us spend one extra night at Lobuche, and I think Yoon Su is going to deck him. Last night she announced her plan to go to Base Camp tomorrow, with or without the rest of us. None of us doubt her. She looks so tiny on the trail, and, when the wind blows, she bends almost in half to keep going. She is relentless.

Luckily, Finjo agrees, and today we head up. The path to Base Camp is busy: yaks, porters, and other expeditions crowd the paths, all part of the massive machine that moves humans up and down Mount Everest.

I watch the parade of gear and people to keep my mind from the fact that my lungs burn and my head throbs, and so far we've only been walking. The closer we get, the more it hits me: Everest. Everything I've read, every documentary I've seen is coming to life. I can't tell if I'm terrified or excited or breathless from the lack of oxygen.

But when we pass a memorial to the fallen climbers of Everest, the terror and excitement seem to curl into my chest and hold my breath captive. I put my head between my knees and breathe slowly. Tate walks away from me, turning toward the path behind us as though waiting for something.

The memorial is huge, a pile of rocks and prayer flags and messages looming above our heads, stark in front of the perfect triangle of Everest. My eyes skim over the names that I recognize from climbing books and memoirs: Rob

Hall, a guide who spoke to his pregnant wife by satellite phone as he sat dying on the side of the mountain, too far away to be rescued; David Sharp, the English climber who died on the main trail up to the summit, passed by dozens of climbers who could not or would not help him as he slowly froze to death; Francys Arsentiev, who collapsed on the trail and whose husband tried to return to save her and was never heard from again. I blink back the tears that threaten to overwhelm me. So many names.

Paul puts a hand on my back. "You okay?" he asks. "It's scary, seeing this. Really scary. And anyone who doesn't think so isn't paying attention."

He glances over at Luc, who, after a cursory glance at the memorial, is chatting away to Asha.

"I miss my mom," I say, then stare down at the memorial, avoiding Paul's eyes. I'm mortified that I've blurted this out here, when my thoughts should be on the fallen climbers.

But Paul pulls me into a hug. "Of course you do. This was her dream, and you grew up planning it together. I so wish she could be here with you."

I nod, trying to keep the sobs from building. My instinct is to take deep breaths, trying to control the sadness, but deep breaths aren't possible here. Instead the air catches, and I gasp a little, coughing. So little oxygen, and we have so far still to go.

Paul stares up at the memorial. The wind is strong, and all around us the prayer flags snap and flutter against the deep-blue sky.

"You know you belong here, right?" Paul says. "It's as much your dream as hers, and while I don't have kids, I know, from all the parents I work with, that seeing your child succeed is truly a parent's biggest dream. Bigger even than Everest." He falls silent, and we both stare at the list of names. A knife-twist of fear hits my stomach. If something happened . . . If Mami got a phone call about me and she hadn't been here, it would kill her faster than this disease ever could.

I am grateful Paul is here, but his words open up a hole in my chest. Do I belong here? The closer I get, the more I want this, whether for Mami or me, I don't know. Maybe it doesn't matter. I want this. But staring at those names, I want something even more than the summit: I want to survive this mountain and get home.

• • •

Base Camp is chaos. It's the Tower of Babel with a million different languages all being spoken at once. It's the highest, most exclusive party in the world.

Luc turns to me. *"Incroyable!* It is a small city!"

I nod, too out of breath to speak. The camp is colonized by small outposts of different colors, each climbing outfit sporting their own flag with their logo as well as the logos of their corporate sponsors. Unbelievably, the Starbucks siren waves merrily from one of the big tents. While I know I should be rolling my eyes at the thought of their corporate reach, I can't help dreaming of real coffee.

We get settled in our tents, then quickly regroup in the Mountain Adventure tent, which is enormous and houses dining tables, computers, thick rugs, and even a stereo system. We greet Ang Pasang—who acts as head cook and sirdar, or head Sherpa of Base Camp—and the rest of the Sherpa staff who will be supporting our climb. There are assistant guides, porters who carry endless loads of oxygen tanks and tents and food up to the higher camps, cooks, and more. It's amazing how many people it takes to get the six of us to the top.

"Can you believe this place?" I pull Tate's arm.

Tate doesn't answer. He's been moving faster than me today, staying ahead with Yoon Su while I walk with Jordan and Paul.

"You okay?" I ask, peering at him.

He gives me a quick grin and turns away, moving toward the food. "Sure. All good. Just, you know . . . soaking it in," he says.

I stare at his back as he walks off.

"Going to grab something to eat," he says, over his shoulder. He lets his eyes catch mine for a second, and his smile shouts at me, so loud I look around to make sure no one else is watching us.

Once he leaves, I head to the computers to check email for the first time in days. There are dozens of new messages, ranging from flash sales at my local sporting goods store to e-cards from my grandmother. Seeing them all is like a wave of surreality—in my inbox, my life is flowing on, uninterrupted by the fact that I'm not there. There's one email, almost a week old, from Dad, and I open it eagerly. He's not much for email, typing badly and usually only forwarding terrible jokes. But this time he's written his own words. Words that tell me Mami is doing great, that the physical therapist is really impressed with her strength and that she walked two miles on the treadmill the other day. I know he means this to be good news, to cheer me up, but the image of Mami struggling on a treadmill, when she used to climb up rock walls like gravity held on to her less than most people, feels sour and wrong.

"Everything okay? You look as though you got bad news." Yoon Su has come up behind me, so quietly I didn't notice.

I look up from the email. A churn of guilt and worry and anger washes over me. How am I supposed to answer this? Should I try and sound excited, like this isn't a horrible consolation prize that feels more like a punishment? I look from Yoon Su's concerned face to the busy tent around me, then back to my email. With a click I close the browser.

"No, everything's fine," I say.

Before she can answer, Finjo walks in and claps his hands until we all fall silent and gather around him. He is grinning, his mirrored glasses reflecting back our patchwork of colorful Gore-Tex.

"You're here! Excellent. Now it's time to start the real work. I hope you are ready because your best night of sleep was sometime before you arrived here. Here, you get used to being tired, cold, breathless, constipated, and bored. Enjoy."

He smiles his big wide Cheshire Cat grin, and it's hard to say if he's joking or not. Regardless, I smile back. This is what I came for. To be here. To climb. And to get home again.

Chapter Nineteen:

Tate

April 23
Everest Base Camp
17,600 feet above sea level

*E*verest Base Camp. Launchpad for hundreds of elite-level dreams and final destination for tens of thousands of tourists, who haul themselves up here to be within touching distance of the glory of Everest. I have no idea why they'd bother, unless they're impressed by a giant garbage dump with oxygen canisters flung everywhere and dozens of tent villages. It's massive, like multiple-football-fields massive, and we walk for twenty minutes through a city of snow and wind and tents to find our spot.

Altitude-wise, I'm rocking it. As always, altitude bothers me way less than most people. I barely have a headache, and unlike Rose, who lost weight she really couldn't afford to lose, or my dad, who looks downright skeletal, my appetite's all good. Ang Pasang, the head cook, loves me.

Still, even with the good food, loud music, internet, and party vibe Finjo and the other expedition leaders try hard to keep going, it's freaking brutal here. Wind howls constantly, and a shitty icy fog swamps us every few days, blocking all views of the mountains and making it an actual legit danger to get lost between the main tent and our sleep tent. With temperatures way below zero with windchill, you could die of exposure trying to get to your tent, which is honestly not the way I want to go.

Over the next few days, I try so damn hard to make myself belong here. Rose is distracted, focused on the summit and the training: climb up to higher elevations to push our bodies to acclimatize, then descend again to sleep at lower altitude to recover. Then push higher the next day, then rest; repeat. Repeat again. Finjo's schedule, like all the other guides up here, is pretty locked down: they've got a system of acclimatization, and we follow like breathless, exhausted sheep. But Rose has turned inward, talking less, and when we are alone, she curls against me in her sleeping bag, shivering and quiet. I get it—EBC isn't what anyone would call romantic, what with the cold and the thin air and the stank. But it's not only that we're not jumping each other like sex-crazed monkeys. We've both gone into our own heads, our own thoughts too loud for much else to make sense. She's super focused on the climb ahead, like she's already halfway up the mountain, pushing forward against obstacles only she can see. And me? I'm stuck, every day making it clearer that I want to be anywhere else. It's like a nightmare where something's rushing toward me and I can't move my feet to get out of the way, except I'm awake. And what's rushing toward me is a once-in-a-lifetime climb that I used to want. But no matter how many times I tell my mind to shut the fuck up, to remember when I was so pumped for this, I can't seem to convince myself to want it anymore.

• • •

Today's another slog across the Icefall. We're trying to get to Camp One, a temporary setup of tiny tents at 19,500 feet where we'll acclimatize for a night before heading back to Base Camp. The camp's grim and freezing, but it has to be better than getting there. The Khumbu Icefall is infamous, a frozen Niagara Falls of ice, booby-trapped with crevasses and strung up with rope and metal ladders set by Sherpas at the beginning of the climbing season. They're the Icefall Doctors, the ones who lost four of their own before the season even started. Apparently, they had enough workers to get the ropes strung up and tidy before the big-money climbers showed up.

The Icefall is fucking treacherous, always. Seracs, chunks of ice larger than houses, can break off, dropping with a wrath-of-God crash on whatever's below. Finjo told us the Icefall *moves* several feet each day, a slow churning of ice and rock, which to me is straight out of a horror movie—the idea of a slowly creeping killer wall of ice. The Sherpas check the ropes and ladders, making sure the shifting ice hasn't collapsed a ladder here or left one hanging over a newly widened crevasse there. But that's no guarantee there hasn't been a change since they last checked. There's no being safe—there's only being lucky. And the Icefall's at the start of the climb. We're going to go through it again and again and again.

Despite the insanity of what we're staring at, the Icefall doesn't really require much technical ice climbing. The ropes and ladders change it from a serious climb to a fucked-up tap dance across open crevasses. We're not roped into each other, responsible for keeping our partners safe. Instead each climber clips into the fixed rope that's anchored along the route and moves as fast as possible in a deadly game of musical chairs, hoping to be far away from danger when the music stops.

"God, it's beautiful," Paul whispers as we trudge across the gravelly moraine to the edge of the ice. "It's almost painful to look at, like some mythological sight that bewitches all who see it."

Dad snorts and tries to reply, then coughs before he can say anything. He bends over double, resting his hands on his legs and coughing until he chokes. He swears he feels as good as new.

Paul wraps an arm around him. "Easy, there. Take slow, shallow breaths. Don't try to breathe too deeply."

Dad manages a small smile. "I thought you were a shrink. What are you doing imitating a real doctor?"

Paul laughs and claps him lightly on the back. "Real enough for you. Med school is med school, even if I did sleep through most of the pulmonary stuff." He steps away. "You ready to keep going?"

Dad's smile is gone, and he looks like a sick old man. But he nods and starts forward again.

Paul looks at me, and even with his goggles and hood, I can tell he's worried. "What do you think?" he asks.

What do I think? I think my dad looks brutal—like those medieval paintings where a skeleton's there to show Death at the feast. I think this place is hell on Earth. I think it's the most beautiful thing I've ever seen. I think I want to leave, now, and never come back.

I glance over at him. I want to call bullshit, point out that Dad's dying by inches, and Rose is distant and withdrawn, and we should all call it and go down and drink tea and play Uno instead of trying not to die on what's barely the first step on this treacherous disaster of an idea. But I don't say anything. I give him the thumbs-up, plug my earbuds back in, and start to move.

My head's hunched to keep the wind from blasting me off the ladder. We're near the most dangerous part, known as the Popcorn Field, where the four Sherpas died earlier this season. Speed is the only thing that can help at this point; it's just a matter of moving faster than the ice so that we're out of the way whenever the next big crash comes along. I push ahead fast, grateful that my lungs are strong. For a minute I don't care that Rose and Dad and everyone else is slower than me; I want to get myself out of here. Now.

I taste how humanity dies in this place. I can't make myself care about anyone but myself, and I just want to get through this. Fixing Camp One in my sights, I forget everything and everyone. My world narrows to ice and snow, blue and white and endless and deadly, and I move fast, faster, until my muscles scream.

I don't care. I want to move even faster, to get out of this shit before it swallows me, before I become another corpse along the route.

I need to get out.

Faster.

I get so far ahead that I barely hear Rose screaming.

Screaming for me, screaming about Dad collapsing on the ice.

I turn, and way behind me, he's down, a small crumpled dot on the ice like something dropped from way up high. There's a screaming in my ears, and suddenly I am falling-fallingfalling

inmyhead

butalsohererighthere

"Tate! Can you hear me?"

It's Rose, and she needs me, but

fallingfallingfalling

I drop to my knees.

Press my head against the ice.

fuckfuckfuckfuckfuckwhatthefuck

iswrongwithme

breatheinbreatheout

breathe in breathe out

flower candle

in out

in

out

I catch my breath. I get back to my feet. My neck and back prickle with sweat, and spots dance in front of my eyes, but I stay standing. I look back, and Finjo has an arm around Dad, lifting him up.

Flower. Candle. Breathe in. Breathe out. I move my feet, nightmare-slow through my panic, rushing to get to them but really rushing to get away from here, to get away and never ever come back.

Chapter Twenty:

Rose

April 23–25
Khumbu Icefall
18,000 feet above sea level

*J*ordan is standing in front of me, then he's not. He sinks to the ground like he's fallen asleep, the clatter of his gear hitting the ice loud and terrifying.

"Jordan!" I scream. "Paul!"

There's no running here, on the cracked and death-trapped ice, and no oxygen to scream above the wind. But Paul and Finjo arrive as I crouch, trying to understand what's happened. Finjo pushes me away and puts an oxygen mask over Jordan's face. Jordan groans around the mask. My heart slows slightly. He's awake.

"He will be fine. You should keep climbing with Dawa. We will bring him down to the med tent."

I stare at him, unsure what he means. Keep climbing? I

don't even know if Jordan is conscious. Before I can answer, Tate is here, gasping.

"What the hell? Dad? *DAD*?" His face is a mask of horror.

Jordan groans a little louder and tries to sit up.

Paul puts an arm around Tate, but Tate stands like he's made of rock. "He's going to be okay. They're getting him down to the doctor right now."

Jordan's trying to get up now, and Finjo and Asha are on either side of him, supporting him. I stand too but don't move, unsure.

"Finjo, I think we'd prefer to go down with you and see how Jordan's doing," Paul says, his doctor voice calm and reassuring.

Finjo frowns slightly but nods, distracted by the work of keeping Jordan upright.

"It is as you wish, though you will need to return here tomorrow. No matter what, you must keep training."

I stare at the ice around me, watching Jordan struggle to move down the mountain. Next to me, Tate is silent, his face still frozen.

When we get down to the med tent, a friendly Canadian named Dr. Celina tells us that Jordan's suffering from acute mountain sickness, where the body reacts to reduced oxygen with hangover or flu-like symptoms. The best treatment and the only way to avoid it growing worse—and potentially life-threatening—is to descend to lower altitudes. So he needs to head down to the clinic in Pheriche, immediately. It is decided that Bishal will bring him down. After a heated discussion with Finjo, Tate insists on going with them, and thirty minutes later he hugs me so hard that I can't catch my breath, then they're disappearing into the fog.

Base Camp without Tate is Base Camp unplugged, no energy, no warmth, no heat. Even though they will be back in a few days, everything feels different, wrong. As though to make sure I notice the wrongness of it all, bad weather has blown in, snow squalls and wind and the screaming and groaning of ice moving in the Icefall. I spend the night alone in our tent, unable to sleep, wondering how it all changed so fast.

At least in the main tent, I am just another person, lost in the noise and bustle. There Luc and Yoon Su and the Sherpas congregate, playing music, checking email, dealing up the Uno cards. When I walk in, the brightness almost chases away the Dread. Almost.

"You want to join me for something hot?" Luc calls from the table. He's sprawled on two chairs, his giant down parka thrown on a third. He waggles his eyebrows. "I mean tea, of course."

I roll my eyes but walk over. Luc's casual flirting seems as foreign here as it would in a bomb shelter, but he has continued with his signature banter as though we're all at a party.

"Tea sounds great," I say, sliding in next to him.

Yoon Su is over at the computers, madly typing. She is still live-blogging the expedition for her students back home, and I wonder what she's writing, how she can put a positive, kid-friendly spin on this combination of grueling training and endless downtime. My notes to Mami have gotten shorter and shorter, often just a string of emojis with the video attached. I can't capture how I feel about this place, and I've given up trying. The waiting feels endless.

As though reading my mind, Luc speaks. "I do not like all this waiting around. The brain, it starts to go in circles, and . . ." He makes a gesture like he wants to sweep away all his thoughts. He smiles, but it doesn't reach his eyes. "When I climb, my brain quiets, but now, when we sit around, there is no escape."

I nod. "Can you write to Amelie, at least? Is she excited for you to come home?"

At this he looks more cheerful. "She is missing me terribly, she says! Which is good news, yes?"

"Definitely!" I high-five him, and we sip our tea in silence —or, at least, I'm silent, while Luc talks on about Amelie's most recent email, how he promised her climbing lessons in the Alps this summer, and where he will take her to "dazzle her with my skills." My mind stays stuck on the computer. I haven't checked email since that first day, haven't responded to Dad's good-news email that felt more like a grim reminder of how much Mami's lost, haven't told them about Jordan's collapse. I comfort myself knowing that they would call Finjo's satellite phone if they really needed to reach me, but the thought is sour and ugly. Cowardly Rose, chewing on her tail and hiding behind a smitten Frenchman.

Standing abruptly, I head over to the computers. "Be right back," I say to Luc.

Logging in to my email, I stare at the names filling my inbox: notes from friends and family wishing me good luck, emails from Yale with logistics and details about my housing for next year, junk from stores and bands I love. And one from Mami. My heart stutters, anxiety and excitement warring in my chest, and I have to blink back tears—stupid, Waterworks Rose—just seeing her name. In some ways it's even worse than I imagined, being here without her. She is the one I want to follow so that I can be led, confident and sure that my strong always-climbing monkey mama will guide me through the Icefall, up the Western Cwm, all the way up to the summit. But that wish is useless, a wasted wish, not worth birthday candles or shooting stars or lost eyelashes. Better to save the wishes for what might come true: a safe climb. Me and Tate at the summit. Mami strong enough to travel to Kathmandu. A reunion with Mami and Dad where I tell them all about it, watch the pride and excitement blaze in their eyes.

I open the email.

Rosalita, you must be at Base Camp already. So exciting! Who knows when you will read this, since I don't believe all those stories about cushy Base Camp tents with computers and movie screens. If I know you, you are missing food from home more than anything! Know that I am cooking up a storm already, freezing it all so you can return and have everything your sweet heart desires—

I stop reading to blink back tears.

I feel fine and much steadier. The medication is super helpful! And I love having exercises to do. You know me—I am always best when faced with a challenge. It is hard not to be with you, but I am okay. I promise.

Anyway, my love, I don't want you to worry. Focus on the climb ahead, and remember that you are STRONG, WISE, AND BRAVE. You can do anything. Be safe, mi cariño.

Besos—Mami

I stare at the email so hard that my eyes could be lasers, beaming through the monitor tubes and wires, across the miles and the oceans and straight into her brain. It sounds so much like her that the missing threatens to swallow me. At least, unlike Dad, she's not pretending her slog on a treadmill is something to be happy about. And she does love a challenge. But the scope of what she has lost—of what *we* have lost—makes me dizzy. She should be here. And the unfairness of it undoes me. Never mind the unfairness of the Sherpas who died on the Icefall or of the poverty all around me. Those greater injustices *should* matter more than my problems, but I can't move beyond Mami. I feel like a toddler, stomping my feet and screaming *NOT FAIR*. I am stuck.

My fingers hover over the keys, but I don't know what to write. Cowardly Rose, indeed. Before I can write anything, Finjo bursts in, the door banging and slamming behind him.

"Okay, attention, everyone! This storm is more serious than we thought. It is nothing to worry about. But we will halt all preparations for now." He looks around.

He catches Yoon Su's eye and anticipates her question. "Once the weather clears, we will have to wait for them to go back up and finish setting up the high camps, it is true. But there is no rushing the weather here. We all must wait until the mountain offers us a chance. IF it offers us that chance. As you know, there are no guarantees."

Yoon Su sighs so loudly we can hear her over the wind flapping outside. "I heard that some other expeditions are continuing to set up," she says.

Finjo frowns. "They make their own choices, but I do not risk the lives of our staff because someone is in a hurry." When Yoon Su stays quiet, he continues. "For now you can rest, write letters, try to eat as much as you can, and wait out the storm. That is all you can do, so you might as well enjoy it." He heads over to the cooking area and starts muttering with Ang Pasang.

Paul comes over. "It's wild out there. Even walking across Base Camp, I can barely see anything." He shakes his head. "I'm glad Jordan got down before the weather hit." He squeezes my shoulder. "He'll be fine, Rosie. Descending and getting to the clinic is the best thing that he can do. And you know Jordan! He's going to be fighting this infection with everything he's got."

I nod. "Sure. I know. It's just . . . weird being here without him and Tate. And the storm, it's so loud . . . " I let my voice trail off. Really what I feel is far away from everyone and everything that keeps me grounded, keeps me safe. But I don't know how to tell him that. I clear my throat. "It's all going to be fine, though, right? I mean, the weather, the Sherpas, Tate and Jordan . . . It's all going to come together. Isn't it?"

Paul's arm is heavy and comforting, but his words—spoken in his quiet, honest voice—don't reassure me. "I hope so, but we don't really know, do we?" he says. "There are so many variables that go into these expeditions, and we control almost none of them. But I'll tell you something. I'd rather we find the problems down here than up above the death zone. As bad as it is to imagine it all falling apart, this is the best place for that to happen."

I want to agree, but the thought that we have come so far, worked so hard and it might end before it begins makes me almost physically sick. My mind flashes back to the day Mami came home from the doctor's, newly diagnosed with MS, the dream dying in real time in her eyes and voice as she told us. Before that day, Everest was another item on the to-do list—an exciting one for sure, but I was following Tate and Jordan and most of all Mami's dream. They wanted it so much, all I had to do was keep up. But now . . . Now I'm so close, and I want this more than I ever imagined.

I blink back tears. It's not over. It can't be.

"How can you be so calm about it?" I ask.

Paul smiles. "A lot of practice. I don't know if I ever told you, but Drew and I had some pretty intense discussions before I signed on for this trip. He's never been crazy about my climbing, but he knows how important it is to me. And before we got married, I told him that I thought big trips were a thing of my past—that I'd keep climbing locally but that I had gotten the big peaks out of my system." He sighs. "And then I got this chance at Everest."

I look up. "Was he mad?" I've met Drew a few times, and he's cool, a little older and nerdier than Paul but pretty easygoing.

Paul rolls his eyes. "You could say that. He accused me of being selfish, reminded me that it wasn't just my life I was gambling with. You know we're on the waiting list to adopt, right? He asked point-blank if I loved climbing more than him. I said, no, of course not, but then . . ." He trails off.

"But then here you are," I finish.

"Yup. And we're okay. I mean, we talked more, and I told him how careful I would be, how I would limit my risks and do absolutely everything in my power to come home safely. So I left with his blessing, sort of. And in convincing him, I managed to convince myself that I'm okay with whatever happens, that if we don't get to summit, it's still all good. But right now that feels like total BS. I want a shot at this mountain so badly that I think I'd leave right now if Finjo let me." He grins, lightening the mood. "So I guess it's a good thing we're paying him to make smart decisions for us."

He squeezes me and lets me go. "But it's not over yet, Rosie. Not by a long shot."

As though to prove him right, Yoon Su charges up. "So. I talked to Cameron in the weather tent—"

Cameron is our weather god, the one who monitors all the computer models and satellites and tells us what's happening. It's not surprising that Yoon Su has become fast friends with him.

"Anyway, he tells me this storm will blow out within a few days and we should have clear weather coming in. 'Perfect Everest weather,' he calls it. So Rose, wipe that sad-girl look off your face! We'll be climbing again straightaway!"

Paul and I both smile, but we must look unconvinced, not enough grit and drive and push for Yoon Su because she flashes her fast smile and pretend-shakes me.

"Hello? Is Miss Rose there? We're climbing tomorrow! Get ready, girl!"

This time my smile is real. It's not over. Not yet.

Chapter Twenty-One:

Tate

April 23–26
Pheriche
14,300 feet above sea level

*P*heriche's still cold and grim, but the lower altitude and perks at the clinic make it feel like a spa. Dad's hooked back up to an O2 monitor, with Bo changing out his drugs yet again. Me, I'm chilling out, trying to forget the sight of him crumpled on the ground, the shotgun crack of the ice shifting above and below me, the fucking constant terror that's been flooding my brain for the past few days at Base Camp that I'm only noticing now that it's gone. Trying to forget the way panic wrapped around my neck like a rope when I saw him lying there. Being down here, away from the mountain, is like someone stepped off my chest, letting me breathe again. And I realize: there is absolutely no fucking way I can do this.

It was easy to leave. Dr. Celina's cool and funny and seems like someone you'd meet surfing or at a beach barbecue, except for the fact she's a high-altitude specialist and the most senior doctor at Base Camp. But there was nothing chill about her when she ordered Dad to get down to Pheriche, for the lower altitude and the medical clinic, right away. Dad didn't even argue with her, which is how I knew he was seriously wrecked. He nodded like that was the most he could manage and closed his eyes again. It wasn't even something I thought about, staying up there. I told Finjo I was leaving, that I didn't want my dad to be alone, and after arguing for a minute, he agreed, saying that, with my level of acclimatization and fitness, I could miss a few climbs. I didn't bother to tell him I wouldn't be back.

It was so simple to walk away.

But Rose . . . Rose looked lost, and I wanted so fucking badly to tell her to come with us, to get off this deadly and miserable chunk of ice, but I know she wouldn't. I wanted to tell her not to worry, that I'd be back soon and we'd be chasing our dream up the mountain in no time, but I didn't say that either. I grabbed her and hugged her goodbye. And said nothing.

"You'll . . . Jordan will be fine, right? And you guys will be back in a few days?" Her words were muffled into my neck, and I pretended not to hear them. I just held her tighter, whispering to her to be safe, to take care.

Then I left her there.

•   •   •

Physically, I'm great. Dr. Bo calls me an absolute unit because I've barely lost any weight and my oxygen levels are strong. In theory I'm the ideal candidate to try for the summit. In theory I should be back up at Base Camp, getting ready. In theory I should be with Rose. But I stay.

I don't know what the hell is wrong with me. I mean, our whole lives are only built on luck and timing and good instincts—my ice axes caught in the crevasse in Rainier, Dad didn't collapse anywhere too dangerous on the Icefall, there are a thousand near misses I've already survived—so why can't I do this? I'm fine, which means I should do this; I should climb, gear up, and take my spot next to Rose. Back up. Back through the Icefall, again and again, until we push farther up, into the death zone, past the bodies of climbers who died there and were left behind.

And yeah, Maya might have been the driver of this whole plan, but I was *so* there with her, so ready to claim bragging rights on the tallest mountain in the world. Before my fall on Rainier, it never occurred to me *not* to want to climb it, not even when friends told us we were nuts or we watched those hard-ass documentaries where someone's nose freezes off and shit. Even then, I wanted this.

But not anymore. I know, *know* deep in my core, that I will die if I try this. It's not me being dramatic, it's a fact. There are so many ways to fuck up on a climb like this, but having your head in the wrong space is a sure one. The panic that swallowed me whole on the Icefall will wait until we're in the death zone, until there's nothing to do but keep pushing to stay alive, and then it'll show up and play with me like a cat with a mouse until it decides to chew me up and spit me out.

It's over. I know it's over.

• • •

For three days Dad's been resting and getting stronger, and I'm in limbo. I spend most of the time walking through the village and toward the mountains, then turning around and walking back again. Bo and Dad think I'm training, making sure not to lose my edge before heading back up to Base Camp.

I don't say anything.

I know I need to tell Dad I can't climb, but the words won't come. Even thinking about it makes my mouth dry and my gut clench, and I do everything I can to avoid eye contact, avoid conversation. The hours and days slide by, and I stay silent, knowing that a shitstorm of epic proportions is closing in, inevitable.

And finally it hits. Bo and I are in the main room of the clinic, discussing whether the NCAA is a bullshit league or not, when Dad walks in.

"Tate! Behold! I'm back and better than ever," he says, making pretend muscles.

I force a grin, all thoughts of college basketball gone. "That's great. So . . . the infection's gone?"

He nods. "Lungs seem clear, I gained back a pound, thanks to Bo's secret stash of high-calorie foodstuff . . . I'm ready." He looks at me. "What about you? The good doctor gave you a green light, yeah?"

Bo gives a thumbs up. "Tate's in great shape," he says. "If we could replicate his vitals for everyone who wants to summit, the percentage of successful climbs would go way up!"

I swallow and look down.

My dad grins. "Tate got lucky with his strength and stamina. Though you know we call him the Master of Disaster, right? He's a bull in a china shop sometimes. You need to be incredibly careful on this climb, buddy. There's no way to be safe in the Icefall if you rush, and we're going through it at least six or seven more times—"

"No." I squeeze my eyes shut.

"What's that?"

I'm trying, trying to keep the words from coming, but they burst out, ignoring the DISTRESS! AVOID! DISTRESS! calls my brain's sending.

"I said no. I'm not going to go through the Icefall six or seven more times. I'm just . . . not."

Dad's mouth is open, and if it weren't so awful, it would be funny how confused, completely and utterly fucking baffled, he looks. "I don't understand. Bud, there are no shortcuts—"

"I don't want a shortcut. I want out. I'm sorry, but I'm not doing this. I'm not going through the Icefall or the Western Cwm or the Balcony or trying for the summit."

Now Bo and Dad are staring at me. I need to get out of here. I start to push by them, heading for the door.

"I can't. I'm out. I'm sorry. I'm sorry I wasted a shit ton of your money and that I'm not going to be there for the big father-son moment you've been dreaming of. But I can't do this." I am nearly at the door by now, nearly out in the fast-approaching darkness and gloom, and I want to go, to move, to get the hell out of here and walk until my legs give out. My chest hurts and my palms are sweating and I need to *move*, but Dad puts out a hand and hauls me back. I shrug, hard, but he won't let go; he holds on, staring at me.

Silence.

"Well now—" Bo starts to talk, his face worried. Dimly, in the back of my mind, I feel bad for the guy, but mostly I want to get away.

But Dad interrupts before he can go on. "Why?" One word, almost whispered.

It's the shock and hurt in his face that undoes me. Like I'm doing this *to* him, like this is breaking *his* fucking heart.

All my shame and guilt get buried under a wave of rage, pure and energizing. I want to stab my thoughts right into his brain—let him thrash around in my nightmares, feel tightness in my ribs, which still ache from the fall in Rainier, relive my memory of falling and the loop of panic and terror that hit me whenever I let my guard down.

"Why would I?" I yell. "Who ever said that 'Hey, Tate, just because you're strong and have good lung capacity, you should break yourself to pieces climbing the world's deadliest mountains?' Did you ever think, *ever*, that me almost dying again and again—being the Master of Disaster, as you call it—is a reason for me to rethink this? Did you even think about that?"

"Climbing is all you wanted to do! You pushed for this!" Dad starts.

But I keep going, like a faucet's been turned on and I'm powerless to stop it. "Did I? I don't know about that! Did I want this? Or did I just want to be decent at something so I didn't disappoint you yet again? I fucking tried, I really did! I know you think I'm a fuckup and a loser and a failure, but I tried. And I. Cannot. Do this."

"That's bull! You can quit if you want to—I can hardly make you climb—but don't try to pin this on anyone else!" Dad says, and he's yelling too. "Christ, Tate, what else are you going to quit? College? If you even get in?" He flings his hands up in the air. "You are so smart. So damn smart. Smarter than me, smarter than your mother . . . but you won't work for anything! What the *hell* is your life going to be? I'm worried about you! I am really, really worried about you!"

He swallows, coughs. "I swear if you quit this, you're going to feel like such a goddamn failure. Don't do that to yourself, son. You need this climb. You need to do this!"

The words feel like rocks hitting my gut, and my vision narrows. For all his nagging and bitching, he has never said this before. He's never told me exactly how pathetic he thinks I am, how big a fuckup he thinks I'm going to make of my life.

He takes a breath, his chest rattling, ready to keep going. "Now listen," he starts, and I can tell he's trying to calm down, trying to be the helpful parent who will help me pull the right tool out of the toolbox to fix my fuckup self. But I don't want to listen.

Cold, clean anger takes over.

"NO. I don't want to hear it. Maybe you're right. Maybe I could do this if I really tried. Maybe I'm one big failure after another. But I. Don't. Fucking. Want to."

Chapter Twenty-Two:

Rose

April 28–May 7
Everest Base Camp
17,600 feet above sea level

*H*e is not coming.

He is not going to climb.

It's like vertigo, hearing the news, like being back in the hospital with Mami, like free-falling before the rope catches.

Tate will not be here with me.

Jordan handed me a letter Tate wrote, but the words mean nothing. He can't. He's so sorry. He wants to be there for me but. I crumple it up and drop it. Only maybe I throw it. There's a sharp *craaack*, and I realize my phone was in the same hand as the letter. And it's now on the ground, smashed.

I race away from Jordan, whose face is tight and angry as he tries to explain how Tate needs some time. I push past Paul, whose eyes are too kind. I need to get away from all of them. In our tent I curl up as tightly as I can, trying to protect myself from the Dread and hurt and fear that want to attack. Rose Unplugged, losing power by the minute. A noise I barely recognize as my own sob squeaks out before I silence it. The tents are thin, and today the wind is quiet.

No one. I have no one.

Like the low, terrifying rumble of an avalanche, a wall of desolation so huge I fear it will bury me threatens to break free. Who am I without Mami? Without Tate? Will I really hang my life off a rope 8,000 miles from home without the people who keep me safe?

I bite down on my cheek till I taste blood, then force myself to breathe, coughing in the thin air. I count my breaths, stare at the pile of gear in the corner, quiet my mind. I retrace our climbing route, think about our upcoming trips to Camp Two and above. I picture the glory of the peaks in the blazing morning sun. I don't know how long I stay there, eyes closed, picturing the rock and ice above me.

This is Mount Everest, the mountain we have trained for and dreamed about for over half my life. It started with Mami, with Tate, with our group, like a little family, but that was then.

And now I'm here, and I've trained, and I've spent days climbing through the most jaw-droppingly beautiful mountains I've ever seen. I am here to climb.

I am ready.

No. I am *eager*.

I want this more than I have ever wanted anything.

I force the Dread back. I am not afraid, not this time. I am fucking furious. Tate might be having a tantrum, or he might be freaking out, or he might want to hang out and watch basketball with Dr. Bo at the clinic.

I don't care. Because his path no longer has anything to do with mine.

I stay in the tent as the sky darkens. I don't want dinner, and I definitely don't want to sit around the table with Paul and Jordan and Luc and Yoon Su and discuss why Tate's not here, what he might be thinking and how he might change his mind. The Dread claws at me, but I push it back.

Alone. Alone. Alone. I make it a threat, a drumbeat, a promise. A fierce self-righteous anger warms me, and alone in my tent, I go over Tate's transgressions: he kissed me even knowing this trip is a knife-edge of challenge and focus; he's quitting, despite the fact that Mami would literally give any-thing to be here. He's leaving me alone after swearing he wants to be with me. The anger feels good. Strong. Like building a wall, brick after brick, that will keep the Dread away and keep me fueled and powerful.

· · ·

The next morning I'm staring at the dead remains of my phone, which won't even turn on, when Paul corners me. "Do you know what's going on here? Jordan's barely coher-ent on the subject. Why is Tate not climbing? Did he talk to you about this?"

I shake my head, ignoring the pounding headache that has been constant since we arrived. The wind is quiet, and all around the noises of Base Camp buzz and clatter. "No. I had no idea."

Paul looks worried. "I hope he's okay. This is . . . unlike him. He's been so excited about this for so long."

I nod, the anger right below the surface. "Yeah, well, apparently not."

Paul shoots me a look, but all he says is, "Though if I think back more recently, when we all talked about the climb, Tate's been pretty quiet. Those last few months, he didn't seem too interested in talking about it. Mostly it was Maya. And you."

"That's because we did all the organizing, like we do for all our trips!" I burst out. "Tate never thinks about anything unless it's right in front of his face."

Paul doesn't say anything, but his eyes are a little too understanding.

"Not that we minded," I say, trying to sound more casual. "We loved planning and researching. It's just that Tate's never been one to plan much beyond his next surf session or video game." I try to keep my voice steady. "What did Bishal say?" Bishal, who went down with two Russos and returned with one. Bishal, who liked to bet Tate he could win his favorite ball cap from him in our Uno games. Bishal, who is Tate's friend.

Paul shrugs. "He told Finjo that Tate would be staying in Pheriche for now. Jordan keeps talking like he thinks Tate is having a tantrum and will show up when he gets over it." He shakes his head. "But I don't know. So much of this climb is in the mindset, in how we mentally prepare for what's ahead. If he's not in that headspace, if he doesn't think he can do it, well, I think it's brave of him to admit it. This isn't a place to fake it and hope for the best."

Paul looks at me for a long moment, and I imagine he can see everything: Tate's panicked face at Namche, right before he kissed me; our first astonished kisses; the way he curled around me in our tiny beds along the trail like I was something infinitely precious; his promises that we belong together.

I keep my face blank, not letting the anger show. Tate has left me here. *Brave* isn't the word that comes to mind. "Sure," I say finally. "If he doesn't want to be here, it's better that he's not."

"Rosie, can I ask a nosy question that you can refuse to answer? Are you and Tate . . . Did things change between you on this trip?" Paul asks. "Because I know he's your best friend, and that's hard enough, but—"

I interrupt. "There's nothing between me and Tate," I say. The lie—is it a lie?—feels thick and sour and painful in my mouth.

Paul holds my gaze, and I force myself to look back. I trust Paul, I do, and his honesty about him and Drew echoes in my head, but this is different. Whatever there might have been between me and Tate is over, and I am here alone.

I push down at the Dread that wants to surface. I remind myself that this is MY climb, not Tate's. Not Paul's or Jordan's. Mine. There's a reason people are selfish on Everest, because they have to be. I think about Yoon Su and her relentless training. She is here alone, pursuing her dream. For a second my mind flickers to Mami, but I push it away. She can't be here, but I can, and I will climb. For her, yes, but also for myself. I touch the folded photo of me and Mami that's been in my jacket pocket since we left California, the one I'll hold up at the summit. I imagine telling her about it, curled up under blankets on the couch, Dad leaning over to see the photos as I describe every detail.

I try not to think about the fact that Tate *could* be right next to me. And he chose not to be. He doesn't want to be here. He doesn't want *me* enough to be here.

My climb.

Paul looks at me. "Are you sure you don't want to talk about it? I think Tate should do what he feels he has to. But I know you were counting on him. Are you—?"

"I'm fine," I cut him off. Try to smile, a real smile. "No, seriously, I am. This is exactly where I want to be." With or without Tate.

• • •

We are in our last weeks of training, moving our bodies up the mountain and back down again to acclimatize. Then it will be time to cross our fingers and hope that the weather window opens to let us attempt the summit. We are so close. Life at Base Camp is semi-hideous, semi-awesome. The hideousness comes from how hard it is to breathe, how frozen I am as soon as the sun goes behind the peaks in midafternoon, how dirty I am using only a semi-functional solar shower. The awesome is just that. The mountains are awe-inspiring. They are jagged and ghostly and vast and oh-so-beautiful. The ice on the glacier cracks and sings songs that echo through the tents, and the wind bites down on us and reminds us that even as we drink coffee and watch DVDs, we are far, so very far, from home. It's glorious.

I can barely make myself eat. The altitude kills my appetite as thoroughly as the endless coughing, caused by the dry air and cold, kills my sleep. We are all hacking, and I now know why high-altitude coughing is called the Khumbu cough. I love it, but really, humans don't belong here. And we are barely at the edge of Everest, with so much farther to go.

We're going back up the Icefall again today. Jordan moves

slowly, but he is moving, coughing less and keeping pace with me and Paul.

"God. This still scares the crap out of me," I say to Paul, staring out at the deadly and beautiful seracs of blue ice. The first ladders are right ahead.

"Well, scared is probably about right." Paul looks ahead at Luc, and I wonder if he's thinking what I'm thinking: that Luc isn't scared enough. He's strong—probably the strongest climber I know, other than Tate—but he's fast to the point of recklessness. I've thought of Luc's words in Namche again and again—that climbing drives away all unimportant questions—but if he's noticed that we're walking side by side with death, he doesn't show it. Yoon Su of course is nowhere in sight. She was, like every day, the first person up the ice. Despite her early starts, we usually catch up with her toward the end of the climb. There's only so fast she can move at this altitude without having to eventually slow down.

"You feel okay?" Asha asks. She is behind us, matching our pace.

I nod without saying anything. I'm approaching another ladder, actually three ladders strapped together and laid horizontally across a chasm.

"Not much like a ladder at home, is it?" I say to no one in particular.

"No. Can't hold on unless you want to crawl, and that seems a little undignified." Paul isn't looking up either. Luc has gone on ahead with Finjo and another guide.

"No crawling," I vow and put my foot on the first rung of the ladder. The metal spikes of my crampons clatter against the metal rung. It is not a reassuring sound, nothing like the solid crunch of crampon into snowpack or ice. I steady myself and keep walking, slow, deliberate steps that slide and clink on the swaying, bouncing ladder. I try not to look down, to look only ahead to where the ladder lands on the far side. But my eyes drop downward, as though to spite me.

I stop moving. The colors are mesmerizing, every shade of blue, from the most delicate barely-there turquoise to the bottomless near-black of a night sky. The crevasse is wide enough for sunlight to dance through the ice along the side, sending out glittering prisms of color, before narrowing to endless darkness. I am transfixed.

"Rose. ROSE! You need to keep moving!" Paul's voice, ahead of me on the ice, startles me back into movement, and I lurch, almost losing my balance.

"Sorry," I say and quickly start walking again, keeping my eyes up as though my life depends on it.

When I get to the other side, Asha hops on, light as a fox, and moves quickly to meet us.

"That was good!" she says, and I'm glad my hood and goggles hide the sweat dripping down my cheek. "It is easier each time, right? There are many ladders, and we cross them many times. Lots of time to get good."

I try to swallow past the fear in my throat. She's right. There is no way up the mountain except through the Icefall, through the beautiful, terrible skyscrapers of ice. We are here, in this beautiful alien place, and home is a distant pinprick in my memory. The most frightening part is that some sliver of me wants to stay here forever.

• • •

Time seems to repeat and fold back on itself. Climb high, sleep low: this is our mantra, our one guiding principle. Every day we push through the Icefall, and it never gets easy. In the afternoons, when we are done climbing for the day, we listen for the crash of collapsing ice, wondering what crevasse opened up since our last visit. We climb back to Camp One at almost 20,000 feet and then turn around to come down. A few days later, we climb up again and spend the night there. We repeat this process with Camp Two, which is farther up the mountain at 21,000 feet. From there we can stare up the vertical wall of blue ice of Lhotse Face. We will need to climb it to reach Camp Three and, of course, when we do our final summit push. It looks like a playground for gods. It looks endless. My body is tired, so tired, all the time. I make deals with myself to keep walking, promise myself sleep and rest and sips of water if I can go ten more steps, then another ten. I dream about the summit.

• • •

We have been at EBC for almost three weeks. Tate has been gone longer than he was here, and I wonder: Was he a dream? Were we together, was that real, or did I imagine that we kissed each other, held each other, touched each other like we were explorers traveling sacred paths? It is only at night when I can't sleep and the wind pulls and bends at my tent that I let my mind drift to him. Otherwise, he is as distant to me as California. During the day, when I am reminded of him, because everything reminds me, I force myself to think about the next day's climb. I think about standing at the top.

With my phone dead, it's easy to stop filming, stop capturing every moment for Mami. I log in to the camp computer and send one email, telling her and Dad that I broke my phone and that it's too hard to get online on the shared computer, so they should follow the official expedition blog, which updates in real time. Then I log out. I stop charging my GoPro, sick of fighting the cold to keep it alive for more than a few minutes in the wind. It's easier this way.

Each morning we leave before sunrise to minimize the dangers of being on the Icefall in the heat of the day. Here, the temperatures swing from well below freezing to over eighty degrees within a few hours. When the sun peeks over the mountains on the Icefall, it is blindingly beautiful—and scorching.

In between climbs we rest. Today's another rest day, and Yoon Su is zipped into her tent back at Base Camp. The winds have picked up again, making weird howling noises through the fabric. I stick my head in. Yoon Su is writing furiously.

"Do you want to go and see if the guys will play Uno?" I ask. I'm restless, unable to read anything or write anyone. I don't think of writing Tate, because there isn't anything to say. I don't want to be this angry. But I am.

Yoon Su looks up briefly and shakes her head. "No, thank you. I will finish writing this, then try to rest." She bows her head back to the paper and continues to scribble.

Yoon Su is disappearing in front of my eyes. She wasn't very big when we got here, and her appetite, like mine, is down to nothing. I try one more time.

"Why don't we go into the dining tent at least? You can write there, on the computer, and we can get some tea. And try to eat something."

Yoon Su throws her hands in the air, looking annoyed. I flinch.

"Would you leave off! I need to finish this. It is for my

family, not the blog. I need to concentrate! You go. I'll meet you there, I promise."

Embarrassed, I pull on my mittens and head out into the wind. Base Camp is mostly hidden in swirling snow, orange and red and blue tents disappearing and reappearing as the gusts swing the flakes around. Even though there are hundreds of people here, I can't help feeling like it's the loneliest place on Earth.

Chapter Twenty-Three:

Tate

April 25–May 9
Pheriche
14,300 feet above sea level

*P*heriche is now my home away from home. I'll be here for the foreseeable future, mostly because I have no-where else to go.

After my word vomit at the clinic, I ran until I got to the lodge and avoided Dad's attempts to talk by locking my door and plugging into my iPod. In the morning we faced each other, stone-faced and silent, over shitty instant coffee and oatmeal.

Of course, Jordan Russo didn't give up easily. He offered up a few different variations of "I'm sorry that I got so frustrated. Parents get frustrated too, you know." Followed by "Do you want to talk about it?" and "How can I help?" as though this is just a bump in the road and he can fix it.

I'm not interested in fixing this. I nearly died climbing, except for the dumb luck of my ice axes. I can't even make it through the Icefall without a full-blown panic attack. As he talked, I reminded myself that I sure as hell don't owe him anything, that he doesn't get automatic access to my brain, my emotions, my whole fucking heart, opened up and laid bare for him to judge. But the shame threatened to swallow me whole. *Pathetic. Quitter. Weak. Lazy.* The words he didn't say still managed to fill the space.

Eventually he wound down and left me alone.

The next day he was cleared to return to Base Camp, so as Bishal packed up their gear, he tried one more time to capital-T Talk before giving up. Finally he told me he had arranged for me to stay here under the I'm-sure-baffled eye of Dr. Bo, for now. The way he said it made it clear he's hoping that I'll change my mind. After more back-and-forth over logistics, he was gone, off to EBC.

His final words? "I worry that you're going to regret this for the rest of your life. I have no idea what's going on with you, Tate. But I still love you very much."

Awesome.

It's actually not bad being here with Bo. The first night he said, "So, do you want to talk about all this?" and I said, "Nope," and that was the end of it. He nodded and told me that if I changed my mind and wanted to talk, he'd be cool, but otherwise he'd leave it alone. And he has.

We eat dinner together at his place, which is attached to the clinic and is slightly less smoke-filled than the lodge. And sometimes if there are no patients and we can get internet, we'll go online and check out college basketball standings. But a lot of my time is spent staring out the windows, watching the ugly gray clouds drop more snow on us.

I'm left wondering how the fuck I got here.

Mostly I miss Rose so much I actually feel sick. I know she needs to be focused on the climb, and her training, so I don't let myself worry that there are no texts or messages. After that first letter I sent up with Dad, I try texting her a few times then leave her alone. I try to remember how much I *don't* want to be climbing that mountain, but all I think about is her. I have hit a new low. Bo busts my chops for moping. When he found me listening to some bad eighties power ballad on the radio at the clinic, he threatened to do a med check to see if I still have my balls. I do. They're a deep indigo blue.

On the tenth day in Pheriche, I get into college. The internet's up, and I check my mail to find one from Mom marked urgent, with five smiley face emojis in the subject line. Mom loves emojis. The contents is a forwarded email.

It's an acceptance from my first-choice school. Rhode Island School of Design. Holy. Shit.

"Bo. Dude. Check it." I gesture to the screen, still not believing what's written there.

"'Dear Mr. Russo, We are pleased to offer you a place in our class of 20—' Man, you're in!" Bo grabs me from behind the computer desk and tries to high-five, fist-bump, and hug me in a kind of bromance free-for-all.

"Here you've been, all emo-boy-in-the-mountains, and now look at you! You're in, BABY! With all those preppy types with their yachts and Kennedys and . . ." He trails off, apparently unable to think of any more New England stereotypes.

"Oysters. And cold winters. And cute little mountains. But who gives a shit? I'm in at the best design school in the country!" I'm grinning like an idiot.

"And hmmmm . . . Yale. That's somewhere around there, isn't it?" Bo says. While I tried not to talk *too* much about me and Rose, I may have mentioned she's going to Yale, that she wants to be an architect, that she loves Twizzlers and necklaces, that she always scouts a line for five minutes—no more, no less—before lead roping. Stuff like that.

"Yeah," I say. "I've been trying not to think about that, since I figured I was going to be matriculating to fry cook community college and living at home in the basement."

"You've got to tell that girl!" Bo says. "And your daddy. This is going to put a big smile on his face."

A little bit of my excitement dims. Dad's words still hang over me like the yak shit smoke in the lodge. But Rose . . .

"Yeah. Maybe I can try the sat phone. It's not that hard to call Base Camp, is it?"

"Go for it." Bo looks at his watch. "I'd say to try her now. They might be in for tea, since they should be down from whatever climbing they did today. Here." He pushes me back toward the computer.

"I'll give you a little privacy. But, you know. This is a public space. So no . . ." He makes a series of lewd gestures and backs out of the room, ducking his head to get through the door.

Ignoring him, I dial the number he gives me, my heart flying faster and faster in my chest. RISD! I'm in! A wave of exhilaration, and utter relief, races through me, and I want to announce to the world: SEE? I'M NOT SUCH A FUCKUP, AM I?

After seven rings I'm ready to disconnect, when someone's voice, crackly and loud, blasts into my ear. I nearly drop the phone. "Hey! Hi, this is Tate Russo. Is Rose around?" I ask.

There's a garbled noise, then the voice—maybe it's Bishal? It's hard to tell—says, "Rose? Yes. Rose is here." And a second later, I hear her.

"Tate? God, I wasn't expecting you. What's going on?" Her voice, slightly delayed and wobbly sounding, comes through, and I miss her so badly for a second that I have to close my eyes.

"Are you there? Tate? What's wrong?" Rose says, and her voice sounds small and exhausted.

"I'm here! Nothing's wrong! I'm great! I . . . I miss you," I say. It doesn't even seem to make sense, these words. It's so much more than missing her, this guilt and hunger and need. Now that we're talking, I'm frozen, unable to find words. "So how's it going there?"

She doesn't say anything for a minute; then her voice changes. "Awesome! Training's been going well, and we're all feeling pretty strong. And the views are gorgeous." She pauses again, then changes the subject. "How are you?"

Something is off. Her voice is too bright, too impersonal, like she's talking to someone in the school office. Not the voice that gasped my name, that breathed it into my mouth while she held on to me like I was the rope keeping her alive.

The smile slides off my face. I tried to explain to her in a letter that first night, after I told my dad I wasn't climbing, that I couldn't be there with her, that it wasn't a choice. I simply *couldn't* do it. But I'm not sure I said it right, and now, hearing her voice, I don't know that she believed me—or that she cared.

I know this is my chance to tell her about RISD, but my throat's tight and the words stick.

I find myself saying, "Things are chill. I've been helping out at the clinic. That's about it."

There's a scuffle, and I hear Luc's voice in the background.

"*Alors*, it's La Rosinator! Are you speaking to yourself?"

"No," Rose says. "It's just Tate."

Just Tate. I try not to let it sting. There are more muffled noises, and I've had enough.

"Look, I'll let you go," I say. "Sounds like you're having a blast with your team and the views and all, so, you know. Enjoy."

"Tate," she begins but stops. When she speaks again, her voice is cold. "Yeah. It's an absolute blast." She pauses like she wants to say something else, but then she says, "I need to go. Goodbye."

Bo comes back in, grinning, to find me pacing around the office. His eyes widen.

"Dude. This doesn't look like the face of someone who was barely avoiding phone sex." He looks at me in disgust. "Did you piss her off?"

I shrug, trying to slow down, trying to slow my pulse, which is pounding. I don't even know what happened. "It was like I was talking to a stranger," I say finally. "Like she was someone else."

He sighs. "Yeah. Everest Base Camp is a weird place. It's a world of its own, you know? Maybe let her be, let her focus on the climb, and wait to talk to her when she comes down. Right?"

I nod.

He smiles. "Good. Leave her alone, celebrate that you're going to a fantastic school, and when she gets here, you can look right at her and give her the sexy eyes and actually talk to her. Once you're together again, you'll be fine."

I nod again, hoping so damn hard that he's right.

* * *

Another week goes by in Pheriche, and there's nothing from Rose. Dad calls to congratulate me, since I guess he got an email from Mom up at EBC, but I'm out of the clinic when he calls, and I don't bother to call back. I ignore everything that has to do with Rose, Dad, Everest, climbing, and the rest of my life. Bo and I reorganize the office space, and I haul all the random crap they need to get rid of into one big pile for porters to bring down. I sketch some new health manuals, all related to dental hygiene, which is fucking disgusting. I learn Texas hold'em and lose two of my favorite shirts to a Sherpa named Ang Dori who works in the clinic.

But this empty time is about to end. Soon all of the Mountain Adventure climbers will come back to Pheriche for a last medical checkup and an "oxygen vacation" before they head up for the final push.

Five days.

Then four. Three. Two.

One.

* * *

I'm sitting in the lodge, waiting in the same tiny room Rose and I shared just weeks ago. Rose kissing me. Rose holding on to me, like I'm the only thing that matters. I want to get up, move, get to her, but I make myself wait. She'll be here any minute, but all I can think of is that she'll leave again to go up that hellish mountain where everything can go wrong and nobody can promise to be safe.

There's a bang on my door.

"Tate? You in there?" Dad's voice is hoarse and raspy.

I jump like I've been tased and throw open the door.

Dad and Rose, standing there. If Rose looks way too skinny and tired, Dad looks like shit on toast. He's lost around twenty pounds. His beard is almost completely gray, and his eyes are sunken and dark. I can't stop staring.

"Well, not even a hug for your old man?" he says, holding out his arms. "What's the matter, don't recognize me on the Everest diet?" He stands sideways and pats his stomach, as though showing off his impressive weight loss.

Rose laughs, giving me the cue to follow. Dad's clearly going for the let's-not-mention-the-elephant-in-the-room version of our reunion. Thank God. I step forward and hug him, wincing a little at how frail he seems. He notices.

"You look fantastic. I guess a doctor's life agrees with you. Who knows, maybe you'll follow in Dr. Bo's footsteps," he says, and his voice is thick with a kind of faked cheerfulness.

I don't know how to respond. Telling him I nearly puked when Bo needed help restraining someone with an abscessed tooth doesn't seem to be the right thing to say. So I laugh again, like the village idiot.

"And RISD!" He slaps me on the back. "I tried to call you! Did you get the message, at least? I'm so proud of you! Damn! I knew you had it in you!"

I grin, looking at Rose, but she's already moving down the hall.

"I'm going to get some tea," she says, her back to us. "I'm so glad it's not too crowded with trekkers. We heard the April and May tourist season is almost as busy as October and November nowadays."

Rose keeps talking the whole way to the dining room, which gives me a chance to pull myself together. I don't know what I expected. Dad still pissed and silent, waiting for me to get over my tantrum? Rose throwing herself into my arms? They feel like strangers. Vertigo hits, and for a minute I'm lost, wondering who we are, wandering away from each other in these mountains so far from home.

When we're finally chilling out in the dining room, Paul and Luc and Yoon Su looking all gaunt and tired but happy, everyone cheers and whoops over RISD, and Luc insists on a round of disgusting Everest beer to celebrate. But in a few minutes, they're back to the topic of the mountain and the climb. And in their excitement and discussion of all the details, it sounds possible, doable, even reasonable. They sound so *sure*.

My eyes stay on Rose, but she's looking everywhere but at me. As the sky gets dark and everyone moves from tea to dinner to their books or games, I stay near her, but she ignores me, without ever making it obvious. When I sit next to her, she stays until she needs to refill her water bottle or get something from her pack, then she takes a new seat. When we gather near the fire for Uno, she sits three chairs over, not across from me, where she'd have to look at me, not next to me. Finally, when the game wraps up, I grab her arm as she walks by. She pulls it away but stands waiting, looking down at me in my seat.

"Hey. You okay? Are we good?" I ask. My chest clenches. I hate that I'm asking her this.

"Sure, why wouldn't we be?" she says, and before I can answer, she goes on. "But I'm going to room with Yoon Su. I figured you'd have your stuff all over the place in your room, since you've been here a while." She smiles, but it's not a real smile, not even trying to be a real smile.

I open my mouth, then close it again. Before I can think of what to say, she walks away.

All the next day, the climbers cycle through the clinic to get checked out and take their solar showers and do whatever it is they need to do before heading back up.

I hide out in my room. Fuck this. Fuck Rose and her passive-aggressive "everything's fine, but I won't talk to you" vibe, and fuck Dad, who is determined to pretend things are great between us and that he's so proud because I got into college. I pace around my room like it's a cage. Seeing Rose was supposed to make it better. We're supposed to be RoseAndTate. I'm supposed to be able to hold her and touch her like I've been thinking about for weeks.

It's not supposed to be like this.

Finally that night I can't stand it. I listen for her footsteps outside my room and throw open my door. She startles and pulls back, making sure not to touch me.

"Whoa! You scared me. I've got to go grab my—"

"NO!" My voice is too loud in the dark hallway. "Can we talk? Now?"

Her eyes meet mine for the first time since she arrived, and I flinch at the coldness.

After a second she steps into the room. "Fine. What do you want to talk about?"

"What do I . . . Why won't you talk to me? What the hell is going on with you?"

It's like I turned on a fire hose. Rose slams the door behind her and steps toward me. "What's going on with *me*? Are you kidding? You get into your dream college and you don't even tell me? You decide not to bother climbing the mountain we've been training for our whole lives, and you don't bother to tell me *that*? What the fuck is going on with *you*?"

I get it, she's angry, but God, I'm angry too, and the frustration builds until I punch the bed, again and again.

She yanks my arm back. "No! You don't get to be the one to throw a fit. Not this time! You kissed me! You kissed me and had sex with me, and then you disappeared! This was our trip! Remember when this was what you wanted to do more than anything?"

I yank my arm free of her. "Yeah, well, things change! But not like you or Jordan ever fucking notice. No, the train just kept charging down the track, never mind if Tate's a little fucked up and broken and dragging behind! You kept on going, ignoring anything but your fucking need to be the best, so that you can race up the mountain and tag it and add one more thing to the list of Rose's Incredible Achievements—"

"What the hell is that supposed to mean? Are you actually pissed that I'm still planning to climb? That I'm doing the thing that we've been training to do for ten years? Because you choose to walk away means I'm supposed to feel bad and sit this one out? No! You left. You *chose* to leave me. So you don't get to be an asshole because I'm still going for it."

"It wasn't a fucking choice!" I scream at her. "I don't want to disappear! I don't fucking want any of this! I wish I'd broken my leg or hell, my neck, back on Rainier! Because then maybe you and my dad would think that maybe, just maybe, it's okay for this poor bastard to take a break!"

She stares at me.

"You think you had no choice? You wish you were hurt worse? Do you have any idea—any idea at all—what Maya would do to be here, healthy and able to climb?" Her voice is rising.

I shake my head. "I'm sorry, okay! I'm so fucking sorry that I won't be there in my usual spot as Rose's top cheerleader! But this isn't all about you! Jesus, you're selfish!" I look at her. "Did you ever think to ask why I can't climb?"

She shakes her head, her eyes red and her cheeks blotchy, but she doesn't cry. "You fucking coward. You could climb. You don't want to. And you don't care whose hearts you break on your way back down."

She storms out of the room, and I slam the door behind her so hard that the walls rattle. Rage pulses through me, beating in time with my heart, but I make myself stay in the room, ignoring Dad's knock on the door, Paul's soft questions, everything. I am hollow, empty, nothing. I have nothing to say to any of them.

In the morning, they head back to Base Camp, and I come out long enough to mutter goodbye before disappearing back into my room. Then they're gone, and I'm alone again.

Chapter Twenty-Four:

Rose

May 10–12
Everest Base Camp
17,600 feet above sea level

*B*ack at Base Camp, I am somehow Rose Recharged, my anger driving me like a motor. I do not think about Tate, not about his eyes when I called him a coward, not about his mouth on mine. It's as though he was never here. Neither Luc nor Yoon Su seem too curious about why he's not climbing, and I realize everyone here is so focused on their own summit that everything else fades into background noise. It's only for me that his absence is an abyss.

Paul stays close to me, sensing the hole, and tries to make me smile, sharing photos that Drew sent of their dog in a variety of ridiculous hats, and we joke and laugh and pretend everything is normal. From the other side of the table, Jordan coughs, loud and wet. As much as he tries to believe otherwise, Jordan came back from Pheriche no better than he went down.

We all pretend we don't hear him, and he carries on talking to Luc like nothing's wrong. There is a lot of pretending happening.

I make myself check email, promising myself that I will respond no matter what. Sure enough, there's a new one from Mami.

Rosalita, we follow the EVEREST news on the Mountain Adventure blog and website, and we are SOOOOO excited for you! The BIG DAY is coming. I know without your phone you are not getting email often, so I will just say we LOVE YOU so much and can't wait to hear your voice after the summit. We will be waiting by the phone!!!!!!!!!!!!!!!!!!!! Give big hugs to Paul, Jordan, and of course the amazing TATER-TOT.

All is well here—xoxoxoxoxoxoxxoxoxoxoxox Mami

I don't say anything for a minute. Guilt churns in my stomach. I should be writing more. I should be bringing Mami with me, every step of the way. I promised.

Paul looks over my shoulder. "Everything okay? How's Maya feeling?"

I shrug. "She's okay. Doing physical therapy." I try to keep my voice level, but Paul gives me a sharp look.

"I know it's an enormous shift, this diagnosis, but don't write her off. MS is a strange beast, and many people are able to live symptom-free for a long time. Your mama is one fierce woman. She's going to find the best possible way to make her life work as well as it can, Rosie."

"I know." I answer quickly, trying not to shout out the obvious: her life will never let her climb Everest or any other mountain again. But his words give me courage. I hit reply and type:

Mami and Dad—internet very spotty, so I can't be on for long, but I love you both so much. SO SO SO SO much. Trip has been incredible. Summit should be in the next week or so— WOW!!! A million zillion besos from your Rosalita

Then I press send and log out. I feel better. Stronger, somehow. I can do this.

I nudge Paul. "Hey. Thank you. You know, for everything." I don't bother to say what we both know, that being here without Mami or Tate would have been unthinkable without him.

He grins. "'What can I say, except . . . You're WEL-COME!'" he sings, channeling the god Maui from *Moana*.

I shake my head. "How can you even remember all these songs? Do you study them at night to torment me?"

"Come on! These are some seriously catchy tunes. You're being a hater," he says. "But in all seriousness, despite all the commercialism and, yeah, some problematic body image stuff, the themes of these movies *are* universal. Themes of identity, pushing back against parental expectations, staying strong in the face of adversity, trying to understand and accept yourself . . . These are big! I use them as an entry point to hard conversations with the kids I'm treating, and, trite as it may be, we can all connect with these heroes' journeys."

"If you say so," I say, shrugging. "But I think you just want a chance to channel the Rock."

He laughs. "Okay, that might be part of it."

We join Luc and Yoon Su at the big table, where they are playing Connect Four and trash-talking each other, while Bishal and some of the porters watch.

Yoon Su looks up when I come over. "Finally! Some female reinforcement! Maybe you will convince him that the definition of insanity is repeating the same steps and expecting a different result. I'll beat you every time we play! Haven't you learned by now?"

Luc laughs and shakes his head. "I am lulling you into a sense of security, *chérie*. You are unable to understand the higher strategy I—"

"I win again!" Yoon Su crows, dropping a red piece into the game with a clatter, and the porters applaud.

I can't help laughing along with them, patting Luc on the back as he drops his head in shame.

"Ah! Wait until we are back in Kathmandu. I will challenge you to a road race. Or a tennis match. Or cycling! High jump!" He continues to think up contests where he might win while Yoon Su takes a photo of her winning board.

Luc leans against me. "Tell the truth. Do I seem less manly now that I have been beaten in this way?" he asks, and I can't help it, I laugh harder.

Yoon Su walks over and squeezes me in a fast hug. "You're on my side, right?"

I fist-bump her. "Totally," I say. "Sorry, Luc. Sisters before misters."

He whoops and repeats it, his accent rendering it hilarious. *"Seesters before meesters! Alors,* I can never win against such women!"

Yoon Su winks at me, and I grin, the excitement of the room driving out all thoughts of Mami, of Tate, even of the mountain above. For a moment at least, I am right here.

We are so close. At this point we are all on different schedules, climbing or resting based on Finjo and Dr. Celina's assessment of our readiness, so it's rare and wonderful to all be together for the night. It is almost time. Now we wait on the weather.

• • •

Two days later I wake up early and head into the mess tent to find out: Jordan is gone. I slide onto the bench next to Paul and Yoon Su, listening as Finjo fills them in.

"He was bad again in the night. Dr. Celina looked him over and did not like his O2 levels. She tried the Gamwow for overnight, but this morning she decided he needed to descend."

Two nights ago we all slept at Camp Two, our tents bending and folding in the screaming wind. Jordan was with us, but he looked bad. I hadn't seen him since we stumbled into Base Camp the following morning.

Finjo is still talking. "So there is nothing we can do for Jordan. Now we must focus on our next steps, not his."

I glance up from the coffee one of the porters had brought me the minute I sat down. This sounds a little harsh. Paul seems to think so too, judging by his look of concern. But Yoon Su nods vigorously.

"Yes. Now we must think about ourselves."

I shoot her a dirty look and she looks surprised.

"What?" she asks. "Cameron in the weather tent says the weather window is going to open and close early this year. Much earlier than usual. There may only be one chance. We—"

I cut her off. "Stop and let Finjo talk."

Yoon Su looks annoyed. "Why are you angry at me? I'm preparing for the summit. I care about Jordan, but the lungs of your friend aren't within my control."

This is the part of Everest I hate. Yoon Su has been a woman possessed. She climbs mostly with Luc, and even though she weighs around a hundred pounds, she stays with him step for step. She sometimes stops to throw up but then stands and keeps climbing. I've never experienced a team that climbs the way this one does. Usually team members are, quite literally, holding each other's lives in their hands. There is a kind of trust that takes years to build. Here, each climber is on her own. Unbidden, my thoughts fly to Tate, who is the most loyal partner I know. Except that he left me here.

Before I can say anything more, Paul speaks up. "Yoon Su, Rose is concerned about a teammate's health, which affects all of us who are supposed to climb together. Rather than listening to Cameron in the weather tent, let's worry about today's climb, okay?"

Yoon Su looks annoyed, but she nods. "Fine," she says. But she won't look at me.

Finjo smiles his cat smile and puts an arm around each of us, including Paul in the hug. "We are a team! All of us! Let's make sure we get along, right? Right."

We all nod, sort of.

"So. Yoon Su is right, we must keep going and take advantage when the mountain gives us a chance. In fact, Cameron wants me back in the tent to look at more weather reports. But Rose is also right. We cannot rush. We must take care, okay?"

Again we all nod. Like a well-meaning parent, Finjo has tried to please both of us but has only managed to annoy us. I barely grunt as he tells us to meet in an hour, ready to climb, and I stalk off to get breakfast.

I've been sitting for almost the whole hour, trying to lose myself in my book, when Asha walks over.

"Big day, no?" she says.

I am not sure what she means, but I smile and nod.

Before she can say anything more, Yoon Su rushes back in, a brilliant gleam of the sunrise cutting through the dimness as she opens the flap of the tent.

"Rose! Is Finjo back?" she asks. Her voice is loud and excited, her eyes flashing.

I shake my head and she mutters something. "Stay here! I'll find him and come right back." She disappears again.

I shrug, wondering what's up now, but my mind is drifting. We are so close. An itch of anxiety runs through me, but I don't know if it's excitement to climb or impatience to be done: with the bloody noses that come most days, with the cough that has cracked one rib, with my bleeding fingertips, with watching my teammates' faces get gaunter and grimmer—and knowing I look just as bad.

Asha's voice startles me. "So will we go?"

"Huh? Go where?" I ask.

"Summit push. Peak Experience and Adventure Experts are both heading up now. The weather window is good, Cameron says, and it won't last long. This season is likely to be a short one."

I am stunned. A kind of vertigo sweeps over me, though I haven't moved from my seat by the fire. Today? Is that what Yoon Su is talking about?

"Now?" I ask. "What about Jordan?"

Asha shrugs.

I stand, my tea forgotten. Where is Paul? Are we really going to climb before Jordan gets back? He will be crushed, when he comes back, if we're all gone. If he comes back.

I nearly walk right into Paul, who is walking toward me.

"Rose! You're hearing the same rumors I am, I guess," he

says, his face tight and concerned. "I tried to find Finjo, or anyone, frankly, but people seem to have scattered." He stares ahead, his face tight, before continuing. "According to Bishal, who got his information from Yoon Su—Jesus, this is like high school—Cam says the weather window is going to be early and short this year, due to unusually high temps in the Bay of Bengal leading to an earlier monsoon season. Or something like that. Anyway, point being that the weather often isn't optimal until later in May, but here we are on May eleventh with an open window of a few good days, and that might be all we get."

"But what about Jordan?" I ask. "I'm sure he's still hoping to recover enough to make a summit bid. He thought he'd have another week."

Paul is quiet for a minute. When he speaks, I lean close to hear him. "I don't know why any of us thought we wanted to climb this mountain, but we did. And now we're here, recognizing that we had no idea what the hell we were in for. And I'm listening to you, thinking you're right; this is Jordan's dream, and we would be heartless to carry on without him."

"You don't want to go," I say flatly. I don't know if I'm relieved or horrified.

"I *do* want to go," Paul says. "I want to go more than I've wanted almost anything. It is literally painful to think about staying here, being the good pal, the rare all-for-one-and-one-for-all guy on the mountain, and missing the window. I want to go. I want to climb this thing. But I don't know if I like the kind of climber . . . the kind of *person* . . . that makes me."

We're silent for a minute. The summit pulls at me, every image I've ever seen flashing in my brain. My climb. Not

Mami's, not Tate's, not even Jordan's. I want this so much. Does that make me a horrible person?

I try to take a deep breath, but a fit of coughing overtakes me. Finally I look up. "I want to go."

Paul nods. "Yeah. Me too."

We head out into the icy blister of the wind, the mountains blazing glorious and white above us.

Chapter Twenty-Five:

Tate

May 8–13
Pheriche to Base Camp
14,300 feet above sea level

I didn't watch Rose and the rest of them leave. Instead I locked myself back in my room after saying goodbye, trying to ignore the feeling that my vital organs were walking away from me. But after around ten minutes, I left the lodge and walked up the trail until I could see them in the distance. I stayed there, watching Rose laugh at something Yoon Su said, shove Luc when he interrupted them, walking farther and farther away. Before they rounded the trail, Rose turned, and I pressed myself into the shadows. She looked around at the jaw-dropping valley view that spread out beneath her and flashed a grin that nearly turned me inside-fucking-out. Even though it wasn't for me. Then she turned and was gone.

For the next two days, I'm basically a zombie, wandering around Pheriche trying to imagine a world where we're down off this mountain, away from dust and cold and burnt-yak-shit smell, where fresh fruit and ocean breezes and electricity are once again part of my everyday life. Bo leaves me alone once he realizes that I can't even suck it up enough to watch playoff basketball with him.

I'm so untethered I feel like I could float away and no one would notice, like everything holding me to Earth—Rose, school, parents, music, surfing, friends, chores—has disappeared. For the first time, I miss home and Mom with an ache that feels bottomless: I realize that after this trip I'll have only the summer before I leave for college, coming home a few times a year. Even when we get down from here, even when this is over, everything will be different. Not a climber. Not Rose's best friend. Not a high school screwup fighting with my parents. Who the hell am I, after this?

I'm sitting in the lodge, sketching sad homesick drawings of beaches and Rose and Rose on the beach when the door bangs open and Dad and Bishal walk in.

This isn't good. We stare at each other, and I try to hide my shock at how he looks.

"Dad," I start, unsure what to say.

He shakes his head, every motion looking painful. "Not sure this is going to happen," he says, his voice flat. "I . . . " He breaks off into a coughing jag that leaves him doubled over.

Bishal takes off his pack and leaves it in the corner. "Let's go to the clinic, yes? It will be better if the doctor can see you."

I get up. "I'll walk him over," I say, shrugging into my jacket. "You're probably tired after the trip down."

Bishal smiles and shrugs. "I am okay. But maybe it's better to be with family."

Dad doesn't say anything, and we walk out into the afternoon chill. "So what . . . Did something happen?" I ask. Then I want to slap myself. "I mean, obviously *something* happened. But what—?"

Dad shakes his head. "I went up to Camp Two—only Camp Two! Twenty-one hundred feet! And just . . . felt like crap. Could barely make it down." He shrugs, a weird, helpless move that I don't think I've ever seen him make.

I slow my steps, like I'm walking at a funeral. But even at that pace, he lags behind. I feel like my strength is another fuckup, another way that I'm a disappointment to him. I stay silent until we get to the clinic, then mumble something about checking in later before handing him off to Bo.

• • •

When I come back an hour later, Bo's in the front room, organizing papers.

"You here to see your daddy?" he asks, stepping over a big pile of donated blankets. "He's doing okay. Resting and taking fluids. But . . ." He shakes his head. "I don't think I can send him back up. He's cracked a few ribs coughing, and he's too weak."

I sigh, imagining how pissed Dad must be. He's a strong climber, one of the best. On climbs in Switzerland, Chile, all over the world, he's rocked it. And here of all places, his body, like his son, is betraying him when he needs it to be tough. Too bad we can't mind-meld—with my stamina and his force of will, we'd be up and down that mountain in record time.

"Tate," Bo says, interrupting my sci-fi imaginings. "Go see him. He feels like crap and could use a visit."

I shake my head. "Dude, you have to know by now I'm only going to make it worse. I mean, come on. He can't climb, but having to stare at his perfectly healthy fuckup of a son who refuses to? That's not going to help."

Bo stands over me, a bemused look on his face. "You don't get it, do you? This isn't about you fucking up. This isn't about you at all. He's feeling like a pretty big failure right now, and believe me, this mountain is very good at making people remember that they're insignificant little parasites on this planet. How old are you, man?"

I blink at the change of subject. "I turned eighteen right before we left."

"Eighteen. You're a man. You're going away to Rhode-Freaking-Island in the fall, right? And then what? Let me tell you something. Remember what I said about climbing this mountain, about how small mistakes can snowball into big-ass catastrophes? Well, that's not only true on Everest."

I start to say something, then shut my mouth.

Bo shakes his head. "Shit. Just talk to the man." He walks over and claps me on the back, hard. "You got this."

My chest is hot, and I want to tell Bo to go to hell, that he has no idea what the fuck he's talking about, except that I know he does. So I nod and walk down the narrow hall toward the treatment rooms.

• • •

When I open the door, Dad looks like he's sleeping, and I'm chickenshit enough that I debate tiptoeing out again before he sees me. But then his eyes open.

"Hey. Just checking on how you're feeling," I say. I try to keep my voice chill, but my feet are shuffling, begging me to get the hell out of there.

"Like crap." He's silent for a second. "How are you?"

I shrug. What am I supposed to say? I'm great? I'm finally sleeping again? I have absolutely zero regrets about not climbing?

"Fine." I stand there. "Look, Dad . . ." My voice trails off. I have literally no idea what to say to him. I want to be anywhere but here. But I think about Bo's words and try again. "I know this is shitty, and I'm sorry, but—"

He puts up a hand. "Tate. Son. I love you, but I can't do this. I can't deal with you right now." His eyes shut, and he rolls away from me. "Close the door when you go, okay?"

Oh.

He wants me gone. I'm making things worse. He can't. Deal. With me.

Fuck it. That makes it easy to leave.

I shut the door quietly, even though I feel more like slamming it.

Whatever. It's not like I wanted to sit there and attempt to make him feel better about his pathetic trying-to-outrun-death midlife crisis or whatever this is.

I almost run into Bo in the outer office. "Whoa! Slow down. Where are you going? What's up with your dad?"

"He's sleeping," I say and leave it at that. I slow my breathing, trying to push away the anger and hurt. I need to get out of here.

Bo shakes his head. "He's in rough shape. And the timing couldn't be worse. I was talking to Dr. Celina up at EBC, and she told me the weather window's starting to open. Expeditions are scrambling to get ready for the summit push."

I pause, halfway to the door. "They're heading up? Rose and Paul?"

"Not sure who's going when, honestly. Sounds like Peak Adventure climbers were already gone, but maybe Finjo's group is waiting? It's always a shoving match, who gets to summit when. Crowds on the mountain have gotten so bad that some operators are trying for less optimal weather in order to miss the lines." He shakes his head. "Much respect for those folks, but no thank you."

I look at him. Bo's kept his word and hasn't asked me about climbing or why I quit. But now I'm curious. "Do you ever want to try for it? You know, the summit?"

Bo perches on the edge of the desk, his long legs stretched out. He laughs. "Hell naw. Nope. I love hiking, and living here in the mountains is pretty amazing, but yeah, no way. I've tried climbing a few times, and it's not my thing. There's just too damn much of me to haul up the rock."

It's true, he's ridiculously tall. "But you'd have a hell of an advantage with that reach," I point out. "And you're obviously strong."

He shrugs. "Maybe. But I don't like it enough to keep hanging myself off a rope and praying it holds." He looks at me. "You know, there's nothing wrong with *not* wanting to climb. Most people in the world don't want anything to do with this crazy shit. But when you hang out with a few people who make it their whole life, it can feel like *you're* the weirdo for wanting no part of it."

He pauses. "But that's not to underestimate the effort it takes for the people who really commit to this, who pour their life savings and years of their life into training for it. And the bone-crushing disappointment if they fail." He's quiet, and I know we're both thinking of Dad. He looks at me. "It's good you're here, man. He's going to need some family time."

My thoughts fly to Dad's voice, telling me to leave him alone. Bo's cool, but he's dead wrong. I'm the last person Jordan Russo wants to see right now. I shrug and continue out the door.

When I get back to the lodge, Bishal is gone. The lodge owner tells me he's expected back at Base Camp, so he's going to head up as fast as he can, hoping to get there before dark. A familiar churn of guilt sucks at me. There are literally hundreds of Sherpas working to get our bodies up and down the mountain, and for every time one of us is sucking wind, exhausted and cold in our state-of-the-art microlight down jackets and expensive boots, they're doing twice the work, twice as fast, in half the gear.

I know there's a ton of money coming into the country from tourists, and I know Finjo and Mountain Adventure are good guys, but still. As shitty as it feels to bail on this climb, I could walk away. I wonder if Dawa and Asha and the rest of them see it as a choice at all. Summit Everest and you're always guaranteed a spot in the next expedition. What for me is a whole lot of angst about pissing off Dad and feeling guilty about Rose is a matter of job security for them.

The room darkens around me, and I sit in smoky silence, thinking about Dad—hooked up to oxygen the next building over—and about Rose.

Rose, who'll be leaving any day now for a summit push, climbing into the death zone, spending the nights breathless and freezing in a tiny tent on an ice face. Rose, who I called selfish. Rose, who's climbing without Maya, without me, and now without Dad.

I never even said goodbye. Suddenly a rush of pure, unadulterated fear rushes through me, not for myself, but for her. We are RoseAndTate, best friends since long before I could have found Everest on a map. What happened to us?

What did I let happen?

I'm awake all night, and when the sun comes up, I leave a note with the lodge owner, asking him to give it to Bo, and head up the trail for Base Camp.

Chapter
Twenty-Six:

Rose

May 12–13
Everest Base Camp
17,600 feet above sea level

$\mathcal{P}$aul and I try to find Finjo but finally give up, going back
to wait in the warmth of the kitchen tent. We stay silent,
watching as the sky brightens outside the plastic windows.
Morning is coming, and we have missed our chance to climb
anywhere today. Soon the sun will bake into the Icefall,
melting and moving the ice, and no one wants to be there for
that. There is no sign of Yoon Su, but I don't go looking for
her. I wait.

Finally Finjo comes in, his face bright and wreathed in
his usual grin.

"Okay! Okay, okay, we are back to work. It is all good.
You two will leave tomorrow, with me and Asha."

Paul and I both jump.

"What? What about Jordan? What about Yoon Su? What's happening?"

Finjo's smile dims a little, but not totally. "I spoke to the clinic. Jordan will not be back soon, if he comes back at all. He is stable but in no shape to climb. And Yoon Su left an hour ago, to meet up with Luc. They will be ahead of us, but that is okay! We all go at our own pace."

He pauses when he sees my face.

"They are the faster climbers; they will push for the summit one day, maybe two days, before you. It is dangerous for you to try and go too fast, dangerous for them to go slower. You will each have your own guides."

I can't speak.

It's happening, and Yoon Su left without saying goodbye, charging up the mountain to tag it like it's a race. I feel stupidly hurt, like this is some kind of betrayal, even though I understand that we move at different speeds. But the feeling of being abandoned, left behind, threatens to overwhelm me. We were supposed to be together: me, Mami, Tate, Jordan. Then Yoon Su and Luc, my friends, my partners for the past months. And now it's just me. And Paul. Thank God he's still here.

Paul puts his arms around me. "Hey. This is okay. We knew this. Groups don't stay together on Everest unless they happen to move at the same pace. Better that we all move safely, right?" His voice is calm and soothing, and I try to swallow my panic.

He's right, of course. I exhale and picture the route up the mountain. This is my climb.

My summit.

"Yeah." My voice is quiet, and I clear my throat and speak louder. "I'm in. Let's do this!"

"Okay? Yes, Rose says yes! She's ready. We must take advantage. It is auspicious, really, this early window. This is very good. You are both strong and well acclimated. It will be good." Finjo smiles again and starts to turn. "So today you rest. You eat as much as you can. All kinds of calories, especially for you!" He points at me. "Time to get excited! We will get to the top of the world!"

• • •

Today we leave for the summit. It's still dark in my tent, but I am awake, have been all night. And even though I thought I had buried it, Tate's absence is everywhere.

We'll leave at first light, back through the Icefall, past Camp One, and up to Camp Two. Paul and me and Asha. And Finjo, though Finjo will run ahead to scout the trail, then run back to us, always keeping in radio contact with Dawa and Bishal and their climbers. In theory the weather looks good. In theory I will be fine. Two nights at Camp Two, one at Camp Three, then a few hours trying to rest in the death zone at Camp Four in the South Col before leaving in the middle of the night for the summit attempt. If it all goes to plan, we'll summit early on May 17 and be back down to Camp Four or even as far as Camp Two that night. If all goes to plan, I will stand at the summit of the world.

My heart pounds with excitement.

Sleep isn't happening, so I finally give up. I get dressed, filling my pack with PowerBars, water bottles, goggles, and everything else I will need these next few days. My tent is a lived-in mess of my stuff, a few fashion magazines from Yoon Su nearby. I remember laughing with her over the articles, pretending to write a report on Base Camp fashion. I can't wait until we're back together, celebrating.

I walk out of the tent, zipping it shut behind me. The sky above is a crowded bowl of stars. The cold bites any part of me it can reach: my wrists, my neck, my forehead. I move toward the kitchen tent, ready for tea and ready to be on our way. To begin.

I'm not the only one up. Several of the Sherpas are by the fire, and Paul is there, bleary-eyed but upright, staring into his coffee like he's searching for secrets in the inky blackness.

He looks up when I enter. "You too, hey?"

I nod, gratefully taking the cup that Devi hands me.

I sit down next to Paul, and my smile feels so huge it might break my face. "It's happening," I say. "I can't believe it's finally happening!"

We look at each other. No Tate, no Jordan, just us. As if thinking the same thing, Paul reaches over and puts his hand on mine.

"No matter what, I'm glad we're climbing together, Rosie. If I had to trust anyone to be on the line with me doing this, I'd choose you. Again and again." His eyes are warm and, despite the exhaustion, I see excitement brimming up.

I squeeze his hands. "Ditto," I say. "So let's do it."

Chapter Twenty-Seven:

Tate

May 13
Everest Base Camp
17,600 feet above sea level

As I race up the trail toward Base Camp, I can't help wondering if Dad's awake, if he's wondering where I am. If he read the note I left and is relieved that his fuckup son isn't around to be another exhausting thing to deal with. I wonder if he knows that the climbers are heading up. If he's heartbroken. But I push myself to walk faster, my body, as always, rising to the challenge. I make it to EBC in under five hours, my blood pounding in my head as I half stumble into the main Mountain Adventure tent.

But I'm too late.

Rose and Paul are gone. I find out they left before dawn this morning for their summit push. If all goes well, they'll be back in five days, having been to the top of Mount Everest.

I can't believe they're gone.

And I'm here, left behind. I didn't get to say goodbye. Disappointment floods through me, and I realize how much I was counting on seeing Rose, on telling her I'm sorry. Fear of what she's facing sucks at me, but I push it away. It's Rose, the most focused, organized, careful climber I know. She'll be fine.

She has to be fine.

I sit in the main tent, unsure what to do next. Dr. Celina, with no one else to mess with, radios over to say that Bo told her I was coming and to see her for a check-in. It takes twenty minutes just to walk through Base Camp, past all the different expedition tents, mostly empty now as climbers head up for their big push.

"Come on in," Dr. Celina says from the door of the infirmary. "You want something for that headache?"

I peer into the med tent. Seeing it makes my gut churn, remembering Dad barely moving after his collapse.

"What are you, psychic? How'd you know I have a headache?" I say, then realize I'm clutching my forehead with one hand. "Oh."

She smirks at me. "Yup. Psychic. Have a seat." She moves fast, grabbing Tylenol and a water bottle. "So now will you stay up here, enjoying all that Base Camp has to offer until they come back down?"

I shrug. "I guess so. At least I'll see them when they get back. And there's more to do here than in Pheriche." I drink, gulping the whole bottle in seconds.

She nods. "It's wild, isn't it? This is my third time as expedition doctor, and I still think it's great. Those guys have a massage therapist and taco night," she says, gesturing to a particularly large tent with a Starbucks flag on top. "And the Aussie group Mountain Monsters play the Beach Boys from giant speakers on Saturdays. Call it a beach party." She shakes her head a little. "They're all whistling in the dark."

"What does that even mean?" I ask. But I think I know.

"It means they're hoping not to notice, with all the good food and loud music and fun, that this is the waiting room to risk their lives."

She looks at me. "Your dad talked a lot about you while he was in here, you know."

My heart lurches. "What . . . Really?"

"Oh yeah. He told me you were his youngest. That you were an amazing artist. That you and Rose—who's pretty great, by the way—had been best friends since you were little, but he thought things had changed on this trip. He thought you were head over heels. Those were his words."

I look down. "Did he talk about *me* climbing?" I feel like a tool. "Never mind," I say, starting to move toward the door. "I should go."

But she reaches out and stops me. "Tate, he did talk about your climbing. He said he wished you had never come."

Her words cut more than I expect. My stomach rolls as I think about him up here, wishing that his fuckup son was nowhere around. But she's still talking.

"You know he spent a lot of time in here. The altitude was not kind to your father, and he kept trying to push higher, only to get turned back again and again. He felt pretty rough. And the last night, as he lay here throwing up into a bucket and trying to keep the oxygen mask on, he talked about you. And he said how he hoped you would listen to your heart. 'I don't want my son to go through hell.' Those were his very words."

Outside the tent door, another group is out in the sun, sorting their gear into massive piles, probably in anticipation of their ascent tomorrow. The buzz of their voices reaches us, but I don't listen. I'm thinking of Dad, talking to this nice woman. He must have felt so shitty and so fucking sad to realize this adventure was ending before it ever really started. He must have known, on some level, that I was never going to climb.

She holds my gaze. "I'm curious, if you're willing to tell me. What changed, for you? Why didn't you want to climb?"

I try to figure out what to say. I think about the nightmares, the way panic held me down on the Icefall. "A few months ago, on a training climb, I took a bad fall that could have been way worse. I got lucky. I went into a crevasse, but my ice axes held, and I was okay." I tell her about the fall, about the terror, about the way it circles and loops and comes at me just when I think it's gone.

"But it's bullshit, you know? I've had plenty of gnarly near misses. You heard my dad, I've got that whole 'Master of Disaster' thing. So I was fine—"

"Tate," she interrupts me. "You weren't fine. Obviously."

"But I've fallen before! I mean, scary crap-your-pants falls. And this wasn't even that bad . . ."

She shakes her head. "You don't get to make that distinction. You've heard of PTSD, right? Post-traumatic stress disorder?"

I nod. "Sure, but—"

"But nothing. Again, you don't get to choose if what you experienced was 'bad enough' to deserve it. We don't know why people react the way they do, but what you experienced is classic textbook trauma." She looks at me. "Did you tell anyone about how you were feeling? About the panic attacks?"

I shake my head. I don't bother telling her that between extra tutoring and special accommodations at school and having to see Jimmy the shrink as a kid because of my temper, I was reallyreallyreally *done* with being that guy, the one who couldn't hack it, who needed extra help. "No, with Rose's mom getting her awful diagnosis—you know she was going to climb but got diagnosed with MS?—and everything else going on, it didn't really seem like the time."

Dr. Celina smiles and shakes her head. "My friend, you seem like a smart guy, but let me give you a little wisdom, part medical, part personal. This isn't the kind of thing that you can outmuscle. You can't ignore it and hope it's going to go away any more than you can ignore cancer. You can fight it, and beat it, but not by pretending it isn't there. Trauma is real, Tate. And requires treatment."

I can't quite process her words. My chest feels tight and my head throbs. "What are you saying? That I'm fucked up? That I'm nuts?"

"No! Not at all. But nearly dying in a crevasse a few months before heading up on an incredibly challenging climb is going to take a toll on you. You're not nuts . . . I can tell that after ten minutes with you. But you've got some powerful demons dogging you, and it probably would have been better to face them than try to run."

She looks at me, and I don't know, something about her eyes makes me bite my lip, hard, to keep from crying.

"I'm so sorry, Tate," she says quietly. "I'm sorry that happened to you."

I breathe. Chew my lip. Try not to picture the falling, the terror. When I'm sure I can speak normally, I ask the question. "Do you think if I had gotten help and talked about it, I would have climbed?"

"Who knows?" she says. "Are you sorry? Does any part of you wish you had stayed with the expedition?"

Finally, it's easy to answer this question. "Not even a little bit," I say. "It's weird, but I don't want it. Not at all. I love climbing, or at least I did, but this kind of expedition, with all the crowds and the waiting around? Nah. No part of me wishes I were climbing this mountain."

"Okay then." She nods. "There you go. Climbing this thing . . . You have to want to, so badly you feel a little crazy." She laughs. "Let me be clear, Tate. If anyone's nuts, it's the people who *want* to do this. Not you."

I laugh a little. "Well, I don't want to, so I guess I'm cool." And saying it straight out, to this smart doctor, it stings a little less.

I don't want to do this. It's too bad I didn't figure it out a while ago. Like five years or so, before we planned it all. But then I think about Rose, alight with excitement, her hands flying in the air while she describes some massive cornice of ice. Would she be here if my dream had died all those years ago? Would she have done this without me? Maybe my getting this far is part of what will get her to the top.

"Huh?" I say, turning back to Dr. Celina. "Sorry, what did you say?"

"I said that I talked to Rose before she left. She's doing really well, and wow, is she driven. No ambivalence there! She wants this so badly."

"What did she say?" I ask. It's pathetic, how much I want her to have said something about me. But Dr. Celina's answer is even better.

"She said, 'I really, *really* want to get up this mountain. But I'm sure as hell going to get down it.' Smart girl, that Rose." She smiles. "You know, you could probably get a hold of her. To say good luck."

"Get a hold of her?" I repeat stupidly.

"On the radio. They're only going to Camp Two today. It should be pretty easy to talk to them."

My pulse speeds up a little. To hear her voice . . . to tell her how much I love her, how safe she needs to be . . .

I thank Dr. Celina and head out, back to the Mountain Adventure tent. I want to talk to Rose.

Chapter Twenty-Eight:

Rose

May 13–14
Camp Two
21,000 feet above sea level

*I*t is almost noon when I flop into my tent at Camp Two, where Luc and Yoon Su are already resting. The heat is appalling, over ninety degrees as the sun cooks us in the solar bowl of glacial ice. Sweat drips down into my eyes, and my tongue is swollen with dehydration. Paul isn't much better. And of course there's the chance that the temperature will drop into the single digits if the clouds roll in. Still, even with a woozy head and cramping feet, excitement blazes through me. We have made it through the Icefall, and now there is only one last reason to pass through it; on our descent.

I shake my head to clear it and sit up slowly. Finjo and Asha are outside, melting snow and ice so we can rehydrate.

The water is warm and metallic, but I make myself drink, filling my cup again and again until some of the dullness in my head fades. Then I collapse in my tent, grateful for the rest. The summit is still two vertical miles above us, and thinking about it exhausts me to my core. I am so close to this goal that I have wanted for so long, that I am convinced will make me stronger, forge me like steel. But the Dread still hovers, whispering horrors of Mami's sickness and Tate's anger and everything else I can't control. Even here I can't outrun it. I make myself breathe. Remember that this is *my* climb.

Asha sticks her head in. The slash of sunlight startles me.

"Rose! Good afternoon. There is someone on the satellite phone for you."

I sit up, panic clutching at my chest. "Is there bad news?"

"It is Tate. He is at Base Camp now and wishes to talk."

I freeze, remembering our last conversation. I called him a coward. He called me selfish. We walked away from each other, not even saying goodbye.

"Tell him . . . Tell him I'm asleep," I say, finally. "I'm not feeling great."

Asha's eyes stay on me, but I look away, down at my sleeping bag. Finally she withdraws, the tent falling into darkness as she closes the door.

My climb. My summit. I won't . . . I *can't* talk to Tate right now, can't try and survive his voice. Not now. Now with the mountain waiting.

• • •

Later Yoon Su, Luc, Paul, and I cram into their tiny tent, and it feels like a celebration. I forget how abandoned I felt when

Yoon Su left without us and instead focus on the fun of being all together, at least for tonight.

"Wait until we're back in Kathmandu!" Luc says as we clink our cups of water. "There will be champagne, even if I must storm the French consulate to get it."

Yoon Su hits my cup so hard my water splashes out. "To champagne!" she shouts.

"To showers!" I answer.

"To plumbing," Paul adds, and we continue, each adding things we miss.

Finally Luc holds up his hands. "*D'accord*, let us focus on what we *do* have. To my amazing companions and ze mountain, which offers us this challenge! May we emerge victorious!"

When I climb back to my tent, my cheeks hurt from smiling. Excitement builds hot and fierce, and I wish more than anything we could leave with them in the morning instead of taking a rest day. But Finjo insists.

I am not delighted with this plan. I want to move, want to start actually climbing again. Hunger like a fire burns through me, and I remember reading about Everest fever, a kind of crazed ambition that can take over on the mountain. I get it now. This breathless waiting is enough to kill us without any help from the mountain itself. I'm ready. But Finjo makes the rules, so we will wait.

● ● ●

The next day we rest, the camp newly quiet with Luc and Yoon Su gone. The radio chirps again and again as Finjo and Asha get updates on weather, on other expeditions, on climbers farther up the mountain.

"Luc and Yoon Su are still at Camp Three. They should get to the South Col by tomorrow, and tomorrow night they'll start for the summit," he reports after yet another call. "They are moving fast. A rock fell and hit Luc on his helmet on the Western Cwm, but he is okay." The Western Cwm is a massive ice-walled valley that leads from Camp Two to Camp Three. We climbed through on an earlier acclimatization run, and the thought of a rock hurtling down while we hang there on the fixed ropes like sitting ducks is not a happy one.

"Was he hurt at all?" I ask.

Finjo shrugs. "He says he is still grooving. Or groovy. It was difficult to hear. But he is still going up."

I do quick calculations in my head. If they are heading to the summit tomorrow at midnight, we might pass them heading down as we head to Camp Four at the South Col. Camp Four is our last stop, where we'll attempt to rest at 26,000 feet until nighttime, when we make our push for the top. They could be back down at Camp Two celebrating before we even summit.

Almost there. Almost there. The words loop in a refrain as the night wears on. I roll over in my sleeping bag, but I can't sleep. My mind drifts back to Tate, again and again. Should I have taken his call? What did he want to say? A tiny sliver of fear needles me; when will I next hear his voice?

Paul's med school training still holds; he's snoring. I count my breaths and try to rest, listening to the distant moan and crash of ice far away on the mountain.

Chapter Twenty-Nine:

Tate

May 16
Everest Base Camp
17,600 feet above sea level

I replay my conversation with Asha. Rose was right there, she had said. But then . . . She wasn't. She couldn't speak to me. Or maybe wouldn't. Did she know I was on the phone? Did she know I had come here, trying to find her? Did she care? Our angry words fester and push against my brain, and I wish, for the hundredth time, that I had gotten to Base Camp before she left. That I had gotten a chance to wish her good luck, to tell her to be so fucking careful in the ice. To tell her that I love her.

But I left it too long, screwed up the timing again, like always. And she's gone up higher than I'll ever go, and I'm stuck here, praying she makes it back down, trying not to think about all the things that can go wrong.

It's possible that Cam wants to kill me, but I don't really care. He's the great and powerful Oz, the man behind the curtain who controls Rose's fate. Okay, maybe not entirely, but he tracks the weather on the summit and forecasts what the coming days will bring. And his word dictates Finjo's choices, which dictate when Rose climbs. So he better be fucking excellent at his job.

"You're excellent at this, right, Cameron?" I ask, a few days after getting back to Base Camp. There's nothing to do here but track the climbers, who stay in touch via radio. So far everything is fine, though plenty of things have gone wrong or forced changes in plans: broken crampons, malfunctioning radios, horrible crowds on the fixed ropes . . . all typical Everest situations. Still, I think about Bo's words, how small things can snowball, and wish more than anything that Rose and Paul were safely down already. "Let me ask another way: If there were an Olympic sport of Everest weather forecasting, would you be in the middle of the podium? 'Cause I'm not going to lie, I don't want the bronze medalist reading the tea leaves on this shit."

Cameron, luckily, is unflappable. An extremely low-key Canadian, he mostly ignores me but occasionally takes pity on me and tells me again about how much he knows. He knows a lot.

Rose and Paul left Camp Three, at 23,500 feet, this morning and should be heading to Camp Four to get ready for their summit bid. Luc, Yoon Su, and around twenty other people from Adventure Experts and Peak Adventures summited today; the Sherpas sent down announcements in the afternoon. Luc, Yoon Su, Dawa, and Bishal didn't summit until 3:30 p.m., way later than most people. Ang Pasang, who's in charge in the Mountain Adventure tent now that Finjo is climbing, is pissed.

"It is too late. They should have turned back earlier, even if it meant missing the summit. It is dangerous. The summit, it is not the end! It is halfway. The hard part remains . . . coming down." He shakes his head and stomps back over to one of his assistants, Devi, who silently hands him tea.

Cam shrugs. "They were making good time on the descent and planning to motor down as far as they can. Yoon Su's oxygen regulator isn't working right, and they don't want to get stuck in the death zone."

I shudder. From everything I've read, the idea of spending the night after a summit climb stuck at the South Col sounds brutal.

"It's almost dark. When are they supposed to get in?" I ask.

Cameron grabs some tea and swings his legs over a bench, sitting down. "Dawa's radio was dying and he didn't want to stop and put in the spare batteries, so I'm not sure. I'll try him again in a few."

It's almost dark out, and I'm back in the kitchen tent, eating some of Ang Pasang's food. He seems delighted to cook for me. Probably because I'm the only one happy to eat his ambitiously planned pizzas, noodles, and soups.

Cam and I talk surfing. Then he tries to convince me to take a year traveling around the world before college, while he attempts again and again to get Dawa on the radio, with no luck.

"He might have crashed once they made it down," Cam says. "I'll check with some of the Camp Two guys and see what's up."

It takes a while, but finally Cameron gets a hold of one of the Peak Experience guides, who confirms that shortly after dark four Mountain Adventure climbers stumbled into camp exhausted and immediately fell asleep in their tents. Cameron kicks his feet up, looking relaxed.

"There. Two clients safely down, two cuddled up at Camp Four. This wind should blow in and out pretty quick, and hopefully Finjo and the crew will get their shot. Otherwise they've got a shite day of waiting at Camp Four. Still, looks like the wind could quiet in time . . . This is going to be fast and furious." He leans back. "But meanwhile, time for grub!"

The sun's fallen behind the mountain, and the temperature's dropped hard and fast. Still, the kitchen tent's warm, and I'm happy enough listening to the conversation around me and dozing on the bench. Rose and Paul are safe, and hopefully they'll be trying for the summit tomorrow; soon everyone will be down, and we'll be able to get out of this place once and for all. I try not to think about where she is now, about the cold, the thin air, the endless, screaming wind. She's so far away, and there's nothing I can do for her.

"Yo! You alive over there?" Cameron asks, kicking my chair. "Do you want me to deal you in?"

I shake my head and get the images of the ice and rock out of my brain. "Yeah. Sorry—deal 'em," I say. And we start to play.

• • •

Hours later in my tent, I wonder what new hellscape we're in. The wind's monster strong, pushing the walls of the tent in so far over my face that I'm afraid of being smothered. The scream and howl's so loud it's like trying to sleep next to a jet engine. I squint at my watch, the icy air freezing my wrist. Midnight. Hours until daylight. I lie down again but immediately sit up as the tent nearly folds in half. Screw this.

After throwing on all the clothes I can find, I grab my headlamp and head out to the kitchen tent. I'd rather sit by the fire and drink tea than pretend I'm going to get any sleep. Luckily I moved my tent closer when the climbers all headed up, or I'd be afraid of getting lost in the wall of snow that's slanting sideways. As it is, I nearly get frostbite on my face in the two minutes it takes to dash over. When I get there, Devi's dozing near the fire, but Ang Pasang's awake. He nods at me but doesn't speak, and I bring a chair by the heat and stare into the flames.

● ● ●

I lose track of time, not quite awake but not sleeping, when the tent flap opens, bringing in a scream of icy wind and snow.

"Hey. Ang Pasang. We may have a problem." It's Cam, and he doesn't sound happy.

I stand up so fast my chair falls over. "What's wrong? Is it Rose?"

He doesn't look surprised to see me. "No. They're fine. Waiting out this wind, which is way worse than the forecast called for. But I was monitoring the forecasts—and it still looks like it's going to end in an hour or so—when a radio call came in. It was garbled . . . Couldn't tell who it was. But . . . "

A spike of terror, as sharp as if I were the one on the mountain, hits in my chest. "Do you think . . . Is someone in trouble?" I ask.

The radio in his hand crackles. Cameron jumps.

"Hey, it's Cameron at Base. Who's this?"

"Allo? Anyone?" A voice, faint and static, comes through.

Cam presses the button and brings it up to his mouth. "Who is this? Is this Dawa?"

There is an unintelligible crackle, then silence.

"Dawa! Are you there?" Cameron says.

The radio comes back to life. "It's Luc. Dawa is trying to help Yoon Su. We're—"

Silence again.

"Luc! Luc, buddy, what's going on? Aren't you at Camp Two?" Cameron's voice is calm, but his knuckles are white on the radio. I don't realize I'm digging my own nails into the table until one of them breaks with a crack.

"No! Ah . . . somewhere on the South Col. I do not know. We had tried to get back to Camp Three, but we got lost and the radio would not work. Bishal went to find help. Now we're—"

Abruptly it cuts off again.

"Fuck. FUCK! Luc! Come on, man! Give us some landmarks. Can you keep talking to me?" Cameron says.

An agonizing moment of silence, then more noise. "I don't know. It is bad. Yoon Su, she has collapsed, and Dawa is trying to give her a shot of Dex to keep her going. But we don't know *where* we are going. We are just moving."

For a moment the radio is so clear we can hear his rasping breathing and the howl of wind around him.

"Okay, Luc. Can you remember if you went left or right over the ridge?"

Silence. Crackle.

"Luc?" Cameron's voice is loud.

"*Oui?*"

"Keep looking for landmarks, mate. See what you can see."

"*Alors, on ne vois rien!*" Luc's voice is stronger, for a minute, and he sounds annoyed. "It is black out here."

My heart rises a little at his voice; he sounded normal, like he was pissed off at a bad hand in Uno. But a look at Cam and Ang Pasang makes it clear there's nothing good here.

"Tell you what," Cameron says finally, "I'm going to stop using the radio now so you have some juice left when the wind breaks or the sun comes up, whichever comes first. And I'll keep trying to raise someone at Camp Two or Three to come out and look for you. I'll radio you at the first chance to mobilize and guide you in. Sound all right?"

His voice is upbeat, but his eyes look haunted. It doesn't sound all right, and we all know it.

Luc's voice comes through faintly. "*D'accord.* But . . . this is . . . not good."

I have to turn away from Cameron's face as he answers. But his voice is bad enough. "I know, man. I know."

The radio crackles once more, then goes quiet as Luc disconnects.

The silence in the tent is thick and awful.

Chapter Thirty:

Rose

May 16–17
Camp Four/South Col to Summit
26,000–29,035 feet above sea level

For the first time, I wonder if I will die here. We are thirty minutes above Camp Four, a barely-there camp at 26,000 feet on the edge of the mountain where the winds pound us constantly, threatening to pull the tents right off the edge. And that was before the storm.

We arrived there in the last of the afternoon sun, planning to try to nap for a few hours, force some calories down, and prepare for our summit bid. I thought we might see Yoon Su and Luc as they descended, but we missed them. Finjo heard from Cameron that they were safe down at Camp Two. We left as planned at 11:00 p.m., heading out into the darkness with our headlamps glowing, hoping to see the top of the world shortly after the sunrise. But now the wind is rising fast.

I hold on to the fixed line, knowing Paul is right in front of me, Finjo in front of him. But I can see nothing. Nothing but blackness cut with white when gusts of icy snow blow into my face. The next gust is so strong it knocks me over, and only the rope holds me to the mountain. Fear grabs me, and an icy sweat burns me through the freezing night.

"Stop! STOP!" I shout, but no one can hear me. Asha is right behind me, and she wraps an arm around me to keep me upright. After a moment she releases me, gives me a kind of thumbs-up, and pushes me to keep walking. I check my altimeter: 27,000 feet. Taking another step, I try to move forward, but once again the wind pushes me off-balance and I nearly fall.

We have barely been climbing for thirty minutes, and it will take hours to make the summit. I squint into the blackness, and a hideous, nauseous horror begins to sink inside me.

I cannot climb this mountain. I won't even get close.

Trying to push away all thought, I take another step. My promise to myself replays in my mind. I will get down from here. I will get down. But a burning, gnawing part of me wants so badly to get up it first. Step. Step.

Finjo and Paul halt above me. Asha and I climb until we are right up against them, pushed together by the storm.

Finjo pulls his oxygen mask away from his face and speaks, his words barely audible in the howls. "Okay, I am changing the plan. This is too strong, this weather. We go back."

Paul nods, his face invisible through his goggles, hood, and mask.

I pull my own mask away. "Back? Back to camp? What about the summit?"

"No way to summit now. The wind is getting worse. We have to get down. We will wait a few hours and see. If the storm blows out quickly, we may be able to try again."

"And if it doesn't? What then? Do we have to go back to Base Camp?" The Sherpas stock a generous number of oxygen canisters at Camp Four, enough for us to wait out the weather and make a summit attempt, but the supply isn't endless. At some point we have to go back down. And if Cameron's right, if the weather window is really brief this year . . . Could it be over? A wash of panic overrides my exhaustion at the thought. We've come so far!

But Finjo ignores me. "Don't worry about that now. We're going down." He puts his mask back on and turns to head down the mountain as though there is no more to discuss.

And there isn't. He is the leader, and we paid him to make our hard decisions for us. But I want this summit so badly that I am tempted to push past Finjo and keep going. Some animal part of my brain is telling me to go, to pursue this at all costs. The idea of waiting in the tiny, wind-battered tent at 26,000 feet is almost unbearable. But there is no alternative.

We all turn around and carefully, painfully, try to retrace the steps we just took. Step, clip, hold. And again. Again. My brain slips into a kind of robot mode, only noting the strange rasp of the oxygen in my ears as I continue to move. I might as well have my eyes closed for all I can see. My goggles are coated with a rime of ice, and I stop to rub them with my mitten to clear them, but it only lasts a moment.

Slowly, slowly, we make our way along the rope. The wind pushes me down the mountain again and again. My eyes are heavy, and more than anything else, I want to sleep, to rest. My steps get slower and slower.

"Keep moving!" Asha says, her voice muffled. "You have to go faster."

But I can't, not now that we are walking straight into the wind. It somehow whips through tiny cracks in my goggles and manages to blast ice and snow inside against my face. My toes are wooden blocks in my boots, making it hard to know what I'm stepping on.

We have been walking far more than thirty minutes back to camp. A sliver of panic cracks my robot brain, and I scrub my goggles again and peer around. Finjo and Paul are two lumps ahead of me on the line, and there—mercifully—in front of them are the dim, rounded shapes of the tents.

We've made it.

I stagger into the tent behind Paul, pull off my crampons, and lie down on my sleeping bag. The wind is barely diminished by the thin nylon walls, and the whole structure bows and billows in the wind. I look at Paul.

"That was bad," I say. "That was really bad." I have taken my oxygen mask off for a moment, somehow giving in to the illusion that I can breathe better without it constricting me. But after a few minutes, the sick, breathless feeling builds and I replace it.

Paul nods. "Yeah. God, I didn't enjoy that at all. I'm glad we're back here, safe and sound." He smiles and rolls his eyes at his words, and I try to smile back.

Safe and sound. Not how I'd describe being in a tiny piece of nylon lashed to the side of the mountain at 26,000 feet in a blizzard. Still, compared to the icy, screaming blackness of the open path, it does feel like some kind of safety, no matter how illusory. I pull my sleeping bag hood over my head; even in the rated-minus-forty-degree bag, I am freezing, my body refusing to stop shaking.

"Luc and Yoon Su were lucky. They hit the good weather," I say. "I can't believe they're already at Camp Two."

"Luc was even talking about paying one of the Sherpas to bring some beer up. The bastard," Paul says, and we both laugh for a second, but it peters out quickly. They've done it. They've climbed Mount Everest and will be back at Base Camp by tomorrow. I am so jealous I can't bring myself to say anything because it will be sour, whatever it is. The tent is silent other than the scream of the wind.

It is frightening, the weakness of my body. We barely left camp, but my toes are freezing, my muscles painfully tight from clenching them against the force of the storm. And here we are losing brain cells every minute, even with the supplemental oxygen. We are in the death zone. To some extent, our hope of getting to the top is a race against the clock: How long can we hold here, brain cells and muscle dying off, until we scramble up there?

"That was way worse than I expected," Paul says. He has turned off his headlamp, and his face is in shadow.

I nod. We are more than eight miles up in the sky, at an altitude where planes fly. We don't belong here. As if in answer to my thoughts, the storm lashes against the tent more strongly than ever, pushing the nylon against me and sending a flurry of ice crystals falling on my face. I blink them away.

Realization floods through me that this thing we're doing, this climb, is beyond hard, a challenge almost no human on Earth would want to do. Finally, a knot of hurt deep down inside me relaxes, and I let go of my secret thought that Tate should have been here, that he should have done it for me, just because he promised.

Nobody should be here for someone else's dreams. It's too vicious. Everest is for people who know how much they will have to suffer and choose willingly to do it. Whatever his reason was, Tate made the right choice for himself. As I lie in the darkness, shaking from the cold, all I can think is how desperately I want to be one of the few who make it. I think of Mami, asking me again and again if I'm sure I want this, then pushing me to train harder. She understood me, sometimes better than I understand myself. I *do* want this, more than anything. Does she know that? Did I ever tell her? It's a guilty, slippery thought. I think Mami would love it here, that she'd gladly suffer this punishing place for the reward waiting at the top. She'll never have the chance to know. But at least I know why I'm here.

• • •

Asha rouses us at 1:00 a.m., not that either of us managed real sleep. We will head up again. I don't ask what will happen if we have to turn around. I don't want to know.

Finjo is a mummy in his yellow down suit, but I can see a smile crinkle his eyes. "I cannot get Cameron on the radio; the winds are maybe still bad farther down. But I talked to the guides from Adventure Consultants, and they said the storm is finished. We have a small window. So up we go!"

Squinting at the ink-dark night, I can see he's right. The storm has blown out and the weather is perfect, bitterly cold but the wind is dying fast.

Once again we push up the slope in the blackness, Finjo and Paul in front, Asha behind. Crunch, stomp. Crunch, stomp. I move my crampons slowly but steadily up the ice. We are higher than I have ever been, probably higher than

I'll ever be again. It's hard to care. I keep moving only because of that law of physics: a body in motion remains in motion. And of course the corollary: a body at rest remains at rest. If I stop here, I don't think I can start climbing again. If I stop here, I will die.

Of course we do stop, periodically. We suck on snow to try and rehydrate ourselves, and I jam handfuls of peanut M&Ms down my throat. I try to give Paul some, but he looks at me with empty eyes.

"Paul? You okay?" My tongue is thick and stupid in my mouth. "You should eat."

But he shakes his head. "I don't. Not sure. No."

I stare back at him, almost unable to understand his garbled words.

He looks at me like I'm a stranger. "Can't. I can't. You go." He sags on the ropes.

Above him, Finjo motions me to pass him and keep moving, but I stay.

Paul is done?

He's quitting?

There is nothing left in me, nothing except the deep animal drive to climb. I am ready to keep moving, to walk away and leave him behind.

My climb.

I want this summit. So badly.

But it's Paul.

Keep. Moving.

Selfish.

We hold each other's lives in our hands.

I want to climb.

Who am I in this place?

I reach for his shoulders. "Hey, come on, we got this! You

can do this!" I say, and my voice sounds high and panicked, even to me.

He stares, his eyes hooded. I grab his oxygen mask and bang it, hard, with my mittened hand. "It's blocked with ice!" I say. "Asha, he's not getting anything!"

Asha nods and comes over. Paul crouches, his head down toward his knees, and I watch him, barely aware that a parade of other climbers are passing us now, not even acknowledging our group huddled off to the side. She smacks his regulator hard, once, twice, and a huge chunk of ice falls out. His breath has frozen it.

"Better now," she says and puts it back over his face.

But Paul barely moves, even after taking a few breaths. He seems to have sunken inside himself, the exhaustion taking over. I think again of the corollary: a body at rest stays at rest.

I pull off my own mask again. "Paul! Think about the kids who are waiting to hear about this! Think about . . ." I pause. "Think about the hero's journey. Moana wouldn't quit!" I try to sing, even with my throat dry and painful. "'And the voice isn't out there at all, it's insiiiiiiiide me! And no one knooooows how far I'll GOOOOOOO!'"

His eyes blink, and it's like someone turned on a dim light in an empty room. He coughs a little. "It's *the call* isn't out there, not 'the voice,'" he says, pulling his mask aside. Then he nods and puts the mask back on.

He's back. He's with me. A surge of relief and gratitude almost sends me to my knees. We will do this together.

But we still have far to go.

Paul gives a thumbs-up, and we start again. Climbing with oxygen doesn't mean it feels like sea level. It doesn't even mean it feels good. It gives us just enough to feel like we're a few thousand feet lower than we are, just enough to keep us going.

"We need to keep moving," Finjo says. "It will be crowded on the Balcony." He starts back up, clipping into the fixed rope in the brief moment before the next wave of climbers arrives. We follow.

The snow level is low this year, and there is bare rock under our crampons, making us slide and clatter. It is exhausting. The darkness still presses against me, and I am frightened that the sun will never rise, that the summit will never appear, that I am in some endless loop of cold and dark, stuck putting one foot in front of another.

I am slowing again, barely moving up the rope, when Paul stops and points. I gaze up, almost too tired to bother. The wind presses me against the bare rock, screaming in my ears. It reads -40 degrees on my thermometer.

"The moon! Clouds are gone!" he says triumphantly, and his voice is stronger now.

He's right; a beautiful waxing gibbous moon is out now, low in the sky. It adds more light than I would have thought, enough to see our shadows on the snow.

He points the other way. "And the sun's coming soon."

Again I look, and this time it is harder to see, a barely there stripe of something. Not light, but less-dark, a tiny bit of hope that the sun might rise. I smile beneath my mask. We are getting there. Step by step.

We arrive at the Balcony, a long, steep run that means we are close. The Balcony is famous, among other things, for the crowds. There are horror stories of climbers waiting two hours or more to hook into the fixed ropes and make their way up. Today is no different. Dozens and dozens of climbers line up, slumped against the rock, stomping their feet to try to ward off frostbite. I stare around me while I wait, the darkness fading imperceptibly. I have no idea how long we are there, only that it is getting lighter.

Finally it is our turn, and we start up. The Balcony is grueling, steep and long, with icy bare rock and patches of deep snow alternating underfoot. My throat is dry and my muscles ache as I work to pull myself up along the rope.

It is nothing special, this piece of climbing, something I might do on a Saturday afternoon at home, but here at 27,500 feet, it is the hardest thing I've ever done. Still, it is climbing, something that I do almost automatically. Push, grab, reach, and again. And again. The sun starts to blaze over the eastern edge of the sky, and the mountains around us—some of the tallest peaks in the world, all dwarfed by Everest—light up in a glorious pinkish-orange glow.

We continue up the Balcony, now in the blazing morning sunlight. The view is ethereal. I notice it like it is a faded black- and-white photo in a book, like it must be impressive in real life. But I can't really see it. Paul's red form is in front of me, moving farther ahead. He is pushing faster now, or I'm slowing down. I'm not sure. But I cannot move any quicker.

One step. Pause.

Another. Then another pause.

When I look at my watch, a flicker of panic breaks through my haze. It is already 9:00 a.m. Our turnaround time is 1:00 p.m., no later. If we are not standing on the summit at that point, no matter if we are only 50 feet below it, we have to turn back.

I have to be getting close. We have been moving for eight hours already, and when I stand still, my legs tremble with fatigue. Still, I try to go faster.

The route underfoot gets steeper, then steeper still. I start to see black spots in front of my eyes, but I don't stop. Paul is far ahead now, a red shape in the distance. Climber after climber passes me, unclipping just long enough to move around me, as quick as they can be without the safety of the fixed rope, but I barely notice. My crampons slide and clack against the rock, barely holding me in place as I work the jumar up, ever up. The rock angles out even more steeply, and I cling as hard as I can, fingers cramping in my mittens.

Suddenly I'm there. Somewhere, at least, where the steepness ends and there is a respite. I lower my head and breathe hard. It takes several minutes before I can look up. When I do, Paul is right in front of me. He helps me stand straight and keeps an arm around me, holding me up as I try and catch my breath. I look around.

I gasp. Ahead of me, barely any distance at all, is a narrow knife-edge ridge leading to what remains of the famous Hillary Step after an earthquake shifted most of it and, beyond it, the summit.

"Two hours. Less, maybe," Paul says. He has pulled his goggles off for a moment, and he looks transfixed, energized, almost manic. "We can do this. Rose! We ARE going to do this!"

I nod, too exhausted to speak, but an excitement almost like rage burns in me. I will get there. I will do this.

After a few minutes, we start to move again. The ridge is narrow, and there is nothing but air on either side of us. Should I slip now and the fixed rope fail, I would fall 8,000 feet down the southwest face or 11,000 feet down the north side, into Tibet. For the first time in hours, my mind flickers to thoughts of Tate. I wonder how he would do. He is stronger than I am, and even though he's never been this high, altitude has never bothered him. But we move so slowly, so many different things waiting to kill us. I am grateful he is safe, far away from here. I don't even want him close to comfort me. There is no comfort in other people right now. They cannot save me. They cannot even save themselves.

We have walked by dead bodies, more than one, lying in the snow. The cold preserves them in ghastly and horrifyingly lifelike poses: people who sat down to rest and died there, people who fell and never got up. The first time I saw one, I screamed. Now I walk by them without pausing. No, Tate couldn't help me here.

We are at the Hillary Step soon, so soon I start to wonder if I am blacking out and still climbing. Once again I clip into the fixed rope and start to move. The black spots return. At this altitude the body is in necrosis, dying every minute. I don't think of this any more than I can help it. I don't think of the summit. I don't think of anything but how to reach above me, find a foothold, and move up the rope. Paul and Finjo are somewhere above me, Asha somewhere behind me, and other climbers are around too, but I've never felt more alone. This place has nothing to do with humanity. We are all clipped to a rope, but it means nothing, this illusion of safety. It does not keep us safe.

The sun is far above us now, bright and hot, and the thinness of the air means it burns with an intensity I never could have imagined before this. I suppose it is beautiful.

It is hard to care.

We are above the Step, moving through rolling rocks and bumps in the landscape that keep my eyes focused down and my muscles screaming in pain. I cannot look up, I can only move forward.

Except suddenly there is nowhere to go. The ground levels off, and in front of me are prayer flags, thousands of them, flying out hard and fast in the wind, and behind them are climbers posing for photos. Flags. Mementos, photos stuck into the snow.

The summit.

I am here.

Chapter Thirty-One:

Tate

May 17
Everest Base Camp
17,600 feet above sea level

The sun's up, ending the longest night of my life. We never left the kitchen tent, staying by the fire and dozing in shifts, checking in with Luc throughout the night. At around four in the morning, Cam tried and got no answer. None of us slept after that. The storm was full strength, wind screaming and howling and blowing smoke back down the chimney into the stove that Ang Pasang kept burning all night long.

Nobody spoke, until finally Devi said, "Too cold for them to keep taking out the radio. Better they keep it put away and concentrate on staying warm."

Cameron nodded and didn't answer. And we all sat in silence until sunrise.

• • •

Now the sun has barely risen, and the wind's died down to normal icy gusts. Cameron hasn't been able to get Finjo on the radio, but he says that's common when the wind's bad. Even though I'm freaking out, he assures me that no news isn't bad news. . . . It just means they're holed up waiting out the storm.

No, Rose and Paul aren't the problem.

Luc, Yoon Su, Dawa, and Bishal haven't made contact. That's the problem.

All morning I've been running around camp with Cam, trying to find people to jump on a rescue effort. But everywhere we go, there's chaos, exhaustion, weakness, and, way more than I can believe, indifference.

"No can do, mate, sorry," says one South African guy, barely pretending to look concerned. "We're hoping to start our summit push tomorrow, and I can't be gassed before I even start."

Cameron starts walking away, but I stand there. "You're shitting me, right? You realize they're in real trouble?"

The guy doesn't look up. "The price of doing business on this mountain isn't just your money," he says finally. "They knew the risks."

"That's bullshit!" I yell. "You're telling me you don't want someone to come looking for you if you're stuck at twenty-two thousand feet? You don't check your soul at the door, you asshat!"

He shakes his head. "You want to be a hero, kid, knock yourself out. But I'm not risking my summit on a recovery mission. If they spent the night in that storm, you're looking for bodies, not climbers."

He zips up his tent and disappears.

I have to run to catch up with Cameron, who moved on

without comment to ask at the next tent. But I'm so mad I'm shaking.

"Did you hear him? Did you fucking hear him? He's wrong, right? There's no reason to assume the worst at this point. Right?"

Cam doesn't slow down. "What did he say?"

I swallow. We've stopped outside a tent of Danish climbers. "He said, 'If you want to be a hero, knock yourself out, but you're looking for bodies, not climbers.'"

Cameron coughs and spits a wad of phlegm into the snow. He doesn't look at me.

"Well?" I ask. "He's a soulless dick, right?" But before he can answer, another thought hits me.

"Wait a minute. WAIT A MINUTE! I *can* knock myself out. I can go up!" I'm pumped, all the wonderful ADHD adrenaline that shoots through my veins crashing in hard. "I can go up and search!"

Cameron stares, his sunglasses throwing my own face back at me. "You can't go, bud. First of all, you'd need to acclimatize, and then—"

"I AM acclimatized! And I'm on the permit! That's the point! Don't you get it? I was training to climb. I can head up!"

He looks at me, considering, and I want to shake him. The adrenaline is singing now, begging me to climb, dammit, move out and try to find them. This is not a recovery mission, I tell myself. They might be okay. They will be okay.

As Cameron ponders whatever the hell he's pondering, a sound erupts from his jacket that makes us both jump.

"Hello? Is anyone there? Please, answer!"

The voice is thin and crackly, but it's alive. And it's Yoon Su.

Chapter Thirty-Two:

Rose

May 17
Summit of Mount Everest
29,035 feet above sea level

The curve of the earth swoops away in front of me, clearly visible from this height, and the ring of peaks offers gold and orange and amber and deep-pink layers of color. The air is painfully, eerily clear. It's like looking through a telescope at objects endlessly distant from us. Far below, in the valley, clouds fill the bowl with thick, puffy whiteness. I look down, into Tibet, and China beyond, and wonder what I am seeing, how far my gaze can travel. Paul has his mittens off and is trying to snap photos. Finjo gestures to me to stand next to him and takes a selfie with his phone. I almost laugh. Finjo's cell phone has been with us since Kathmandu; somehow it is strange to see it here.

The exhaustion leaves in a rush, and for a minute I'm so energized, so beyond excited that I feel altered, high on some kind of drug I can only imagine. I feel like I could fly, leap off into the clouds and soar and dance on the winds like a god. It's powerful, overwhelming, perfect.

And then it's over.

We spend only a few minutes on top of the world, taking photos. Paul takes a photo with a few tee shirts and flags that his patients gave him, then leaves a tiny vial of ashes that belong to his father. I hesitate a moment, suddenly so tired that even pulling off my mitten is almost too much. But this is why I'm here. I pull out the photo of me and Mami, along with a handful of tiny seashells from the beach where Tate surfs. I clutch the photo carefully so it doesn't blow away, and Paul takes photo after photo of me holding it. I look at the photo, imagining Mami's pride and excitement when I tell her about this, imagining us together, imagining that she is well and strong and so delighted with my stories of the climb, and I can't help it, tears slide down my cheeks and freeze immediately.

Then I open my hand and let the shells fall, and they tumble and dance away immediately in the wind. I smile. It is a piece of home, a piece of my real life, far from this place. I kind of like the idea of them blowing down into Tibet and startling some villagers there.

I stare out at the view again. Glorious, ethereal, unimaginable beauty.

I did it.

I climbed the tallest mountain in the world. I don't have Mami or Tate or even Jordan with me. All our plans and work toward this goal, and I'm the only one of our original group of four who made it. The earth unfolds below me, and I revel in it, trying to love it enough for all of us.

Chapter Thirty-Three:

Tate

May 17
Everest Base Camp to Camp Two
21,000 feet above sea level

Cam grabs his radio. "Yoon Su? Boy am I glad to hear you. What's going on?"

The radio's silent. I'm ready to grab it from Cameron's hand and shake it, when it comes back to life.

"Help! Someone must help us! We were out all night; we tried to keep moving so we would not freeze, but it was dark, and I could not move. And Luc . . . Luc dug in the snow and made a small shelter, then put me in and lay on me to protect me, but now . . . " Her voice is slow and blurred, and I can feel the fear in a cold sweat down my own back.

"Where are you?" I shout, but Cameron waves at me to shut up. Yoon Su is talking again.

"Dawa was not good, but he gave us the radio and left. He was trying for Camp Two. . . . " Her voice trails off again.

"Yoon Su, tell us where you are," Cam says, his voice strong and loud. "We're heading up." His voice softens for a second. "And, love, I'm sorry to ask you, but we need to know what we're dealing with. Is Luc . . . okay?"

The wind's still racing through camp, and a huge group of climbers are outside meeting in a big huddle, and someone has music playing faintly, but I swear every sound stops as we listen to the radio. For long, hideous moments, there is nothing.

Then it crackles again. "I . . . I don't know." Her voice slurs and falls silent.

Cameron swears softly. "Okay. Okay, we're heading up. Hang in there. Yoon Su, do you hear me? Try to keep moving. We're coming!"

There's no answer.

Cam looks at me. "You don't have to do this," he says, but I shake my head. That's bullshit. Of course I have to do this. I don't want any part of this mountain's horror show, and I *knew* that, I fucking knew that, which is why I finally told Rose and Dad that I wasn't climbing. And yet here I am, and in some sick way, I'm grateful that I have the training, that I can try to help when no one else can. The Icefall's ahead of me, blinding in the rising sun. It's more beautiful than I could have imagined, but I hate it anyway, fucking hate every single thing about it. But that doesn't matter. Now it's my turn to play.

• • •

It takes another thirty minutes to pull together the rescue party. Ang Pasang found two Sherpas with other expeditions who were willing to come with me, so we're a team of three. Not enough to move four people if we're lucky enough to find them, but it's all we have. We head up toward the Icefall, radio securely buckled into my belt, with Kami and Ang Dorji, a Peak Experience head guide who only got down yesterday and is completely exhausted but willing to try. Yoon Su provided some garbled instructions on how she knew they were close to Camp Two, but they had veered left, then stopped, panicked that they'd go over the edge in the darkness and wildness of the storm.

I move fast through the Icefall. A drumbeat of terror started up as we walked away from camp, and with every step I take, it slams through me. The Sherpas are quiet, one ahead of me and one behind, keeping pace. The sun's climbing too high now, and we shouldn't be here, but there's nothing to do but go through. Yoon Su's words replay again and again in my head.

"Sometime in the night, he removed his gloves and started to claw at his face. Now he cannot move, but I can hear his breath. We are dying!"

The fear in her voice was a virus, infecting me. I don't want to find them dead. I sure as fuck don't want to find them dying. But I have to try, because I can. Because Rose is somewhere on this mountain, and Jesus Christ if someone were able to help her and didn't . . . I need to stop my brain from churning.

Ironically, the fear and panic over what I might find has made the actual climbing easier. I move through the ice without thinking.

Kami stops in front of me.

"You drink something," he says, handing me a canteen.

I wave him off. "I'm fine. Let's keep going," I say. But my words come out slow and thick, and he shakes his head and holds out the water.

"Fine." I grab it, almost dropping it with my massive mitten. I glug in huge gulping gasps, surprised by how thirsty I am.

"Thanks," I say. "Let's keep going now."

He nods and starts forward again.

Crunch, step. Crunch, step. Another ladder. I don't look down. I imagine Rose crossing these ladders again and again, imagine walking behind her, watching the ladder dip and sway as she steps on it. Sweat's pouring down my face, fogging up my sunglasses and running into the scruffy mess of my beard. It's steeper here, and I have to concentrate, which is a relief. We're gaining, moving, stretching to get somewhere.

Finally we're up and over. I crouch in the snow, breath coming in gasps, while the Sherpas check their phones and mutter to each other. Ang Dorji is on his radio, talking quickly in Nepali.

"Anything?" I say. It's all I can get out.

But he shakes his head. "No news. Just hearing that others in the Peak Experience group are on their way down to Base Camp. We will likely pass them soon."

Anger like a wave breaks over me. "If they're hanging around Camp Two or Three, why the hell didn't they try and help? Where the fuck were they last night?"

He shrugs, his smile faint. "Climbers work very hard to come to this place. Once they get here, some can only see the mountain summit. Nothing else. They say they cannot help, and many cannot. Most are too tired. Their bodies are exhausted and empty after the summit. If they try and rescue others, it would mean more people for us to rescue. They cannot help anyone but themselves."

"And the others?" I say.

He shrugs. "All say they cannot help. Perhaps some mean they will not, but in the end it is the same thing."

I nod. I know this, I guess. For the people who already climbed, their bodies are trashed. But I can't buy it. Not really. People can do amazing things when they need to—the news is always full of stories about people who lift up trucks to save babies or whatever. These people, like the climbers at Base Camp, aren't willing to help someone else, even if it's life-and-death.

I don't say this, though. I just ask him if he's ready to go, and we start moving.

The climbing's harder now, and the familiar movements are a kind of homecoming, even as the air thins and spots swim in front of my eyes. It's reassuring, carrying none of the terrors of the last few times I tried. Compared to what's ahead, climbing is the easy part. My body knows what to do. The pull of my arms against the rock. The ache in the ball of my calf when I push to reach higher than I can really go. I loved this once, maybe love it still. But not here. Never ever here, at 22,000 feet and praying to find my friends alive.

The sun's hot, even with the wind, and we stop again and again to drink water. Each time we radio Yoon Su, asking her how she's doing. Her answers are single syllables, barely enough to let us know she's alive.

Finally we're near enough to Camp Two that Ang Dorji says we should start searching.

We look for over an hour, combing through rocks and cornices that veer off from the trail. There are no footprints; everything's been covered by snow. I spot a flash of red in the distance and rush over, fast as my oxygen-deprived body can move.

It's not Luc and Yoon Su. It's a body, a fucking corpse,

long dead by the amount of skull showing. The faded red down climbing suit and stiff plastic yellow boots are in pretty good shape.

Turning away, I puke on the snow, again and again, until nothing is left.

"You are okay?" Ang Dorji asks. He puts his hand on my shoulder. I am crouched, trembling only feet from the dead guy. "Do we need to descend?"

I shake my head. "No. I'm fine. I . . . How long has that guy . . .?" I gesture to the corpse.

"Ah." He nods understandingly. "You were surprised by Yellow Boots. We should have warned you."

"Yellow Boots?" I say.

"That's what he is called now. He is a climber from a long time ago, but, like most corpses here, he remains where he fell. Nobody knows who he was, but now he is a marker. Climbers know they have missed the route to Camp Two once they see him."

There's nothing to say. I take the canteen Kami offers and rinse my mouth. I kick snow over all the puke. I'm in hell, plain and simple, and there is nothing to do but find Luc and Yoon Su and get out. Still, I can't make myself walk away from this climber—Yellow Boots—without looking again. I walk over to where he lies and crouch down.

"I'm sorry," I whisper. "What a shitty thing, to die here, be left to rot, and then be used as a goddamn signpost. I'm so fucking sorry."

I stand and go back to the Sherpas, letting my eyes comb the snow, looking for signs of life.

More hours, more searching. We're about to return to the trail and try the other side when I see a flash. It looks like sun on glass, glaring and bright.

"Hey!" I call. "Over there! Is that something?" After Yellow Boots there is no way I'm walking over to check out anything until someone's with me.

Dorji comes quickly and then yells in Nepali to Kami. Together we walk toward the light. As we get closer, we hear a voice, and the sound makes my skin crawl. It's the sound of terror, of panic, more animal than human.

Chapter Thirty-Four:

Rose

May 17
Camp Four/South Col
26,000 feet above sea level

*U*ntil now I never really understood how people could say the summit of Everest is the halfway point. After all, once you get there, you're going down, gaining altitude, working with gravity, not against it. Now I know.

"I need to stop," I mutter for the fourth time since we left the summit. My head is pounding so hard I'm afraid I might throw up, even though there's nothing in my system.

Finjo's on his radio, scowling. I barely notice, too focused on trying to breathe.

Paul hands me water, but I push the bottle away. Swallowing anything will definitely make me lose it. I lower my head between my knees and try to breathe.

Finjo turns to us. "We need to keep moving. Let's go!" He starts heading down again without waiting for an answer.

I groan. Apparently, he's all done coddling the clients. But Paul grins. "Good. I'm ready to get out of the death zone. Hell, I'm ready to walk all the way to Base Camp and celebrate with a beer!"

His good mood is infectious, and I start to move more quickly. After resting at Camp Four we will get down to Camp Two tonight and Base Camp tomorrow. We are so close. As we descend lower, reaching the fixed rope below the Balcony, I can barely hang on. Some combination of excitement and utter exhaustion has taken over, and a weird kind of euphoria settles over me.

I summited Everest. I did it. It doesn't seem to matter anymore how long it takes to get down. I can walk forever, placing one foot in front of another. I am no longer cold either. It's pleasant, this numbness.

Paul doesn't approve, though. Finjo is so far ahead I can barely see him, and Asha stays behind me, urging me forward. Paul seems worried. He keeps stopping to check on me, and several times he waits until I'm down the ropes before moving on. I try to give him a thumbs-up, but I'm not sure my arms actually move. I am fine. We are almost done.

The sun is blazing in the sky and there is no wind, and before too long the tents of Camp Four are in view. Safe. We will be safe. We are less than 500 feet from the tents. I imagine lying down, imagine Sherpas handing me hot tea, imagine letting my body rest, finally. It is agonizing, these last dangerous steps. I want to be there already, to let go of the tension I've been holding for so many days. My legs tremble uncontrollably, and I stop again and again. Falling now could mean a broken leg or, worse, a slide off the edge to a thousand-foot drop. Paul waits for me, and together we walk into camp.

A sense of utter safety and even coziness comes over me. We are safe. We've made it. Without even taking the tea, I stumble straight into my tent, remove my boots, and crash face forward into the sleeping bag. Pulling it over myself, I try and relax, but the more I try, the harder I shiver. I shake and shake until my teeth rattle. Paul comes in and wraps himself and his own sleeping bag over me, and slowly the shivers stop. My thoughts are thick and slow. I whimper a little, suddenly tensing up like I had fallen asleep on the fixed rope.

"It's okay, Rose," Paul says softly. The wind is so loud I can barely hear him. He has gotten into his bag and curled up around me. "Rest. We can rest now."

I nod and burrow deeper. We can rest. We have made it to the top of the world, and now we are safe.

Chapter Thirty-Five:

Tate

May 17
Above Camp Two
22,000 feet above sea level

When we get there, Yoon Su's screaming, trying to wrap herself around Luc, who's lying half-undressed in the snow.

"LUC! Luc man, we're here. We can help. We got this. Don't worry, man, you did great. We can fix this!" I shout. It's bullshit, of course. I have no idea what to do, no way to know how to help them. But I keep talking, repeating myself over and over, trying to calm them, or myself; I don't even know.

Yoon Su has ice caked onto her skin in a sick kind of mask, and her eyes are swollen almost shut. Her nose is a scary blue red. I try to smooth out my face, try not to show the horror.

"You did amazing," I say again. "You're going to be fine."

Yoon Su looks at me like I'm a ghost, like I'm the horror movie monster, not her. "He tried to protect me. All night. He lay on top of me, shielding me from the wind. Then this morning . . . This morning he moved. . . . He tried to take off his down suit. And he is so strong—I could not stop him."

Ang Dorji and Kami rush over. They grab Yoon Su, who's gone limp. I move closer to Luc, terrified of what I'll see. Carefully I pull his down suit back on, zipping zippers and closing flaps, like this will save him. His hands are bare and a hideous blue white, curled into claws. I look around for his mittens but don't see them. Pulling off my own, I try and get them on his hands, but they're so stiff the mittens fall off. I'm too freaked out to rub them or breathe on them or do any of the normal things I'd do for mild frostbite. Luc's hands are nothing I've ever seen, something out of a medical textbook or a nightmare.

He's moaning, the sound coming out of his frozen un-moving mouth. The sound's awful, the soundtrack to night terrors, and my hands shake as I try and wrap the reflective heat blanket from my pack around him.

Over by Yoon Su, the two Sherpas are pulling layers over her, injecting her with a steroid to try and reduce the blood flow. She's moving, though. She lifts one arm, then another, as they work a rope around her, then around one of the Sherpas. They're getting ready to short rope her down the mountain, which is brutal for them but will get her down to where a helicopter can land.

"What about Luc?" I ask, desperate to hear that they have a plan.

"He is too far gone." Dorji's face is hidden. "There is no way we can move him when he is unconscious like this. He has lots of body—we cannot carry him."

It is a strange phrase: "lots of body." I look down at Yoon Su, so tiny. She is barely there, just a small, lightweight shell. But at these words she starts to scream and thrash. Kami nearly tumbles over.

"NO! NOOOOOOOOOO! YOU WILL NOT LEAVE HIM HERE!" she shrieks. She looks possessed, flailing against the ropes that hold her to Kami. "HE WILL DIE HERE!"

I want to close my eyes and disappear. "Yoon Su, you have to go. You can't . . . You need to get down . . ." I try to get her to see sense, but she's beyond hearing, beyond responding.

"HE SAVED MY LIFE! I WILL NOT . . . I CANNOT LEAVE! I WILL NOT LEAVE HIM. . . ." Her voice dissolves into screams that turn into sobs.

My own tears pour down my face, soaking the scruff of beard. I move to wrap my arms around Yoon Su, bracing for her to flail more. But she hangs against me, sobbing.

"You need to go down," I whisper. "Think about your sister. And your parents. They're waiting for you. You need to go down and get help, Yoon Su. Okay? I'll stay with him. I'll stay with Luc. But you need to leave."

Her eyes are rolling, barely able to stay open. "STAY," she says. "HELP HIM." Her voice scrapes against my soul.

"I will. I promise, Yoon Su. But you go. Your mom and dad need you to go down now, okay?"

She nods, barely.

Ang Dorji gets off the radio and turns. "We go down now. If we are going to save her, we must leave." He pauses and looks at me, then down at Luc.

"I am sorry for this. We will say prayers for his soul to move quickly. But he is dead."

As though in answer, Luc moans louder, and his horrible claw hand reaches up and tries to grab me.

I scream. I can't help it. "Jesus, Dorji. We can't . . . We can't leave . . ." I trail off because I know exactly what he's going to say. That we have to. That on this mountain, where you can barely ever rescue survivors, nobody risks their life to bring down a body.

But he's not a body. Yet.

I know he's right. I get it, but I can't deal with it. Can't deal with a place where the best thing to do is to walk away from a dying friend.

Luc moans, and I put my arms around him, trying to lift him onto my lap.

Ang Dorji says something in Nepali, and Kami and Yoon Su—who's now slumped over but standing—start moving incredibly slowly, away from us.

"You need to come now," Ang Dorji says to me. "We will keep looking for Bishal and Dawa, to see if we can find them. Dawa has no radio because he left it with Yoon Su. And Bishal's has been off all night. But we will try."

I shake my head. "I can't. I'm sorry. I know you're right and we can't bring him down, but I can't walk away."

"You can do nothing!" Ang Dorji snaps. It's the first time I've heard him raise his voice.

"I can stay with him. I can—" I try to remember the phrase Paul used once. "I can bear witness. I can keep him from being alone."

"Until when?" he says. "Until darkness comes and we have to come back and rescue you?"

I shake my head. "I don't think it will take that long. I'll come down . . ." I pause. I don't want to say it. "I'll come down soon. We're only around forty minutes from Camp

Two. It's not like I can miss it." It's true. Without a snow-storm, the path down to camp is clear, if treacherous. They were practically there.

Ang Dorji stands for another moment. He doesn't look pissed. He looks . . . tired. Tired and older than his thirty-whatever years. "Fine," he says. "You stay for now. You keep the radio on. You look at your watch and come down before evening."

I nod, and he turns to leave, following the others down the mountain.

Luc's quiet. I wonder if he knows I'm staying.

"Don't worry," I tell him. I hold his claw in my hand. "I won't leave. I promise. I'll stay right here, and you won't be alone. You did it, you know. You summited Everest, and you kept Yoon Su alive. She'll be okay because of you. Her sister and parents and students are all going to be so amazed and grateful. . . . You're a goddamn hero. You saved her." I keep talking. I don't know what else to do.

"I'm here," I say, stupidly. "I'm right here."

It makes no difference. None at all.

Chapter
Thirty-Six:

Rose

May 17
Camp Four/South Col
26,000 feet above sea level

After a few hours, Asha wakes me. "We need to keep moving," she says. "I will melt some snow and get your bottles filled." She heads back out.

I hurt in a way I have never imagined. The closest I remember is when I took a bad fall on Half Dome and had bruises from shoulder blade to calf as well as a gash on my thigh that took eighteen stitches. This is worse. Groaning, I head out to meet Paul and Asha.

When I get to them, my eyes land on Paul's face. He too has lost weight, but mostly it looked good on him. Not now, though. His face is gaunt and almost haunted, and I do a double take. Has he looked like this all along and I never noticed?

"Rose," he starts, and when I hear his voice, I know that, no, he has not looked like this until right now. It is his professional doctor's voice, one that gives bad news to parents about their children, that tries to calm terrified kids in the night.

"What? What's wrong?" I ask.

"Luc and Yoon Su got lost in the storm on their way down from the summit. They spent the night out in the storm, with Dawa and Bishal. They—"

"But they were at Camp Two! Finjo said so!" I interrupt. We thought they were drinking beer last night.

"It was a mistake." Asha's voice is quiet. "Cameron could not get Dawa on his radio because the batteries were low. So he spoke to a Peak Experience guide at Camp Two who said he saw four climbers return and go into the Mountain Adventure tents. Except he was incorrect. The climbers he saw were from a different group."

"But when . . . How . . . ?" I can't get the words out.

"Cameron heard from Yoon Su late late, in the middle of the night. It was too dark to do anything. Then he tried to get Finjo, but as you know—"

"Finjo couldn't get Cameron on the radio before he left for the summit. That's why he talked to the other guides up here about the weather." I feel sick. "When . . . When did Finjo . . . ?"

Asha looks down. "At the summit. When he called Cameron to give our good news."

"At the—but why didn't you tell us?"

Asha shakes her head. "There is nothing we can do up there. There is no way to get to them fast enough. So Finjo says to let you have your celebration, then he will go down, fast fast, and try to help."

At the summit. While I stood there, victorious and celebrating, my friends were dying. That's why he was in such a rush on the descent. I gasp, then getting no oxygen, start to cough and choke.

"Rose," Paul starts, coming toward me.

"They're dead, aren't they?" I interrupt. "Yoon Su is dead." Because suddenly I know. I know Everest won't let us go without taking one of us. Nausea breaks over me, and I gag a little, trying to swallow down the bile.

"NO! No, honey, she's alive. In rough shape but alive. She's being brought down to Camp Two right now, and Finjo's meeting them there, working to get a helicopter to evacuate her to Kathmandu."

I nod, trying desperately to catch my breath. This isn't the worst news, then. But Paul's still talking.

"Luc—he's . . . It's bad." His voice quavers a little.

Asha speaks. "He is unconscious, and there is no rescue possible. He is too far gone."

"Luc?" It makes no sense. It can't be Luc, who made everyone laugh, who promised me a dance party back in Lukla and champagne in Kathmandu.

"You know how very difficult and dangerous it is to rescue people on the mountain," Asha says. "Luc will not survive. He cannot move. It is not right to risk more lives to try and bring him down. Possibly later, a crew will be able to retrieve his body."

Retrieve his body. The words fall like rocks. I nod, tears streaming down my face. "So he's all alone? Dying?"

Paul and Asha exchange glances, and then Paul speaks. "No, honey. Tate climbed up to be with him. And he says he won't leave until he's gone."

Tate? It makes no sense. He didn't even want to be here.

"How . . .?" I start.

"He can climb because he is still on the permit. He can reach Camp Two because he's a strong climber. He's staying with him because . . . well, because he's Tate." Paul puts his arms around me, but I shrug him off.

"I'm going," I say. "I'm going to them. Now."

•   •   •

Moving down Lhotse Face toward Camp Two, every part of me hurts in a frightening way, as though the pain is drilling out from my bones. Even though there's more oxygen here, I can't catch my breath. But even worse is the Dread, thicker and stronger than ever. I am terrified of what I am walking toward. Asha is in front of me, but I feel so totally alone. Once we got to the fixed ropes, Paul rushed down to Camp Two to offer medical help. I want him to come with me, to help Luc, but of course there is no point. A doctor won't help him. If I'm honest, I don't want Paul to help Luc. I want him to help me. I don't want to see Luc dying. But Tate is there. Tate, loyal and brave to his core, has climbed anyway, to be there. Down the rope we move, every step a painful challenge.

It is late by the time we get off the Face and onto the gentler slope, and the sun is low in the sky.

"We start looking now," Asha says. She has waited for me, her radio in hand. "Finjo says he and Paul are down at Camp Two, and Paul helps a lot. But he says Luc will be somewhere near here."

My heart is thick with fear and a kind of horrible anticipation. This is the Dread, every single moment that I have feared since Mami got sick. Everything I traveled around the world to conquer, and it was lying here the whole time, waiting for me.

I scan the edges of the trail but see nothing, so we keep walking. I have been using oxygen at a reduced flow, but now I take the mask off.

"TATE!" I scream into the wind. My voice is pulled away so fast I can barely hear it myself. But I can't help it. I scream his name again.

Asha puts a hand on my arm. "We will see them. I have directions. We will see a big rock on the left, then a cornice. They are near there."

I nod, barely able to believe what we will find. Barely able to believe the Dread is so real.

But soon enough there's a huge jutting rock on the edge of the path and a wind-blown snow cornice beyond it. I move faster now, too afraid, like a kid who throws open the closet door rather than waiting for the monsters to come and find her. But the monster is real, and I'm running as fast as I can to meet it.

"Tate? Are you here?" I cry. "Tate!"

"Rose? Jesus, is that you?"

The voice is so close I scream in surprise. They are a little above me, pressed against another smaller rock in a pathetic attempt to shield themselves from the wind. Tate is on his knees in his down suit, a figure slumped half on his lap and half in the snow. Luc.

Tate looks up at me, and his face, oh, his face is so lost. And Luc . . .

My voice cracks, and I am crying, trying to talk but crying too hard to make sense. "Oh, Luc! No . . . No! Is he . . . ? Tate, I'm sorry. I'm so sorry you had to be here, to do this. Luc wouldn't . . . I'm so sorry—"

He cuts me off. "Rose. You didn't do anything. It was my choice. My choice to come. To be here with Luc." His voice breaks, and he reaches out a hand to me. "But you're safe. You left, and I didn't say goodbye. I wasn't there."

I grab his hand and hold it tight. I want to run into his arms, to hold him until I am warm and safe, but we are 22,000 feet in the air, and there is a dying man already there.

I move to his side and kneel next to him. Luc is still and silent in his lap. He is so large, draped across Tate's lap, but he's not moving.

"Is he—?" I don't want to say it.

Tate shrugs, then shakes his head. "He lost consciousness around thirty minutes ago. Before that he was . . . I guess 'awake' is the best word. I talked, and he kind of responded. That was before, though. He's still breathing. But barely."

I close my eyes for a second, trying to control the rising hysteria. The tears have been pouring down my cheeks since I saw them, and I have to bite down to keep big racking sobs from tearing out of me. I try to think of Luc, of what he might still be hearing.

"You are such an amazing climber," I say softly. "I'm so glad I got to climb with you." I move my head slightly so my tears won't drip on his frozen face. "You worked so hard for this, and you made it to the summit. I hope by now you're feeling okay. I mean, I think you might be feeling warm. . . ." I break off.

"God, Tate, how are you doing this? How can you sit here and not scream? I'm sorry, Luc! I'm so sorry! I wish we had been together. I wish we could have saved you." I stop, trying to control the racking sobs that shake my body. "I promise I'll tell everyone how amazing you were—how brave and funny—how you looked out for me whenever we were doing practice climbs and always shared your chocolate bars, even though you pretended to be mad about it. And I'll find Amelie. I'll show her our photos." Here my sobs threaten to choke me. "If she wants I'll take her climbing someday. Not Everest. But somewhere. Somewhere else . . . "

I can't talk anymore. Putting my face in my palms, I sob for long, awful minutes.

Tate puts an arm around me. "He's gone, Rosie. He's gone."

I open my eyes. Tate's eyes are dry, but dark circles ring them and he looks ancient and broken. Looking down at Luc, I want more than anything to see him look at peace or released or some kind of pretty little lie that will let me stand up and walk away from him. But he looks exactly the same—bluish skin, eyes half-open, ice frozen over his forehead and into his hair.

"We go down now," Asha says, scaring me. I had honestly forgotten she was there, my guide and friend who has been watching two American teenagers hold a dying French man on the side of her mountain. I wonder what she thinks of this, if she is thinking of her brother and whether anyone held him as he died. I wonder what she thinks of us paying enormous sums of money to stomp up and down the mountain they thought of as a god.

I nod. "Let's go," I say.

Tate gently lays Luc's head on the ground, then lifts it again and places his own pack under it like a pillow. I don't say anything, just watch, while the tears fall like rain down my cheeks. The air is colder now, and they start to freeze against my skin. I wipe them away with the back of my mitten.

He picks up Luc's pack and stands, slinging it over his shoulder. "For his family," he says.

I slip my mitten into Tate's and lean against him, but he

∧∧ 272 ∧∧

is tired and off-balance and stumbles with my weight.

There is no comfort to be had anywhere. I start to walk.

"Rose," Tate calls.

I turn, and he holds his arms out to me, and I am in them, trying to hold him as tight as I can with my exhausted, pathetic grip because it seems so important to hold on to him, to make sure he knows I'm here.

"I couldn't save him, Rose," he whispers. "I couldn't fucking save him. He was a hero, and he kept Yoon Su alive, and I told her I'd try, but I couldn't. I just couldn't." He repeats the words over and over, until the words turn into sobs, and we hold each other until Asha tells us we have to go.

Chapter Thirty-Seven:

Tate

May 17–18
Everest Base Camp
17,600 feet above sea level

We're halfway through the Icefall before I even notice where we are. This whole nightmare's almost over.

Except for the part where we get to wake up.

Rose and I, along with Asha, limped into Camp Two, where Paul gave us the news. Bishal had been found by some Adventure Consultant climbers and brought down to Camp Two this morning. He had severe frostbite and would probably lose several fingers, but he and Yoon Su had already been picked up by a helicopter.

Ang Dorji had found Dawa's body, 500 feet from Camp Two. Frozen to death.

This is the one that floods me with so much rage that I want to tear the mountain apart. Five hundred feet. So fucking close, and he couldn't get there. Dawa had summited

Everest before; he knew this mountain as well as anyone in the world. He was smart and strong and knew everything he needed to survive, and still the mountain killed him. I think about his daughter, close to our age, and sons who are already climbing as support Sherpas. And now they'll live the rest of their lives without their dad.

He was close enough to camp that they were able to get his body down in the helicopter, so at least he won't be left on the mountain, like Luc. Like hundreds of others. I hate this place more than I ever knew I could hate something.

Jopsang Sherpa, the last support staff at the campsite, wanted us to stay the night at Camp Two and rest, but there was no fucking way I was staying on this mountain another minute more than I had to. So we headed down to Base Camp, even though it was getting dark, and now we're almost there.

"Last ladder. Last time," Rose says. We're so close we're practically bumping into each other, but neither of us has said anything in hours. Her voice is croaky and weak.

I try to smile. "You're an expert by now."

She shakes her head. "They scare me every single time." She's silent for a second, then speaks again. "I get it now, I really do. This climb . . . No one should be here who doesn't really, really want it." Her voice catches. "And I wanted it, so badly. More than I even realized. And maybe that makes me selfish, maybe only someone really terrible would push so hard for something like this. But you . . . You climbed for Luc, even though you didn't want to. You are so brave, and I'm sorry for what I said!" She bites back a sob and starts to turn away.

I grab her before she can start on the ladder. Grab her and hold her because I need her to hear.

"No! Rosie, no. You're not selfish. I'm the one who's sorry. I'm so fucking sorry I'm not as brave as you, that I didn't tell you what was going on with me. I didn't want to disappoint you! I wanted to be there for you." I make myself breathe—in, out. Candle, flower.

"I'm sorry I wasn't honest with you. But I'm not sorry I came. And I'm not sorry I kissed you. I'm so fucking grateful that I was brave enough to do that." I wrap my arms around her, and even with all our gear and exhaustion and sadness, I have a sense of rightness, of RoseAndTate, fitting together where we belong.

"I love you," I whisper. "I wish I could have done this for you. I wish I could have saved Luc. But I love you so much, Rosie."

Her eyes meet mine, and they're shadowed and bloodshot and exhausted, but still they shine out at me. "I love you," she says, her voice a ghost in the icy silence. "I love you, I love you."

For one beautiful second, everything else in the world disappears.

◆ ◆ ◆

Finally we're on the gray, gravelly moraine, crossing the endless and empty stretch that leads to the tents. It's almost dark. Ahead, headlamps bob around, and in the domed nylon of the tents, lights like ships drift in an ocean of snow and ice. I'm numb, inside and out. The darker it gets, the more I think about Luc, lying alone in the dark, my backpack under his head.

We're still a ways from the tents when a headlamp veers up and starts moving toward us. It's coming fast.

"Please don't let it be Luc's family," I whisper. "They couldn't get here yet, could they?"

Before Rose can answer, there's a shout that cracks through the cold air.

"TATE!" a voice screams. "Tate! Is that you?"

It's Dad. Dad's voice, except it isn't, really; it's a panicked, crazy-sounding thing unlike his usual loud laugh and laid back California drawl.

"Rose? Tate? Who's there? Do you have him? Is that my son? *Jesus, can someone tell me if that's my son?*" He's screaming, and he's moving closer in the darkness until the glare of his lamp is shining right in my face.

"Dad, it's me! It's okay! It's me and Rose. We're both here; we're fine. I'm fine, Dad. I'm okay. I'm fine." I keep repeating the words as he barrels into us, nearly knocking me down as he grabs me.

His arms are wrapped around me like a strap, and I can't move, can't hug him back, can't do anything but stand there, still holding Rose's hand. He lets go and opens his arms wider, trying to grab us both. I reach out and hold on to both of them, not caring if it's too hard. I cling as tight as I can. We're holding each other up, and I don't know who's sobbing, who's talking, who's repeating my name again and again.

• • •

The next morning when I wake up, there's a moment of normal before everything rushes back. I'm alone in my tent, since Dr. Celina had Dad back in the infirmary the minute we got into camp. I never even got to talk to him before she had him hooked up to oxygen and had sent me and Rose away, each with a sleeping pill. Shaking off the grogginess, I head over to the infirmary. The day's bright and clear, and a few groups have already left for their summit push. The business of Everest, still churning away.

When I get there, Dad's lying down but wide awake, staring at the open door. He sits up, groaning slightly, when I come in.

"Hey." I take a step forward, then stop. I don't know what to say. Looming over him makes it worse.

He pats the edge of the bed, an IV line taped to his hand, which looks like it belongs to an eighty-year-old. "Hey, T-Man. Have a seat."

All the fire and strength that makes him Jordan Russo—former college baseball player, peak bagger, extreme marathoner—is gone. And I feel like I'm sitting next to a stranger. Without a live current of competition and frustration and energy crackling between us, I don't know what we are.

"Do you know that when you were tiny, just a newborn, I used to do all the night feedings? Your mom was exhausted after the C-section, and so the first month, the nights were mine. She'd pump so I'd have bottles, and I'd lie on the couch and you'd stare at me with your big brown eyes. I'd tell you about work, about what Hillary was up to, about how tired we were, but mostly about how much we loved you." He smiles faintly. "Back then you loved listening to me talk. As soon as I shut up, you'd start crying, so I'd start up again, babbling about anything I could think of until you fell asleep. My voice was hoarse for weeks."

I perch on the edge of the bed, my weight bending the mattress. "I don't think I ever knew that," I say.

He shrugs, then winces.

I want so badly not to say the wrong thing, not to spark yet another argument. It's like walking on the Icefall, taking tiny, tentative steps and hoping the ground holds. "I'm sorry you couldn't climb, Dad," I say finally, feeling the stupid, pathetic inadequacy of these words.

He shakes his head, not like he's disagreeing but in confusion. "What are you sorry for? Did you sabotage my lungs without my knowing it? If so, you might want to look for a job in the Special Forces or Secret Service or something."

I try to smile at his joke, but it feels more like a grimace. "No, but I fucked this up. I know that."

He shifts so that he's sitting up. "You don't need to apologize, son. But I want to understand." He sighs. "I want to know what's going on with you. What happened?"

I swallow. "I don't know exactly. I mean, that fall on Rainier was scary, and I was freaked out, for sure. We never really talked about it. And . . ." I pause, unsure how to tell him what Dr. Celina had said. It feels too dramatic, calling it PTSD.

"Dr. Celina was saying when something like that happens, it can be traumatic. And yeah, maybe that sounds stupid, but the panic attacks were bad. Really bad."

"Why didn't you say something?" Dad asks, but he doesn't sound exasperated.

"Because I didn't want to let you down! Any of you! You were so pumped, and it was the one thing we still did together. I—I didn't want to ruin it. Then Maya got sick, and the last thing I wanted to do was disappoint Rose. I figured it would get better. But it didn't."

I let my gaze fall to the floor so I don't have to see him pretending he's not disappointed, pretending like he doesn't think it's laziness or weakness.

"Tate. My son," he says, and his voice is rough, from

coughing or maybe something else. "I don't know why *any-one* wants to do this. I wanted it, and God, if I'm honest, I still do, but it's not the kind of thing anyone should take lightly. And I'm sorry—" He breaks into a cough that turns into a sob. "I'm goddamn sorry that I pushed you. What kind of a father . . . What kind of man . . .?" He stops, turning away from me.

Panic floods my chest. I've made Dad cry. "Hey. HEY. I wanted to! Or at least I thought I wanted to. And I'm not even sorry I came," I say. "Dad, I swear—" And now I'm crying too, tears and snot running down my face. "You didn't do anything wrong. I could have said something. I should have. I know that."

We're silent for a minute, and I wipe my face on my sleeve, taking a deep breath. Next to me, Dad coughs again, then quiets. He moves over, shoving his own body against the wall.

"I'm exhausted, buddy," he says, patting the spot next to him. "How about keeping me company until I conk out?"

I wriggle next to him until I'm lying down, my filthy trekking pants and boots on top of the blanket. He closes his eyes. "Talk to me, T-Man. Tell me something I don't know."

I smile a little. "Well. Rose and I—"

"I said something I don't already know," he mutters, his mouth curving into a grin. "What do you think, I'm an idiot? Nice job, by the way. Russo men always hit above their weight when it comes to amazing women."

I laugh a little, shaking my head. I guess we weren't as subtle as I thought. "Okay, then, let me tell you about the kind of lightweight plastic I think could work if we're ever going to make flying cars," I start and talk and talk until his breathing evens out and he starts to snore.

Chapter Thirty-Eight:

Rose

May 18–22
Everest Base Camp to Kathmandu
17,600–4,600 feet above sea level

The trek down from Base Camp to Lukla passes by in a fog. Whole days disappear as we walk in silence, our footsteps barely registering on the dusty earth. The mountains are behind us now, and I don't turn to look at them. I don't want to see them. We cover the distance slowly, my body aching and weak. It should be getting easier. We are heading down into oxygen and warmer climates, down to fields starting to bud out in a coat of green fuzz, alive with new crops. There is no more snow, no ice, just an ever-increasing warmth from the sun as the days lengthen.

No one talks much. Jordan and Paul watch me nervously, anxious for proof that the same girl who went up the mountain came back down. Occasionally they bring up subjects from home: questions about dorms at Yale or whether I'll come home for Thanksgiving. The words are low and soothing, but I can't make myself concentrate on the meaning. My schedule—my famous plan that Tate used to tease me about—is gone. I can't even pretend, anymore, that I have any control. All of the details and facts that make up my life feel so far away from who I am now. Everyone seems to understand. At least, they don't push for answers but let their questions hang in the air.

Jordan is shrunken, still skinny and weak from his altitude sickness. He walks even more slowly than me, and sometimes he calls for Tate to come walk with him, to stay close. And Tate, who can read the panic in his father's face, slows his pace and stays with him for a while. Then he returns and takes my hand, holding it tight.

• • •

Asha and Finjo walk in front of us. Like always, Finjo is on his cell phone, madly talking as he walks, making plans for his next trip. I almost smile at the familiar sight. Asha was successful in her summit, which means that she will be a senior guide the next time she climbs. It makes me shudder. Next time. She will go back up, up through the Icefall, up past the dead bodies. She will climb again and again.

I try not to think about Luc, still up in the snow on the mountain, or his parents, who are in Kathmandu. I try not to think of Dawa, his sly smile when playing Uno, his easy grace as he crossed the bridges of the Icefall, or the funeral that took place in Lukla, his widow and kids stone-faced and silent as we tried to stammer out our condolences. I try not to think of Everest at all.

But the mountain won't let go that easily. Night after night I wake up screaming, nightmares of bodies and ice and endless darkness invading my brain.

Night after night Tate pulls me close, holding me in his arms and whispering softly in my ear, "It's okay. We're okay. We're right here."

My breathing slows, and the sweat on my neck and face dries. I blink, disoriented, in the tiny lodge beds. We're okay. We're right here.

Outside my window, the sunrise hits the peaks and turns them a glorious, blazing orange. I turn away from the view and let my eyes close, my back pressed tight against Tate's chest.

• • •

When we arrive at the airport back in Kathmandu, after another gut-churning flight on the tiny bouncing plane, I am unprepared. Unprepared for the smog, for the crowds, for the French and Korean media crews there to get footage and quotes from those of us who were with Luc and Yoon Su. Most of all, I am unprepared for Mami and Dad, who had jumped on the first possible flight after getting the news. They are standing right outside the restricted area, their faces tight and drawn, scanning the crowds until they see us.

"ROSE! ROSALITA!" Mami shouts, catching sight of us.

At the sound of her voice, something inside me breaks, cracking open like a crevasse on the Icefall, deep and endless. The Dread that I thought I could climb away from claws over me, and I pitch forward, nearly knocking them over as I try to get to them. Sobs pull out of the broken place, so hard and painful that I cannot catch my breath, even with all the oxygen in the air.

Mami holds me tight, so tight that my chest is crushed against the backpack straps, but I don't care. There is no amount of closeness to her that feels close enough, and the Dread rears up again and again, reminding me that it will never go away, that it will loom over me forever.

"Sweet girl, it's okay, you're going to be okay, my Rosalita, my baby," Mami whispers into my hair, but I can't stop, can't slow the sobs tearing out of me.

She is here, holding me, but she is still sick, and even after I did it, after climbing the tallest mountain in the world, even after training myself to fall asleep at the edge of the earth, I cannot bear it. I want her to make everything better; I want to feel safe, compared to the senseless death all around me on Everest, but instead everything feels so fragile.

"It's over. It's all over. You're okay. You're going to be okay," she repeats, and I try to catch my breath, try to slow my sobs. But I can't.

Somehow I know that even with the climb behind me, it's not over. The tears stream down my face, and I can't stop them, can't do anything but cling to her.

Chapter Thirty-Nine:

Rose

July 19
Palo Alto, California
30 feet above sea level

I glance at my watch and slurp my iced coffee. Tate's running late, as usual, but I don't really care. It's warm, and, even after two months back home, I'm still aware enough to be grateful: grateful for hot, sunny days; for my feet in flip-flops; for being hungry and eating my fill of cherries and burritos and fish tacos; for taking a run and having so much oxygen. I slide down the wall and turn my face to the sun, basking in the warmth.

I'm waiting outside my therapist's office, happy for a few minutes to collect my thoughts before Tate arrives. He doesn't ask me what I talk about with Dr. Nathan, and I don't bring it up, not because it's uncomfortable but because my thoughts are messy and fragile and tenuous, still too weak to hold up to the light. But they help, these visits.

It's not like Tate doesn't know that something inside me is broken. It was Tate who watched me, after we got home, and told me that I needed to get some help. He talked about trauma and about PTSD, and it was hard to hear, hard to see myself in what he was describing about his own terrors. I was angry at first, but he was right. The tears that started in the Kathmandu airport never really stopped.

Even now, thinking about those days in Kathmandu makes my chest tighten. Seeing Yoon Su in the hospital, unable to talk or move; meeting Yoon Su's parents and her sister Min Seo, and watching them try to grapple with the fact that, yes, she had survived but would lose toes, fingers, possibly part of her foot. Meeting Luc's parents and trying to hold on to his mother as she fell to the ground, sobbing . . .

Even after we got home and I texted with Yoon Su, the nightmares were constant, and I would wake up with my pillow soaked with tears every night. It was like a dam had burst within me, and the Dread that I'd been working to contain for months flooded out ready to drown me. Nightmares about Luc, nightmares about Mami falling off a cliff and dying . . . Night after night I fought sleep, trying to stay out of the dark recesses of my own head.

I close my eyes and breathe deeply, focusing on the sun, on the smells of coffee, ocean breezes, faint food scents from the restaurant next door.

I am here.

Dr. Nathan and I talk a lot about climbing and why I do it. We talk about the risks and the motivation—attempting to control something in a world that often feels out of control. We talk about Dawa and Luc and how *wrong* their deaths feel, how unfair. We talk about my guilt in choosing to become one of the many Western tourists who pay huge sums to climb a mountain in a country where poverty looms and Sherpas risk their lives for our dreams. We talk about the summit and how I can be proud of what I did, even with all that happened after.

And we talk about Mami. Mami and how guilty I feel that I got to climb and she didn't, especially since she was the one who pushed me to be able to do it. Mami, who endured my bad moods and complaints about training because she knows me and knew what that summit would mean.

Mami—and how terrified I am of losing her.

At first talking about it felt like touching electric wire, painful and shocking every time. But the more we talk, the less it hurts. Slowly I'm realizing that the Dread isn't going anywhere, no matter where I climb. Mami is sick, but she's okay for now. And I have to find a way to be okay with that. I have to find a way to walk alongside her with this illness, to keep walking, even when she has a bad day and my thoughts spiral to an image of her in a wheelchair, unable to hold me up, to be my rock the way she always has been.

Sometimes it seems impossible, like the Dread will always own me. But other days I think I can get a glimpse of how it could be different. I'll tell Tate about it, but not yet.

The beep of a horn startles me, and my eyes fly open. Tate's in front of me, his longboard strapped onto the top of the car, his windows down. He looks like a postcard of a California surfer dude. His smile is gentle as I get in.

"I talked to Paul," he says. "He's freaking out because, according to the agency, they're now next on the list for adoption. Could be months of waiting, or they could get a call tomorrow. He's losing his shit, and Drew is apparently buying out the entire baby department of Target 'just in case.' But Paul says they'll still be at Rockface on time, even if he has to pry Drew out of the Snugli section."

I grin. The thought of Drew and Paul as dads makes every single thing better. Ever since Nepal, Paul's been . . . not a father figure, and not exactly a brother, but family. We shared something that ties us together forever. And the idea of him with a baby feels hopeful in a way that few things do right now.

"I can't wait to be an auntie," I say to Tate. "I'm in charge of all hats." Baby hats are the cutest thing in the world.

Tate rolls his eyes. "You may need to fight Drew," he says, then leans over and kisses me.

It is still a small miracle, kissing Tate. Kissing him in the California sunshine, in warm summer rain, in our houses when our parents are out, in the back of the car when there's nowhere else to go . . . It's the one thing that has returned home from the mountains miraculously intact.

"How are you feeling? Ready for this?" he asks finally.

I lean back in the passenger seat, smoothing my hair, trying to catch my breath. "I'm ready. Or at least I'm glad we're doing it. I'm glad there will be something—I don't know—permanent to remember them." My eyes fill up with tears, but it's sadness, not panic or Dread. Only sadness.

We are on our way to Rockface for the first annual Lucien Cartier and Dawa Sherpa Memorial Fundraiser and Yoon Su Rhee Climbing Scholarship. It was Mami's idea, or at least the idea of a fundraiser was, and Tate and I decided to see if Rockface would let us do something there. So yes, I am ready to do it, except that I know it will hurt.

Tate's hand squeezes mine. "It's going to be fine. Better than fine. You'll dazzle them." He glances at me. "I have a surprise for you when we get there. Not a huge one!" he adds quickly, knowing full well how I feel about surprises when I am in full-on planning mode. "But I think you'll like it."

I raise one eyebrow. "As long as it's not a schedule-changing surprise. Because I'm already nervous enough about speaking in front of everyone." I sigh. I want to do this, I really do. But walking willingly back into the sadness is so very hard.

As we drive, Tate talks about the surf report, Jordan's plans to visit him in Rhode Island for a father-son hiking weekend during foliage season, a recent text from his roommate, a fabric artist named Jorge from Pittsburgh. Jordan's back to his usual healthy self after getting down from the altitude, but he's changed, like the rest of us. He's quieter and less quick to make jokes or lead the conversation. He sometimes trails Tate around the house like he doesn't want to let him out of his sight, and Tate is more patient than usual. They go out paddleboarding together or walk Zizu the dog, which they haven't done since Tate hit puberty.

If I came home from Everest broken apart, Tate came home stronger than ever. *Not* climbing seemed to answer some question in him that he desperately needed answered. I'm so proud and happy to see him like this, even though I can't help feeling even more damaged in comparison.

● ● ●

When we get to Rockface, there's already a big crowd milling around outside: all the climbing gym regulars, a ton of friends from high school, local media outlets, and our parents, of course. Tate pushes through the doors into the lobby, which is usually empty except for whoever's working the desk. But there's a crowd in there too. Tate moves toward the front, where the doors lead to the climbing space.

"There," he says, gesturing to the wall by the door. "My surprise. I told you it was nothing too crazy."

I stare. The wall has always been covered in mostly out-dated climbing-event posters, used-gear-for-sale signs, and lost-and-found notes. But now it's repainted a clean white, with a giant framed photo of our Everest group: Luc in front, head thrown back laughing; Dawa with his hand on Finjo's shoulder; Yoon Su grinning wide. And in beautiful lettering that I recognize immediately as Tate's work is a quote: *"The challenges here are tremendous, and the risks are sobering. But there is no place I would rather be than in the mountains."—Lucien Cartier*

I let the tears fall. Yoon Su had shared the blog posts and notes Luc wrote to her students, and he had written this in her last post, the day before they left Base Camp. I think back to that day, the wind-scoured Base Camp, the desolation and emptiness of the summit climb. Luc had loved it there. That has to count for something.

Grabbing Tate's hand, I stand there, thinking back to our climb until the crowd around us quiets and I realize we have to begin. I turn to face everyone, the climbers and friends and family who have all come to help us launch this scholarship. Yoon Su and I have been texting since I got home, and she loved the thought of Luc and Dawa being remembered this way. We talked to Finjo and decided: we would put half the money toward an academic scholarship for Sherpa kids from Dawa's village of Lukla and half to support Dawa's family. If they don't want to, Dawa's kids will not have to climb. Then Rockface agreed to donate an annual Yoon Su Rhee Accessibility Scholarship at the climbing gym to sponsor a gym membership and classes for a disabled climber in the community who otherwise couldn't afford to climb. When I asked Yoon Su how she felt about it being named for her, she didn't text back for days, and I was so afraid I'd offended her. Everything felt dangerous and unsure, even sending a text.

But then she answered, attaching a video of herself in the physical therapy gym, asking that I make sure and share it today. "Whoever wins this scholarship, just know this: I'm not here to be some inspiration poster you hang on your door," she says in the video, staring at the camera. And there's her quick smile: a flash, then gone. "I'm here to work, and you'd better be too. Because someday I'll come to California, and we'll climb together. And you'll want to keep up."

I think of her now, fighting so hard to reclaim her strength and her power. And I look out at all these people who will make sure Luc's and Dawa's names are known for years to come. It still feels so horribly unfair. This is not what I wanted, any of this. But it's what we have. And it's what we do next that counts.

Tate squeezes my hand, then steps back into the crowd. Yoon Su's video is almost over. It is time for me to speak. I take a deep breath, then another. The air is generous here, unlike on top of Everest. I can breathe here. One more breath, and I begin.

It is not the mountains we conquer but ourselves.

—Sir Edmund Hillary

Epilogue:

Tate

(Six Months Later) January 5
Providence, Rhode Island
75 feet above sea level

So what's it like to summit Mount Everest? I'll never know, and Rose doesn't talk about it. Not yet, anyway. Does it change you to know you've succeeded in something that only a few thousand people have ever done? Make you braver? Maybe. I have no idea. But I do know there's no talk of other peaks. We road trip to hike gnarly ridgelines in the White Mountains of New Hampshire and rope in to hit a technical route sometimes. But she doesn't talk about far-off summits in far-off lands. And neither do I.

And I don't miss it, that drive for the next big mountain. Walking away from the summit of Everest was like letting go of a rope I'd been clinging to and realizing I'll float instead of fall.

Honestly, it was a little like a drug, saying no like that. And I keep going for the high. Since then I've said no to taking a full load of classes first semester because I know I'd only get overwhelmed and fuck it up. I've said no to getting a single dorm room because if I don't have roommates, I'll spend every minute driving down to see Rose. *No* is my superpower, and amazingly, it hasn't blown up anything. Not Dad. Not Rose. Not me. We're all still standing.

Sometimes we talk about the others. Rose texts constantly with Yoon Su, who had to amputate one foot completely, all the toes on the other foot, and several fingers on her left hand. But being Yoon Su, she hasn't slowed down that much. She stayed pretty quiet for the first months of recovery but recently wrote to say she's going back to teaching and plans to take up adaptive ski racing. Rose says we should keep an eye out for wherever the Paralympic Games are going to be held in eight years, and knowing Yoon Su, that's probably a good bet.

Finjo and Asha are preparing for the next Everest climbing season. I asked Finjo, back in Kathmandu before we left, if he wanted to give up climbing. He looked shocked. "Never!" he said. "This is everything I always wanted. Even now."

But Asha might quit after this season, might try for a scholarship to go to college in Kathmandu. And Bishal—we don't know how he's doing or even where he is. When he left the hospital in Kathmandu, he went dark. Finjo said he would look for him, but we haven't heard any news in months. I try not to think about it too much because I hate how powerless I feel, how pointless that a guy like him could be lost just because he had the bad luck to be in a snowstorm on the mountain. It makes me want to rage, want to punch and fight the utter bullshit unfairness of it all. But there's nothing to punch, nothing to fight. So every once in a while, I send texts to his old number, send him a funny photo or a surf shot, since he was low-key obsessed with the idea of surfing. Maybe someday he'll answer.

• • •

Now we're at sea level, trying to study, trying to balance our lives at school with everything we shared, everything we are together. With what happened on the mountain.

Rose climbed Everest like she tackled every other mountain we've climbed, like the natural she is. But there's no smile of satisfaction when Everest comes up. There's just a shadow, like the memory of something lost forever. Then I take her to the ocean and we breathe that awesome thick, oxygen-rich air we both love, and I kiss her and make her laugh until the shadow fades away.

The End

A Word about Sherpa

The region of Nepal where this mountain exists is known as the Khumbu, and the people who live there are an ethnic group known as Sherpa. Originally nomadic, they have lived primarily, though not exclusively, in eastern Nepal for centuries. From the early days of Himalayan expeditions, the Sherpa people were highly valued by the western explorers due to their knowledge and climbing skills in the high peaks of their home. Today the term *sherpa* is used to signify a climbing guide or support staff in the Himalayas, but it is still accurate to use this term to refer to the ethnic group of the region. Adding to the confusion for visitors, Sherpa is often the last name given to an individual, so that Finjo Sherpa (his name) might be a Sherpa (meaning he is from that ethnic group) who works as a sherpa (meaning he is a mountaineering guide).

Author's Note/ Further Reading

$\mathcal{F}$or millions of years, in an inaccessible part of a remote area near India, Tibet, and Nepal stood a looming, massive peak. It was called Chomolungma by the Tibetans who lived in its shadows, which means mother goddess of the universe. Later the Nepali government named it Sagarmatha, or goddess of the sky. Measuring it, climbing it, "conquering it," as the later explorers hoped to do, was unfathomable. It just existed, enormous and wreathed in clouds, high above where humans lived.

But in the 1800s British explorers were aggressively traveling and mapping the globe, hoping to fill in the gaps on their maps of our world. In 1841 George Everest surveyed a part of the mountain range known as the Himalayas, and in 1856 it was measured with what was at the time cutting-edge technology. It came in at 29,002 feet and was designated

Peak XV. Nine years later, the British renamed Peak XV *Mount Everest*, after the western explorer who mapped it. New technology and shifts in the mountain itself have caused the official height of the mountain to be revised several times. In 1999 it was considered to be 29,035 feet, but the Nepali government began a new measurement campaign in 2019 to see what the effect of the 2015 earthquake had on the mountain.

Once named and measured, it did not take long before foreign explorers considered the possibility of reaching the summit. Starting in 1921, massive expeditions flocked to the base of the mountain to launch summit attempts. Again and again climbers headed up into incredibly harsh conditions and bad weather. Some died, many more were turned back by impossible conditions. While it's possible that earlier explorers managed to reach the summit before disappearing on the descent, it was not until 1953 that Nepali Sherpa Tenzing Norgay and New Zealander Edmund Hillary, as part of a British climbing expedition, made the first official ascent.

Since then, a veritable parade of "first ascents" have been attempted. First climbers from different countries, first climber to reach the summit without bottled oxygen, oldest climber, youngest climber, first visually impaired climber, first paraplegic climber, first descent by ski, first descent by paraglider, fastest time to the summit . . . The list goes on and on. In addition to the zeal of holding a record, no matter how esoteric, there are also more climbers who simply want the glory of having tagged the highest mountain in the world and ever more commercial climbing companies willing to help them get there—for a price. The crowds have led to increased pollution, ecological damage, and, improbably, human traffic jams on the mountain. Many fear that this commercialization of Mount Everest will lead to its ruin. But the allure of a place that is both gloriously beautiful and utterly deadly continues to draw people in.

As I wrote *Above All Else* I did a lot of research, and I have traveled to Nepal to the Gokyo Lakes in the Khumbu, near Everest Base Camp. It is a truly extraordinary part of the world. I can't overstate the beauty of those mountains, the improbably blue of the sky against the white peaks, the sense of distance—both physical and cultural—that it takes to get yourself there. The Khumbu region has been transformed by tourism: English signs offering solar showers, pizza (dubious at best), Coke, and internet access dot the landscape. But it is still an incredibly poor part of the world. Twenty-five percent of people live on U.S. fifty cents a day, and rates of disease, malnutrition, and child mortality are high. The contrast between the climbers who pay upwards of $60,000 for a three-month expedition and the local communities is stark and sometimes uncomfortable to witness, even as the Sherpas gain some benefit from the tourism dollars and are welcoming to the global visitors who admire their home. There are no easy answers to this tension. And in Nepal, like everywhere, climate change is irreparably shifting the reality on the mountain. More extreme weather patterns will lead to more dangers, putting more climbers and Sherpas at risk. The future of the mountain, and the region, is unknown.

Most of the details about the landscape, lodges, villages, climbing routes, and camps are as accurate as I could make them. There are indeed dead bodies left along the path to the summit, though the ones I reference in the book are not real. The dangers of altitude sickness and exposure are real, as are the kinds of problems and missteps that befall the characters in the book. Unfortunately, small errors can turn deadly on the mountain. But the beauty of the place, the glory of the mountains, and the kindness of the villagers who host travelers there is also real. If you get a chance, I strongly recommend you wander that way someday. You won't be sorry.

For more information about Mount Everest and climbing, please check out the books and links below. Most of these are adult titles but offer vivid and page-turning tales of life on the mountain.

Annapurna: A Woman's Place by Arlene Blum

Breaking Trail: A Climbing Life by Arlene Blum

The Climb by Anatoli Boukreev and G. Weston DeWalt

Dark Summit: The True Story of Everest's Most Controversial Season by Nick Heil

High Crimes: The Fate of Everest in an Age of Greed by Michael Kodas

High Exposure: An Enduring Passion for Everest and Unforgiving Places by David Breashears

Into the Silence: The Great War, Mallory, and the Conquest of Everest by Wade Davis

Into Thin Air: A Personal Account of the Mt. Everest Disaster by Jon Krakauer

www.alanarnette.com

www.melissaarnot.com

https://www.nationalgeographic.com/adventure/everest/reference/climbing-mount-everest/

http://sherpafilm.com

http://thewildestdream.com

http://www.beyondtheedgefilm.com

http://www.mounteverest.net/expguide/route.htm

There are many global foundations and nonprofits supporting Nepal. You can always look on **www.charitynavigator.org** to ensure that the organization you are supporting is actually doing good work and using the money well. To directly support the Khumbu region and the Sherpa families there, consider giving to The Juniper Fund, a small nonprofit started by western climbers that works directly with Sherpa families impacted by accidents on Everest: **www.thejuniperfund.org**

Acknowledgments

*I*t took me significantly longer to write this book than it would take even the most unlikely mountaineer to train for and climb Everest, and if the perils of a misstep had been even a fraction as deadly, I would have been smashed on the rocks more times than I can say. I am extra grateful for my beloved family—Patrick, Noah, and Isabel—who gazed up at the Himalayas with me and then listened, for six years, while I tried to figure out how to write a book about it. The fact that this book exists is a testament to my stubbornness but also to the amazing writing community I have.

I don't know if I can thank everyone who ever read a draft of this, from those early readers in 2013 to the last saviors a few months before the final draft was due, but I will try. Readers like Sarah Harian, Laura Tims, Jen Downey, Helene Dunbar, Katie Bouton, and others helped me fix the rope and start the climb. Heather Lucas and Willow Monterrosa had to deal with me attempting to write this book on our fortieth birthday trip, and then again on our forty-fifth birthday trip. (They will be relieved that by the time our fiftieth birthday trip rolls around this book will finally be on the shelf!)

Beloved Marietta Zacker roped in and led me up the steep bits, even when it seemed there was no path. Liz Levy, Catherine Egan, Jen Malone, and my long-suffering sister Erica Levy-Ringel set up camp and helped untangle the snarls. Joy McCullough, like a Saint-Bernard with a flask full of whiskey, showed up at the eleventh hour to help identify a character arc problem that had been dogging me for five years. Thank you, Joy!

And then there's the MoB: Rachael Allen, Alina Klein, and, most of all, Kate Asha Boorman. If I had to hang off an ice face at 29,000 feet with anyone, it would be you. Thank you, thank you, thank you.

I also want to thank Mona Shahab and Prabhat Srestha for their knowledge and expertise. I am so grateful for all the information shared, and of course any mistakes that remain are solely my own.

Finally, I am so grateful to work with the Charlesbridge team. Thank you, Diane Earley, who designed this gorgeous book and found the amazingness who is cover artist Levente Szabo, and thank you, Donna Spurlock and Jordan Standridge, for helping readers find their way to my story. Thanks to Jacqueline Dever for copyediting and Mandi Andrejka for proofreading. And mostly, thank you to Monica Perez, for seeing the story in *Above All Else*, for recognizing that it's less about the mountain and more about the people who are drawn to it, less about the summit and more about the journey. Onward and upward . . .